Three Beauties

Three Beauties

John Fraser

AESOP Modern Fiction
Oxford

AESOP Modern Fiction
An imprint of AESOP Publications
Martin Noble Editorial / AESOP
28 Abberbury Road, Oxford OX4 4ES, UK
www.aesopbooks.com

ISBN: 978-1-910301-18-0

Contents

The Beauty from Zagreb

1

Trams please me, no question – they know where they have to go.

My neighbour's book says: 'He walked up the steps of the Pentagon. The admiral on the door said, "The President is waiting for you..."'

She reads very slow. She turns and says: 'Fuck off. Get your own device.'

My stop.

A lady with the voices tries to push me off the sidewalk. You never know how many they are.

Here is my friend.

'We'll drop China,' Damien says. 'They'll have to fight for all the stuff they'll need, and then go bankrupt. They won't make it. Too much wrong geology.'

I'm lost. 'Too little geography?' I say, to keep in step.

'Nice one,' Damien laughs. 'At all events, they're out.'

Does he sell, or does he spy? I wonder.

He leaves, our usual brief meeting, saying, 'This is the end, beautiful friend.'

As we part, he kicks a storefront window. He must have iron boots. The glass shoots up into frosted roots, they call it 'making a rose' if it's a peacock. It's like a snowflake. 'No future there,' he says, 'No, none at all.'

I can't hear what his admiral says when Damien has run up his steps.

*

Here's everybody – friends, chatting in real time, real presences. There's Alvin, Bosh, me, Cayley, and the rest, all words.

'Those Russians never get it right! Communism, and now whatever... never no peace.'

'It seems Homer was a clan. They started off the whole book thing. And hung up on that one war, just like in Europe. Those odd stiff people, stabbing each other. Like families of dwarves, in the circus, or musicians – powerful upper bodies, obsessed. Then comes Christ, and they swallowed him too.'

'He's off to fight, Adnan is.'

'Well, we're all busy busy.'

'Should we stop him. Somehow?'

'He wants to go back, start it from a different history. Think of all the cadavers, intervening, while it was going wrong, he thinks. That evens it out. He'll make some more, the faithless dead, guys who don't count. The wrong side won, he's the redresser.'

'He'll drop in more corpses, till he's done, that's for certain. But if he's to be punished, it'll happen over there. And he'll see it's not so pure.'

'He's not pure, just stubborn. And there's no room here for him. He's learnt to argue, not give in, but he hasn't learnt to reason. They don't teach them that.'

'Everyone's doing something now, not like before, when they only reaped and sowed. Years back, they went into the Underground. That didn't get them far.'

'You mean the subway.'

'We were taken in by China: it's just more exotic food, that ends up here.

'I don't get on with your kid.'

'You don't know how to take him. If he torments animals, tell him "no". Obnoxious is the same all over.'

'I feel they're all fragile and evil.'

'It's so, but there's no one else to love. And they're indifferent to you.'

'Once there were lots of human species, side by side. Clumsy, stupid, painters, starwatchers, all roaming. Firing at the elephants. Maybe there's a better crowd arisen among us now, facing down challenges, not giving in. They don't laugh at us. They need our cash. Damien is surely one of them.' That's me, that's what I think.

'Often, Damien steps out his frame. That big voice! Kicking things. He says, "If the rich won't run everything, we'll need another of those rebellions. The false revolutions – our generation's been full of them. Or else we'll need to shut the bottom classes up....they'll not find work to suit, and I'm not paying them to lounge. We'll need to set the cops on them, poor things, there's nowhere they can go, and as for their horizon....!"'

'Damien knows it can't be fixed. We'll never be again what we once thought we were.'

I say again, this time to Alex, another of the new, the coming, species, when we are alone. 'It can't be fixed... Damien'll fix it. They write books about him. Waves of angry people, classes that rise and fall, and then are battened down. That's what he sees. He's the guy – they listen to him, follow his advice. Is he a superior one, the better sort, emerging species? Or just a louder voice?'

Alex says, 'You can't stop Damien. Besides, it's just ideas. It's all committees, in the end. I'm on them all. And you – it's clear, you aren't the better sort.'

'This Homer thing,' I say. 'It seems there was a pack of them, a family biz. Each one invents an episode, and joins them up, a hero sticks the fancies like a glue. The real protagonist, the "I" – was Homer number one. Maybe he even fought – some skirmish....' and I carry on.

'So what?' asks Alex. 'The Greeks – they didn't make the team. Got it all from Africa....'

'We lesser ones,' I say. 'For us, it's only stories. Animals don't tell them, only us; we hoisted up ourselves, and told them. Tales. Concoctions. Gods and heroes, like you do at school, and good guys, bad guys – maybe you can get to shoot the right set, even keep your cash. That's it, is all! Sure, we're more advanced than chipping flints, but still – we haven't got the brain to solve the real enormous things....'

'Look,' says Alex: 'Remember this, forget the species maybe that's evolved, and gives advice, and wears iron boots. There's always a survivor. Everything goes down... some lizard thing creeps from the pile and starts it off again. It's gardening, my friend.'

Our brains are exhausted. Alex says, 'But you – you did your bit for freedom, in the streets.'

'I thought about all that,' I say. 'For us lay guys, what is there left, but freedom? It's the least – besides, you can't go in the streets and always shout for cash.'

We part. I take the tram: the woman's book says, 'He nuzzles down between her thighs....' I say to her, 'That doesn't turn one on,' and she says, 'Oh no! It's you again! Another book. This one I wrote myself. You can read it when I've done another page.'

I say to Chloe, when I'm in our room, 'This story thing. It really fits, with everything. There's "I" is God, or "I" that's making rhymes, or leading monkey armies, or just sitting there, letting it all drop off like sweat. We primitives, we lay guys – we have Homers, who pretend they are some warrior; who travels round the world, and then it's vengeance, more slaughter. Probably another war. You see, it is all stories. Now, as it all comes to an end, you need some guys that can survive, and maybe solve the business....'

'What crap,' she says. 'You and your friends. It's wishful, all this stuff; and envy. You'd like to tough it through, like Damien.'

'Damien has the ears that matter,' I say.

'You always were more suspicious of your side. Maybe you'd be happier – over there, with the others. It's them that don't want you, though,' and Chloe laughs. That sets it out, just everything.

I go back on the tram. The woman with the little pad is writing – '...looking for a safe and easy ride, he chose an elephant. Then someone thought to spice it up, fired pepper spray right down its nose....'

'Ha!' she says, 'it's you again! People love prose, it's like warm food. It's sitting round campfires. There is no quest; although it has an end – that, you can't twist or fake.'

'I'm sure it's true,' I say. 'It passes time, that's passing anyway.'

We're at her stop. Her bag clinks as she starts to leave. It's full of canisters of pepper sprays. Then, there's an insistent sound, like someone close to you, crunching ice cubes. Behind us – there's a guy, much relaxed, shot through the eye, just sitting there.

There's the noise, and we all act as if we're in Juarez City, and we have some theory, some analysis. There's guys around the guy, being photoed by their mates. The woman says 'small cal, hi vel', and that seems right. I look at her quite close, the first time, her sly sexy face. I guess she's about sixteen. That's ok, you see she knows it all, maybe not deeply, and I say, to fill the space, 'That's real target shooting.'

She doesn't answer, and we stand and look, as if we're partners and she got off the shot.

This was the moment I decide to quit Chloe, go with this arty witch.

I tell Chloe, 'There was this guy, behind – shot through the eye. Like there were snipers.'

'It's fixed,' she says. 'The tram comes round the curve, and you just squeeze the trigger. The people ride that tram – are all the usuals.'

'It seems so out-of-date,' I say. 'Like rock and roll, the fear, the shot from out the heavenly blue. Things are not chance, not now. We've all been told the worst.'

'You could be loud, like Damien,' she says, seeking more fruitful arguments.

'You know how much he gets?' I ask. 'These guys are not amongst us. They buy in, then they're bought out. Their job is all the same, it's talk and dinners. Putting the creatures in the ark, pretending they are saved. We others are invisible. Left in the rain.'

'You shouldn't mind that,' Chloe says. 'I know you'll do a great thing. Losing your work – it's nothing – like when Damien climbs the tree. He knocks the soft fruits off. Like you. Down they go, and make another tree. I'd recommend you where I work, but you don't know colours, can't cut shapes.'

I don't rise to this. 'The middling people – it's their time,' she says. 'Only the communists had some hope, a future – and look where they have ended up! The religious ones – they knew how it all would end, the saved, the damned. Now, it's the turn of in-betweens. The moderns. Dependent, angry. On the streets for petty things.'

Next day, the woman's on the tram. 'You ought to turn your head,' I say. 'Your profile, like you're on a coin – it's dangerous. Makes you a target. Show both your eyes, and look at me.'

I see her page. '... my father kept a hardware store,' it says, 'till he died duelling in the Bois.'

'Where are you from?' I ask.

'No!' she says. 'It's too direct. You pry. And I'll not tell.'

'Far far away,' I say. 'But not where you would want to stay.' She's silent.

'The Caucasus? Balkans? I see a mountain, and the sea.' She reads her book.

'Croatia? I know exactly what you are. "The Beauty from Zagreb". A title that would make you proud.'

She laughs. 'Yes, yes. Exactly right.'

I know her name: Wittgenstein says a name could be sacred. Luisa.

'Luisa,' I say. 'Chloe wants to live on an island. She hates this country too. It means she'd learn some Portuguese.

Putting little turtles in the sea, among the sharks. I'm quite attracted.'

'That's your secret, then,' she says. 'They give us secrets, that way we blackmail them. Then they go after us, to punish. A secret's there to tell, at the right time. The music never stops. You do.'

'You knew that guy, that's dead?' I ask.

'A bit. Everyone on the tram. He used to read what was on my pad, like you,' she says.

'Who gives us secrets?' I ask.

'The state. Sometimes God,' she says. 'Don't sit by the window, if you've spilled your secret.'

'My friend Damien,' I say, 'talks to the President. They're dumping China, their fear of it. No resources. Except people, like the hundreds and thousands they used to put on cakes.'

'People is best,' Luisa says. 'Having only them, you don't need dig the soil.'

'My friend Alex says the future's on the table. You have to disbelieve your friends,' I say.

'Come on!' says Luisa. 'Stop trying to peek at my underwear. This is where I live.'

We leave the tram. It passes by where all of us live. 'Here's my cat,' she says, though first you notice the red flowers, their yellow tongues, the white grass frizzed, the tiny birds. 'See – the birds have blue tongues,' she says. It's true. 'Here's my cat,' she says. 'I have to kill for it. Food,' she says.

'Ludwig was right, where language ends, hunting begins.' She holds an axe.

'A chopper,' I say. 'The "chopper" should be mine....'

'It's underwear again,' Luisa says. 'You live in double senses. It's you who hopes you've got the chopper.'

It's a scalding moment, and I stand nearer to her than I need. 'There's other ways of feeding cats,' I say.

'Jesus!' she says. 'If that's not bonding! Doing its dirty work, fresh kills.'

'You must love real hard,' I say.

'Your friend Damien....' she says. 'You shouldn't just dump countries. There's the people, too. Not their persons, but the quantity. It's not convention, saying that, nor humanism: you can see them all, on trains and stations.'

'You know philosophy quite well, Luisa,' I say, quite at a loss.

'Oh yes,' she says. 'I live in the world, just like you.'

'Let me take the axe,' I say, not knowing what to do. There's the cat, brownish, asleep.

'That's it,' she says. 'Axe. Get the name right. That's the first thing, if you want to be a writer,' and she puts brown cat stuff in a bowl. 'Or a thinker.'

'Is this place yours?' I ask.

'The place, I guess. Yes. But not property. That's an illusion. When you're dead, it slips away, transmogrifies,' she says.

'This kind of talk, Luisa, is crap,' I say. 'Its being true doesn't make it interesting.'

'Well,' says Luisa, 'what you going to do? Do something. You want to chop me up?'

'No. And I wouldn't know how to start with sex. But – there's money here, around?' I make a question of it.

'Money has no place,' she says, teasing. 'And it's not property. Maybe it's an illusion too. And my lover, Franz, as well.'

'We all have people who love us, Luisa,' I say heavily, 'or have or thought they did. But it's good he's left the grass and birds.'

'It's time you went to Chloe,' Luisa says. 'Enough sex for today. I'm quite too young!'

'I have to leave,' I say. 'Leave this city. Do something.'

'We shouldn't sit in the same row, on the tram,' she says.

'Why ever not?'

'Maybe I don't like you. You're so full of your own desires. You should listen to you.'

'Here, Luisa, take the axe. It's yours,' I say, and she does.

Then – here's Alex, on the tram. Like Damien, he's from the species more advanced. 'I don't want to hear about desires,' he says. 'I've seen the President. He reflects. He isn't deep. A Narcissus. And he wants out. The others, round him, against him – they are naturals. Steeped in their desires.'

'Of course, Alex, everything's desire,' I say. 'Like waiting for your stop. Getting off. Having no ticket. You want to hear about Luisa? Precocious. A joker. Fun stuff. Not like Chloe. I'm suffocating in all that. I wonder what Chloe's really like? No one can care, be serious, and plan like her – it must be fake. As for me – if it's by sea you go, the thing is – arriving on some land. It doesn't matter where.'

Alex waves his shoulders at me. 'Damien is everywhere,' he says. 'He pours his poison in the President's ears. And you can't say you'll suck it out....'

Here he comes, Damien, boarding the tram, and pushing through. His sealskin overcoat – that must be hot. It's toe-length.

'Away, away,' he shouts. 'Show me the pedal!' He takes the tram's controls, and throws the driver from the tram, and we accelerate. There goes the palace, there the mint, there the river, yellow-grey. 'There and back again – on no! We're on a loop,' and round we go, the clumps of passengers surge up, to board, then back they shrink. Looking behind – they're matchstick bundles, every head aflame, identical with questions and with rage.

We scramble off the tram.

'I've things for him to sign,' shouts Damien, hoisting quires of onion skin, and showing us the fatal space without... the signature, the cross!

'The President! He's dying on me,' Damien weeps. 'He must confess as well. But we can't think who to.'

15

'I'll cover policy,' says Alex. 'For what that's worth. This chancer here – he does confessions. He loves 'em,' thrusting me forward. 'He thinks they're secrets. No one says what they really did, in case there's resurrection.'

Here we are at the bedside, here the President, unattended. 'Fuck it,' he says. 'I should be the last to go. I am the tops, and now some creep....' and on he croaks and sobs.

'Someone got off a lucky shot,' says Damien. 'Just okay each bundle, and you're done. It's the jobs for all your boys and gals. The heritage. Succession.' He forces the fat files upon the President.

There's bandages. Is that an eye, there on a dish?

'Such promise,' Alex says, 'and then it all jelled down, the only thing that's ever left is boundaries and plinths. Everything always must be finished off by someone else. Or lost and put in store.'

'Sign these!' pleads Damien. 'Not your name, just put OK.' It looks as if it is KO. 'That, I can adjust,' says Damien. 'We'll need to clean our suits, go on TV. Maybe a funeral pyre, an alabaster urn. A mausoleum where the guys can muse. Black horses too, and maybe human sacrifice....' He's cheered. 'The law that says "no funeral smoke" – we shall abjure it for a week.'

'It's not "abjure", you cretin,' Alex says. 'It's something else, that slips my thoughts.'

There isn't much to do: I ask the statesman, as he dies, 'Is there something you would like to tell, regret? One of those cadavers that you spread around – is one particular to you?'

I wonder what you do if someone should confess... forgive? reprove? say we're all responsible, perhaps? But no – I never vote, I don't pay tax I can avoid. They offered us a gun, I never picked up mine. I've never even joined a *manif*... – no, I'm clean.

'Fuck it,' says the President. 'I see no afterlife, no tunnel, no bright light. I should have taken out the guy that shot me,

16

that is all, that's my regret. I paid a heap of guys to do just that.'

It's all unedifying. History.

'The last words have been circulated,' Damien says. 'It's all yours now, the end.'

'Goddam it,' sobs the President. 'I thought I was exempt. Maybe I'll bomb some guys, to make us safer still,' and Alex says,

'No, no! The time has come for noble thoughts... We'll have to take our chance. No more talk now, so we can say you died in peace.'

'No flames. No worms. And no one gawping at me,' the President begs. 'Perhaps a gentle chilling....'

'Oh no,' says Damien, checking the big guy's pants for cash, 'Don't be a feeble, now. Who wants to end up like a box of beans, stretched out, mouth gaping, like a stockfish, dumped in a freezer?'

'Where's his women?' Alex asks. 'His generals?'

'Oh,' says Damien. 'They're with the coffin, down the corridor. Hear them ululate. And the snappers. Gathered round the empty oaken case. All is taken care of. Just the big guy here, with us to send him off – find his successor....'

Outside, there's tanks, and military types with feathers in their hats. Here comes a rocket – Damien says, 'I thought we might send him up, to circle us in space. But then – he's not so fatherly. Too weepy. And besides, there's everyone up there, to spy on us – the corporals and the divas. Then a casket falls, and half Siberia's up in dust and fire.'

In fact, the President is taking death quite personal, as if it happened only to himself.

'Well, now,' says Damien, 'who's next? The empty throne calls out for bum....'

'It could be me,' says Alex, preening. 'I am a hero of the war.'

'So are we all! You, Alex?' Damien scoffs. 'You sop. You bowl of grey, you workhouse gruel. You shot the guys they told you to – it is the ones you're not supposed to that defines. No, no, you're rule-bound, Alex. Rather, a guy like this,' he pokes at me. 'Seems humble, but his head is full of crazy moths. You'd need to read some speeches. Tell some jokes. A song. Perhaps a dance.'

I think – 'Luisa. She'd not fit. Too young to be first gal. Besides, she has a palace of her own. Chloe's too dowdy, she would never do.'

'The music, Mister President,' says Damien.

The near-cadaver brightens. 'That girl – "I'll be your somebody, Your somebody to love." That's what she sings. First I love her. Then – everybody loves me.'

'Exactly!' Damien says. 'That is just right. On brass bands, arranged.'

'Let's settle where you'll put me,' says the President.

'A wall. A pavement – like in Hollywood. A mountain with those faces – we could pack you in your nose – up on the monument. Trees for your ear hairs....' Damien talks on. Alex says,

'You love this, Damien.'

'Of course,' he says. 'I give a skip when it's to someone else and not to me. We'll put this guy here in his box, and up and down the hill he'll go. And he'll not feel a thing.'

We stand, bored, uneasy. Damien says to the big guy, 'You want the kiss, old pal?'

'Only from you, Damien. That Alex – I've seen him skin 'em in committee – don't let him near me!' says the President. He goes on, 'Did I hear "skin"? "Flaying"?'

'That was you,' says Damien. 'Loose phonemes only. We'll be cool.'

'Just chill me out,' the President says.

Damien takes out a hipflask, waves it around.

'And where's my women?' asks the President.

'Oh, you know,' says Damien. 'They have a sense of history. Passes the old and – as they say – "Cosy fanny" for everyone. You want loyalty, you have to pay. Along comes the Heldentenor – and they're beneath the spell.'

Damien fills his mouth from the flask, leans over the body. Liquid passes between them, Alex and I – we turn away. A dreadful intimacy.

It's over. 'Long live somone else,' shouts Damien. 'Now – the end of paranoia, hypochondria too. Hear those old Greek doctors, diagnoses tumbling down the stairs. Now,' he turns to me, 'You don't want it? Too heavy, the job? Soldiers in one drawer, trumpets in another. You're sure?'

'It's choosing the first lady, and the second,' I say.

I don't want the job.

'Right!' says Damien. 'You're an imperceptible loss. I'll start the procession, get the fireworks out. I do love bangers!'

*

'Too bad,' Luisa says. 'No presidency for you and me. We could have sung, even kissed, before the populace. Made the people cry.'

'You swim from the wreck – you don't put on the captain's cap,' I say.

'My sister might take it on – she only screws rich guys,' she says.

'You prosper here,' I say, changing the topic, relieved, and questioning.

'Look around, without romance,' she says. It's true. Without romance, or lust – there is a shrub, a cage with birds. A tall heap of empty pizza boxes. I'd thought they were Kabuki prints. The palace is no more. Perception has misled again.

'Those last words?' Luisa asks.

'They told me they were. 'Hit those high notes, hard and clean.' Nothing discriminates in that,' I say.

'If my sister's elected, I'd need to move house,' she says.

'She should be careful. They say the chief was shot: – the paranoia, he already had that. It came from coca. And the people. That was his generation,' I say. I'm alarmed – no one likes being near to famous people. I say, 'Damien and Alex – are they friends – or partners looking for accomplices?'

'Friends are always weird,' she says. 'The more you stick with them, the stickier they get. That's why I'm more into philosophy. Especially what comes after. How the moral base depends on where you were brought up.'

'I know,' I say, 'you've said it all before. But – best not be in a category that Damien and Alex might not like. And do you really have a sister?'

And a lover called Franz, who eats pizza.

'Those two, Franz and my sister, are my strongest memories,' Luisa says. 'They protect me, they are bulwarks. They mean I can't repeat the things that happened with them. But – I can give you their addresses. Naturally.'

'So, they don't live here?' I say. Of course they don't. Stupid. 'Me – I'm pointed to the future,' I tell her. 'The past's a box you'd better lock.'

'Yes,' she says, 'it's the toiling of the past, the riches of labour, expended in misery. And set down on my pad.'

'Luisa,' I say, 'those are ruins – they're bones. By tomorrow, like every tomorrow – our desire, our hunger, our necessity, starts the totality up again. I used to think like you... Chloe, friends – all with their angles, all wrecked off some ship, paddling along, singing the same old songs. Learnt at mother's scrubbed-out knees. Now, I see that every day, we start it up again from scratch, to throb and thresh. All new.'

'No, you idiot,' Luisa says, 'It's not the bony ruins, it's the people, made yesterday.'

'Oh, people!' I say. 'They should look at things a different way.'

'You're a celebrity,' Luisa says. 'We could start a salon. Go out for cocktails and meet architects. You renounced the presidency...'

'Most people do,' I say. 'Talking of people.'

'Now the funeral's done, you can bring Damien here,' she says. 'And Alex too.'

It's a mistake, I feel. Damien comes – and at once, he whirls her, pokes into corners, roars and plays the nursery lion, the gobbo.

'Hey, what's this?' he shouts, taking her little screen. '"Those smouldering ropes on every corner – that's how I remember Kalicot – on every coil, a spark, left for the smokers, the earth opening up beneath you, carrying you away as if the roads were rivers, rivers of crawling, creeping shit...." Ho, ho,' he cries, 'we have an artist? Or a copier?' And there's Luisa, giggling, tearing the tiny black slab away, and blushing, yielding as he hugs her.

Grey Alex – he's transformed, he says, 'I'll get some guys to paint these walls.... And then we'll have a dance!'

'Oh yes!' Luisa says. 'Me and my sister, we do that – our boyfriends, friends of friends, it's quite a lunching on the grass, with cutlets and tequila....' and she tells about erotic afternoons, and glances at me.... Is there some effect?

I'm dismayed. Perhaps excited too, as if she were another person, scarcely known, who shows a universe remote and peppery. What was her father? Fascist? A brother...? In the war, for sure – first anti-Semites, then the scourge of Islam? And Franz – not the narrator, K, the impotent, writer of the weird, but some powdered baron with a tennis suit, his balls inscribed by Cartier.

Luisa – what are you, where do you come from, now philosophy is ended and the next has not begun, dancing away the afternoon, strip-whirling with your gaseous sister, screwing tanned idlers, stretched out, a long white gutted fish? There's the single bed, no mattress, the knitted springs a net.

'Whoa!' shouts Damien, 'horseriding! This is the spot. Round and round, and change your partners!' And Alex too responds, as if he feels the charge of this quite ordinary room, and Luisa turns from one to other of them, brown soft eyes, a smile.

'I love an orgy,' Alex says. 'Most, when it's unexpected.'

'Remember our clean funeral drapes,' says Damien, backing off.

'Just high school boys,' says Luisa, again that little smile. 'It was. And don't forget my sister for the Office.'

'No one's excluded,' Damien says. 'That's what the system is. Although, this circus needs a pachyderm. I know you're all potatoes in a sack – that's how it seems to each of you – but my eye picks out the winner – colour, timbre, sex – even the past.'

'Maybe you made movies of the fun?' says Alex, his mind fixed in its sexy groove. ''Of all the arts, the cinema's the most important.' That's what Lenin said, and it's the truth for Luisa and her mates, for sure.'

I can't stay here.

I can't imagine staying long with Chloe. It's too dull. And here – there's too much spinning, dressing down and dressing up; in this drab room.

I leave them, Alex, Damien, Luisa, standing there and calculating.

*

Chloe says, 'This island, off Brazil....'

'It's cheap,' I say, 'for everything.'

'Oh no,' she says, 'that price is not the whole. You choose a little lot and build. Then all live equal. It's socialism, but you buy and sell. That way, you come out with capitalism.'

'That's all irrelevant,' I say. 'You mean – no palace, and no slaves? Not Ithaca? Nor yet – a solitude?'

'I would be faithful,' Chloe says. 'There's not much choice.'

'There's hate right here,' I say, 'but people won't shell and bomb each other. We export it, other people take to it, and on it goes. We don't do that, not yet. Maybe we should stay awhile.'

'It's the shopping. Here, you concentrate on that, don't focus on the others,' Chloe says.

'You can't be tricky now,' I say. 'There is no way to win. Since no one sets a trap, you just plod on. There's flat all round. I'd hoped to be a warrior, of the peaceful kind, but now we are all Trojans, waiting for the ships to show.'

I wonder about Luisa. Helen? Witch?

'You idiot!' says Chloe. 'That's the high point, when you could choose between the little island and the continent. You should have run for President – then retired.'

I take the leaflet. 'It says here, "on the little island, that as well as turtles there are stumpy little birds".' I read on. 'They live in wooden boxes, they're suburban. Their parents forage, just like brokers, come home with empty guts and get squawked out. That's no life.'

'Storms, witches, monsters – that's your life! Dodging, running – all in your head, or dozing on your tram,' she says, exasperated.

*

I can't change Luisa's past, or Chloe's future.

I tell Luisa, 'Damien's responsible for security too. He says, 'The tram's as safe as can be. If you're unsure, don't take it. It's the curve – gives a clear sight. Some monster.... We could straighten out the tramlines."'

'It's OK, really, it's OK,' Luisa says to me. 'It's taken care of. Don't be afraid. You can't make the tram go faster – it's not a mule!'

'What's on your screen?' I ask.

'I like you like this,' Luisa says, 'when you're cool, and sound like you're going somewhere. Somewhere I don't want to hear all about, and if you like it.' She shows me.

> Halfway up Kennedy Boulevard, a tall man stands in front of me.
>
> 'Give me to eat,' he says, and holds my shoulders. 'No drink. Eat.'
>
> 'Don't threaten me,' I say. 'I don't care who you are. You should learn to stand in line. They say – the line gives you food, if you wait.'
>
> I give him money. He doesn't speak. I see he's crossed the road, taken someone by the shoulders....

'It reminds me of something,' I say. 'Maybe several things. Who wrote it? You?'

'You're fixed on authors, continuity,' she says. 'Straight lines. Coherence of who does what. You're wrong – nothing is decisive. The storm is followed by lots more, men, women on your path, lots... they don't need be different. You always are. I guess they taught you – persevere, be logical, consistent. What you do belongs to you. It isn't so. The names – they may not change, things do.'

'That's it? The secret?' I say, though Luisa's made it easier for me, seeing her as – just Luisa, described by herself.

'Everyone knows it, except you,' she says. 'Sometimes I copy, sometimes I invent. But it all goes forth, like little ships, off to capture cities. So small, you know they won't come back. That's good.'

*

Maybe it is. Chloe goes off to her island. I don't go. 'You'll come later, when you feel it,' Chloe says.

'Sure. Of course. You won't have a house.'

24

'No. It'll be a container. Off a ship. You rent them,' she says. She's happy. I'll not be there, but pencilled in.

Chloe's safe, I'd know where to find her, though she's destitute. Other people will be there, watching her. Lust on treasure island.

All our friends drop me – I'm quite glad.

Luisa says, 'There! Chloe's settled.'

'Those containers... so hot. Perhaps a little trailer, to push the birds and turtles to the sea. A gun to keep the suitors off. So tough to get there, yet everyone watches the sea, desperate to leave,' I say.

'If you can't dive through the waves, you don't eat,' says Luisa.

'Where's Franz?' I ask.

'Oh,' she says, 'look!'

There it is, written out. 'Someone must have been telling lies about Franz... for having done something wrong, he was arrested one fine morning.'

'It happens a lot,' says Luisa. 'It's a relief when they take you.'

'It doesn't happen to Damien's friends,' I say. 'Not yet.'

'Damien – he's not religious? Nor Alex,' she says.

'No, absolutely, I think.'

'Religion – it's bluster. Or warmed-up chickpeas. Cold knees. Liturgy – it has to rhyme,' Luisa says.

I don't follow. 'What do you do with all your literature?'

'I send it off. It's to make money. Like my songs. And dancing – though with that, there's nothing to show,' she says.

'What do you hope it's for?' I ask.

'For something new. To make something to fight Damien. And all his stuff. The massacres, the law, the snooping. The suburbs, the cities. The gangs. Cows in the fields. The candidates. Everything in Damien's eye,' she says.

'How much money will that take?' I ask, thinking of that dead guy's eye, not Damien's.

'I know you don't think it's a literary imagination,' she says. 'And God doesn't come in.'

'What's left?' I ask. 'Motorcycles? Smoke, acid, China?'

'Adventure. A challenge – like life in a container, throwing birds into the sea,' she says.

'But – your sister...?' I ask.

'A test for her,' she says. 'Worth a try.'

*

Knock, knock. Like the knock on the door of the waxworks cabinet – there they are, in a row, Adolf, Goebbels, you didn't expect to see them again, and why did you pay to view their unpresence? There's Franz. 'I was sure you didn't exist,' I say.

'And I'm sure you are invisible,' he says, pretending to look through me. I laugh, but he never says anything funny, ever. He could do any straight part – gravedigger, high priest, warder. 'I thought you were just written about,' I say.

'I know,' he says. 'You put your love in a bottle and tossed her in the sea. You must have a grand ambition, even wider than Luisa's.'

'I'm not like Luisa,' I say. 'She wants to do something with America, but it's all been tried. Those plots, inventions. The guns, the cash, all those people settled down with yards.'

'She's crazy, it's true,' says Franz, 'and trivial. But if you don't want to pull it down, nor be its big cheese – your ambitions must be greater still.'

Here comes Luisa's sister, up the stairs, stumbling. '*Shit!*' – her voice precedes her, firm and pure.

'I didn't believe in you, either,' I say.

'Oh,' she says, 'I'm with Franz now. Those trams – they're perilous. They threw us off. We had no tickets. We don't believe in them.'

Franz is a cube, with thin legs: the sister, face of an unloved doll – an adolescent in her thirties, I should say.

Liesl. Even more beautiful than Luisa – perhaps a cleaner past, a dirtier future.

'My – this place,' cries Liesl. 'Like a shop that's never sold a thing! What else is it that you do, when you don't loll around Luisa?' She sits, crosses her ankles, asks me sharply.

'I do publicity,' I say. 'You don't need spell. They pay by sentences. It's better if you're white. And as for shops – the blacks and browns don't sell a thing....'

We don't care to sell. Here, it's not a shop, a store, it is Luisa's place.

'Hmmm,' Franz says. 'A shop that's never sold a thing. That's quite a record – it would bring the crowds. Now, since you ask, I used to be a bodyguard, but now I do ecology. I just about preserve the world. Without me, it would just about fall down,' and Liesl cuddles close to him.

'Oh, I believe,' she shouts. 'You bet – Franz keeps it standing!'

'Settle in, you vivid people,' says Luisa. With them, she's more defined, more in the game.

'What's your speciality, Liesl?' I ask politely.

'Franz was my bodyguard,' she says. 'I'm famous.'

'We're all famous, when someone writes about us,' Luisa says, sharply. 'Liesl just comments. And she shrieks. If she ran a store, no one would buy – they'd peer and point.'

Franz takes me aside. 'Luisa's body,' he whispers, breath heavy with *mortadella*, 'is a fantastic instrument. Loud or soft, roars and whispers... play any way, anywhere....' He stands back, eyes like black olives, waits for my response.

Is this how a movement, bound to change the world, begins? Yes, I suspect it's so.

'You know,' says Liesl, seeking comfort in a straggly chair. 'The people here – don't care if those Arabs have democracy. Nor even if their faith is right. That goes for others, too – China, now. Or Russia. What people want – is silence! Silence all around. and doing what they're used to.

The rest is, well, the kind of stuff you write,' and she glowers at me. 'But not the stuff Luisa does.'

I see why Liesl could be Damien's candidate.

'I'm on a voyage, guys,' I tell them, 'not a career. And not a movement. Odyssey, that's me.'

'You will find,' says Franz, pushing me, twisting an arm, 'that Liesl and I have all that's needed for a social mobilisation. Besides, what kind of journey is yours? Where's it end? A cross? Crowned queen? Monkeys turned back into princes? When you voyage, you're transparent. You pass through people like a ghost.'

'No, Franz,' says Luisa sharply, 'you're mixing journeys, quests and epics. This guy – he isn't epic. Epics are lots of people. Rather, he avoids his destiny – some crap island, full of terns.'

'What kind of movement, then?' I ask. 'College boys?'

'Or bombs on trams?' Liesl puts in, although it's Franz's line.

'Oh no,' Luisa says. 'You talk like that, we'll have to carry bombs for Damien all our lives. And Alex thinks up punishments that last your life... Damien rides on terror. We're all terrorised in any case, before there is a bang.'

'Better to go into politics,' says Liesl, turning up her nose. 'The thing is, those social movements are quite cyclical, you can observe them gyre and drop like swans beneath the clouds. In politics, we'd make our names, avoid a martyrdom for our cause. And then depart, fulfilled. We all know Damien – a nest of spiders there... best to keep clear.'

'Those spiders,' says Luisa. 'Is that Turgenev? Or it could be Gide.'

'Screw that!' shouts Franz. 'No finely written stuff for us. We'll push the rock a little higher up the mound, and then before it rolls and crushes us, we'll jump into another life, and off!'

Into my head there comes that girl, dressed in red, with golden coins as earrings, coming down the stairs, showing off herself and costume to the crowd of customers.... Her customers?

Oh, when the days were louche and simple!

Franz and Liesl say they're tired, they'll write the manifesto when in bed. I'm alone with Luisa, no manifesto to set out.

'That's not a chair, you idiot,' says Luisa. 'It's what used to be a couch. That is for you. Sex? No, no, it's far too noisy. There's the neighbours....'

'I could try playing your piano,' I say, losing interest.

'That's gross,' she says. 'I thought you nobler.'

I sleep badly. Franz and Liesl show their document.

It says:

Tired.
Tired of capitalism?
Tired of owing cash?
Tired of new people?
Tired of who you know?
Tired of too little pay?
Tired of losing wars?
Tired of decline?
Tired of waiting for the end?

'We sought our inspiration in Brussels, and Vienna,' Franz says. 'Manifestoes of communism, and of people without qualities. The second, Vienna and Austro-Hungary, seemed the reference most apt for America, and its empire. We composed, invented, made a distance. Then we slept.'

'We have nothing to lose but our tiredness,' Liesl says. 'That's the nub of it.'

I have come to sleepy shores. Sleep – it's a drug. Cheap. I shake Luisa – 'Don't drop off,' I say. 'You might fall for ever.'

'It's more Vienna than anything,' Luisa says. 'The campaign that said the Emperor was not the centre of the

29

world. Called the collateral campaign.. And it's good you've put in no remedy.'

*

Damien is angry. 'What! This musty consensus! Written by a committee to avoid committees. Written by the guilty to avoid justice.'

'Yes,' says Franz. 'I'd hate a trial.'

'You've split the angry and the exhausted,' Damien goes on. 'It's Luxemburg against Kautsky! How will you recruit your troops?'

'Oh,' Liesl says, 'not with those banal messages, popping up like ads. We'll throw leaflets from top floors.... If we feel like.'

'This could be huge,' says Alex. 'Think of all the hungry people.' He thinks 'orgy', but it's true, it's a universal message, a call. Siegfried – the whole scenario.

'You're important people,' Damien concedes. 'Franz and Liesl – always in campaigns. Luisa with her texts, the cuts – making an imaginary, for when you take the tram. But – I sense a moral void. Nihilism, vacationing – a vacuum.'

'We're at home in many tongues,' says Franz. 'Behind the bright things that we say – there is another, an intelligence critical. Behind the word – the thought.'

'I'm for revolution, Damien, if that helps,' says Luisa, 'Though it's not something you can do on your own.'

Liesl says she prefers angling for votes, and Franz says, 'No jail for me! People must take my thinking as it comes – I can't predict the consequence.'

Damien looks flustered. 'We are exactly where we were,' he says.

'It's like this, Damien,' says Luisa, kindly, showing him an opening on her screen. '"There was a depression over the Atlantic. It was travelling eastwards...." only it's not, it's travelling westwards. You're not the centre, Damien. It's stormy weather now.'

Franz goes on, 'We're steeped in German culture, Damien....' But no one else is, no one cares.

'Hold on,' says Alex. 'We have broken through. There's no more panic. No one thought of it before – we had a meeting, and we've solved the awkwardness. We tap into the core, the Earth's hot belly. Volcanoes all round, and all the extra people, – they can go to Greenland, eat the coconuts and spear the purple fish.'

'Oh no!' shouts Damien. 'I had hoped to live in Colorado, hunting stuff. Now there'll be holes all over, malls and such.'

'This time,' Luisa says, 'the whale will tell the story. Then we'll wait, along will come another whale, a metamorphosis, changed utterly.'

'Oh no, my dear,' says Liesl. 'Whales are all alike. That's why a bunch is called a pod – like peas. It's butterflies, that starts off green and wriggly, then they change, and for a day or two—'

'We want to be there, at the death,' says Franz. 'Not caught up in snags and drifts, the trials, the hierarchies – a single shot brought down the Archduke, whittled away my namesake, old Franz Josef. Now, it's a basketful of states involved – will it take more to bring them down? Or less? Each one a shot? A secret leaked? Or deserts made of magma, lizards from the depths, all up and running....'

Damien's concerned. 'A pistol shot?' he asks. 'No, no, there must be more. The guy, sat there on the tram – just nothing special, that's what a casualty is – quite casual.'

*

'It's pizza time,' says Alex. 'When the meeting speaks of depths and holes, then we must eat.' And so we do. The empty boxes stack up on the pile.

Luisa clings to me. 'That guy,' she says to me. 'If he had read a book, his eye would not have been so visible.... I send my samples out – and offers! You would not believe! My little specimens attract – it's just the time I lack to write the rest.... And now – it seems we're stumbling on The End before the middle's told.'

'Those campaigns that they used to have,' says Damien, looking round. 'Did they avoid the end?'

'There's always ends, but people carry on, without beginnings,' Liesl says. 'There's nothing special stands it up, America. Or anywhere.'

'It's true, goddam it,' Damien says. 'Just as I'd discarded China, all the rest that was in baulk is cannoned into holes.'

His hand is raised – he gives a dreadful chop – the pizza boxes split and scudder round the room.

'You see, Damien,' says Franz, 'we three were all together, in the war. Luisa, Liesl, me.'

'That's not possible,' I say, amazed. 'You're much too young, especially Luisa.'

'Oh,' says Luisa. 'The war doesn't end when the fighting stops. It's like musical chairs – it gets going when there's silence. Anyway, I love everyone. I hate everyone. I love it here. I hate it here. Over there, everyone's called Franz. Holy war? Another? That's a good joke!'

'Let's settle down,' says Alex, opening a drawer, looking for Luisa's underwear.

'Enough of that, Alex,' Liesl shouts. 'It's just a tic afflicts you, but you are only tics.'

Franz says, soothing, 'We'll keep off the real bad books, you guys, and bad things, too. Just grumbles about bureaucracy, and keeping dodos flying – all that kind of thing. It's not all Wozzeck...' and we see that Damien's lost his patience.

'You freaks!' he cries. 'You want to spoil my fucking day! And you, my friend,' he bristles up at me, 'your stupid face, just turns from dire to dire, a weathercockup!'

'I'm not a scientist,' I say. 'I only know the tragedies where all are killed, then there's more scenes and acts, and bonhomie as well.'

'How can such idiots be?' says Damien and turns away from me.

'Have no fear, Damien,' Liesl says. 'We looked at the commies, their manifesto. Here, no one joins with anyone, your workers hate the rest, and elsewhere it is neighbour against neighbour. Forget that pistol shot – the system's absolutely safe....'

'You crazy!' Damien shouts. 'Listen to what you say! The system isn't safe. I'm it, and I should know.'

'Come now, Damien,' Alex says. 'We've just saved the world. Relax!'

'It's not enough,' says Damien, who sulks.

'More pizzas! We are on a plateau where we can agree,' says Franz. 'Of course, with the old emperor – we weren't so badly off. It wasn't the modern world, of course. There were ways it might have turned, and some who might be with us still....'

'That's crap, Franz,' Liesl says. 'You should read the book. It couldn't be. It wasn't. History's not pizza – you can't pick the good bits off and leave the crust.'

We laugh at that, Damien most of all.

'It all takes time, to work things through,' says Alex sagely. 'So long, you're often dead by when it's sorted out.'

'How about it, Liesl?' Damien says. 'You'd be the candidate, say everything you like. Forget the manifesto, though.'

Liesl sneers him down. 'It's against any of my principles. If only more were like me, and had some. Besides, Damien, you only want Luisa. She's too fresh for you.'

Franz kisses her: I see their throats working, one a chick getting its parent's food, regurgitated. Luisa stares at them, as if she'd like a half-digested spider too. I stretch out on the chair. I won't do publicity for them. 'Tired' means 'constipated' in adland. I think of Chloe, amid regurgitations, helping the juveniles down the beach, their first waddle.

I say to Luisa, 'This physicality, this being in the world – it'll be the death of us.'

'No physicality from me, my friend,' she whispers back, and between us – there's Damien's face, his ear.

'You Hungry-Austrians,' laughs Damien. 'It's all digestion and assimilation.... Just like Americans and pizza. I know all about it – Sissi and Kafka, Schweik, Hitler, all to the sound of music. Magnificent. We've nothing like it here.'

'You've got it wrong, Damien,' Luisa says. 'We're about the future, how the empire meets its destiny. Us.'

Damien shouts towards me, 'I want you, all of you, on my team. Tough times, you turkeys!' and he laughs, pulls Luisa on his knee, pinches her face as if it's on a biscuit box, him Santa. 'This guy,' he says, grabbing me, 'the best puffer there has ever been. I want him on my team. Alex here – he'll make our automobiles run on Coca Cola, just like God intended. But this guy,' me, that is, '– wow, a sentence is a zinger, every word a million sales!'

'Nevermore, dear Damien,' I say. 'If I can't sell myself, there's nothing left I want to sell.'

Damien slides his hands round Luisa's breasts, but goes on shouting about empires – the Brits, a tatty one, the Romans crumbling inch by inch and clan by clan. The Turks... Mostly they take a patch of thistles, scabby goats, and call it glory.... Germans, Russians – when it ends, you don't want what happens then.

'My empire, America,' Damien crows, 'will go in flame and malediction! I'll take them down with me – they touch one hair, one cell – and down we'll go together. Mine will be the last, the best and brightest. No sharing! No partners!'

He sings about the bombs, bursting in air – 'On land and sea!' he cries. 'Bombs and much much more.'

'Come, now,' says Franz, 'Let's be more systematic,' and Alex says, 'Yes, Damien, just hold on, some guy will come from State, calm things down, and set out all the details,' and I hear Luisa's splinter of a silver voice, 'My novels tell, foretell – all are tests, and some are quests,' but she is snagged in Damien's net, she leans back on him, and his hands go round and round.

'OK,' says Alex. 'It's all clear. It will go on like this for ever.'

'Till it ends,' Damien joins in, his mouth full of Luisa. 'And when it ends – everyone will know. After – there is nothing. Not little states, not socialism, no flags, no trumpets. Fire. Dust in the air. Dust in your mouth.'

'We should campaign,' says Liesl weakly, 'nonetheless.'

'We're in the spiders' nest,' says Franz. 'It's not just going in the door – it's finding the right room. Then – the right guy. The documents. The time. The space. Responsibility – or guilt.'

There, on the strip, the main drag, the trams go up and down, the red, the blue. They're like the row of ducks or Indian heads – and now the turbaned ones – that jiggle up and down in shooting booths.

'You're comfortable here,' Damien says, or asks. 'Even happy?'

'Oh yes!' we say, unthinking. It's the call of a gospel song, a call of the wild we're all trained to answer.

'You see,' says Damien, 'wherever you came from, we'd never send you back. It would be an offence against time, against history. We shipped so many here, it would be crass to send some back. We can put you in jail – that's what we do – for heavy terms. Now, your chains are made of gold. Remember, though – it needn't always be so....'

'I came from here,' says Luisa. 'Where'd you send me anyway, that you won't?'

I think of Chloe: you don't always have to be comfortable.

Damien puts an arm round me. 'And you, my friend. There's hardness here, you know. We live easy, but we're

35

hard. We're not scared, we know all about the end, how it comes to everyone. The good life... after, there could come the bad. Sacrifice. No – better end it all. Pre-emption. Courage from us, a blessing to the rest, outside, the ragged, wretched, who will never know the sweetness we'll have lost. You think – if you see it coming, you can duck. No! my friend. You, my precious jar, you came cracked from the kiln.' He turns to me. 'That's why you're good at puffing – to you it's lies, or stories. That's what you think! But – for us, it isn't lies, it's rhetoric. It's the plating on the rock.'

'It's bluster,' Liesl says. 'They made a movie – I remember. Bring it down with you, your temple. In life, the moment never comes, stuff goes on and on, it's bad, then good, then bad again. You never blow the dams, flood everything.'

'OK,' says Damien. 'You'll be the candidate?'

'I'm unsure,' says Liesl. 'Who'll vote for me, knowing they'll be sacrificed?'

'Oh well,' says Damien, having won, 'they're safer here than anywhere. But – there's bad guys all around, and inside too. You hope, you ride the tram – maybe it won't be your day.... And then there's Franz. We'll find a better guy....' Franz looks cast down, and Liesl rather less.

'It's indeterminacy,' Damien says, elbowing him in the kidney. 'Franz starts attacking from the dee-fence... it won't do. You don't get through the vestibule. Trouble with the doorman and the usher. It's a losing ploy.'

*

We leave them cogitating; Luisa says to me, 'It started off as sex – and now you don't seem keen. What're you after? My novels – they make them into movies, games. A line's enough: then, they make up the rest. Or I do. My fame's assured, my fortune's not.'

'My journey, Luisa,' I say. 'I have to finish it.'

'My birds!' she says. 'I have to settle them! Then you and I, we'll share a wave at least. See if it flattens on a shore.'

She takes the cages, opens them: scraps of unravelling wool, the beaks, the eyes – a flash. A fall.

'Can you imagine that!' she says, looking down into the street. 'They've forgotten what they do. They ought to fly! Look – one is clinging to a tram! How anomalous they were! It shows – you need to puff your muscles up, if you're a traveller.'

There's no wind, no direction. Luisa says, 'We should take Franz. Another hawk here – might finish him off.'

'He's a bodyguard,' I say. 'Let him guard his own.' It's like dragging an anchor, taking him along; lead in your shoe. But – to please her...

'OK,' I say, 'put him on board.'

'OK. No Franz,' she says. I've passed another of her tests. I'm quite indifferent.

'The shooting of the President,' Luisa asks. 'Does it spread bad things around, or is it expiation? '

'Oh,' I say, thinking of Damien, 'I'm sure if you wait long enough, it'll be both.'

'Fuck you,' says Luisa, holding my arm in friendly fashion, 'Your journey! Means you can't tell good from bad stuff.'

'It's true,' I say, 'I need a philosopher, like you, to make distinctions, as you say.'

'I didn't say,' she shouts, 'You cretin. Journeys are like that, you wander in the good and bad. That is the fun!'

We don't talk about the President. We've covered the whole case.

She looks hard at me. 'You look as if you suffer. You're an idiot, and anyone can suffer, but – it's what you do.'

'It's all vicarious,' I say. 'The suffering. It's like you watch a movie, maybe in Hungarian, and all the characters look the same, you don't understand a word, a scene, and then it rains, quite heavily, on the screen. and then you go outside, it's pouring, and there's lightning.'

'No, no,' she says. 'You have to duck and dodge. Be tricky.'

'If it rains,' I say. 'That doesn't work. It just comes down. No, best tell the truth – that way, they'll know you're hiding what's important.'

'What's important... is what we'll get,' says Luisa, pushing me on the red tram, 'Cash. Now.'

We pass the court, a higher court, the mint, on and on.

The casino.

'It's animal snap, no harder,' says Luisa. We win large sums. 'Of course,' she says. 'I'm lucky. I don't make a song of it.'

The Indian on the door says, 'Don't come back.'

It's not his cash. I tell him. 'I'm with the Indians. In their history, at least.'

'Come on,' Luisa says. 'Don't use that word. Liesl – she can be top person. Isn't she terrible? Tiredness!'

'Yes,' I say.

'We'll sleep for ever. Someone will take a shot at her. If not me, then Franz. Your friend Damien – he won't do it, see his wrists a-tremble! I can do it, I'm lucky, as you've seen. Winning's awfully easy, hitting the spot. But – it's a question of blood – mine, not hers.'

I don't want to be involved. 'What would that accomplish? Banality....' I say.

'It would do a lot – if that's what accomplishing means. But – she's my sister. Anyway, Pandora's vase is probably empty. Don't you think the future is a corridor, you have to unlock the doors along the way, and down the middle too.... Let the people out?'

'You sound like one of your pieces, your cuts,' I say.

She laughs. 'See! It's all happened, and yet it still scares you, even to talk of it – you're afraid of jail... and afraid too –

more – of everything coming down. The guy behind us in the tram, the Archduke....'

'It's speculations,' I say, uneasily.

'Oh,' she says. '"Never exclude anything" is my motto. I'm Tosca. *Vissi d'arte*. I lived for art, and then I didn't.'

'I doesn't fit with Franz,' I say.

'No, it doesn't,' she says, quite angry. 'You need a mind to start with, if you never make it up. But guys like him – they have a pistol, it makes an impression on a girl.'

'To make an interesting killer of him would take a lot of work,' I say.

'That's what plots are for,' she says. 'And don't think of a life of conservation with Chloe. I have your future at heart. Don't do it. Never look back and think you're going forward. You may have qualities – no one cares. They're interested in the monsters and the spells. Work on yourself. Be a drama. Murderers abound. Think of something different, that's not involved with animals.' She pauses. 'Franz can ride shotgun for us. And Liesl will be cancelled only if she is a candidate...'

'My!' I say, 'you're ancient, Luisa. Straight from the death-house. Franz – a butler, probably a pig. Liesl, the first Austro-Hungarian President in all of time!'

'We're not really from...' Luisa starts.

'I don't care what you're not – that's infinite,' I say. 'It's what you are....'

'Aha....' she chimes along. 'I'm lucky, but I'm not going back to the casino.'

'Why ever not?' I ask.

'You must keep mastery,' she says. 'Those games – there's only money if you win, only nothing if you don't.'

'You'll find a sponsor, a tycoon?' I ask.

'This tycoon guy,' she says. 'He has a palace, in midtown. Above the door, it says "the best available". It's true. That's what we have. You can't do much about that. This guy – he buys up islands.'

Oh no! I think. *We've hit the tracks that take us down to Chloe.* 'And then?' I say. 'It's golf?'

'He puts his people in. It's sanctuary. He brings in animals that eat the ones that's there – they're all close to extinction, so there's nothing lost.'

'You've seen this guy?' I ask. 'And tapped his source?'

'He's busy,' says Luisa. 'Criminals are, that's how you know. The honest guys, just sit around and clean their muskets. So far, I've done the front steps, and I've seen a desk, inside.'

'That's mastery?' I ask. 'How?'

'Oh, it's the start,' she says. 'When you're in the palace, you can make your spiel, the money comes, the secrets too....'

'It's a delusion, I'm afraid,' I say. 'It's not at all like that: to get your trial, your crime must equal theirs, or they won't recognise it. To enter palaces, you must bring cash that's equal to what they've got inside – and secrets too.'

There's a pause. 'Well,' she says, 'I won't use my luck. Where do your wits help you? Mastery?'

'Oh no,' I say. 'You have to close that out. You shut your eyes, your ears, your nose, and you don't say a word.'

'You made your cash with sentences,' she says, delightedly, scoring a point.

'They didn't mean a thing, Luisa.' I say, assured.

We see Liesl, making her ploy on television: behind her, there is Franz, frogs on his tunic, a musket on his knee. Liesl's talking about empires, and such. 'No, no,' she says, 'it all fell down, but not because of different sorts of people – no, not too many people, too many emperors.'

I ask Damien, 'Is that the right message?'

'Oh, she doesn't connect – but she talks. That's good,' he says. 'They're all watching Franz with his musket, anyway. They remember the picture – spirit of '76. All mercenaries.'

He pauses. 'Remember when we first knew each other. Do you still do drugs? You're still liable, I'm sure, for prosecution – but no one's worrying, I bet. I'll help you out, of course.'

'That wasn't me,' I say. 'Damien – you can be trivial. Luisa's looking to put cash behind us. I'm not sure why.'

'She sees you as her opposite, I guess,' he says. 'It's like me and Alex. I act, he puts the numbers on. She goes up the steps, you cross the road, pull down your hood.'

'Shall we spend our cash, before the end?' I ask.

He laughs. 'It's like your journey. Your journey's into Luisa.'

Can that be so?

He holds me close, and preaches – 'We live a life the best there is, even those with squalid lives – they must think "It won't get any better, this is the best." All people want is passports and a crutch. That we can give. As for the cash – spend, spend, my profligate friend! You must be yourself, just once, before it ends,' and he joshes around.

*

The cottonfields have been ploughed in. 'Let's take the tram, go and drink the green-wine,' Luisa says. 'The vineyards come right up to the city walls.'

'We need more cash,' I say. Luisa says,

'I've put my luck away. It's not fair to use it. On the unluckies. But if I could, I'd buy a golden tree. That's our civilisation – the Romans used it in their orgies, you can make crosses from it, and under its branches, elders gather, decide on war and peace.'

'Have your joke, Luisa,' I say.

'You bet!' she says. 'I love stories that's all about consciousness, really, or filial love. If you can make that out. Behind the words, there's a procession, flagellants, perhaps, or guys with bull masks. You must peer to spot the shuffling. Anyway, if you ask, I'll tell you my story – "I was trafficked and my new father beat me." There! No more curiosity, no more questions. My sister will be President, or dead. My former lover – martyred. Think of the movies – the stars already buffing up their shine, trying to learn their lines. This, my dear, is big time – not the little dusty stuff you wear, the watch that doesn't watch, or time unheeded, lingering on your mantel. Not "ticktock" time – it's "dingdong". Damien's kind. Bells that rock the towers.'

'Have you seen your tycoon?' I ask.

'Nearly,' she says. 'I've lost the taste. He's infantile. He collects big toys. Towers, he makes with blocks. You need to be infantile as well, to knock them down with aeroplanes. I never had a nursery, but that is what you do, it happens there.'

'So, you've escaped from that as well,' I say. I'm not close enough to grasp it all.

She turns on me. 'Your suffering! It isn't worth! You suffer because you are a narcissist....' she laughs, she even screams, a small one.

'Luisa,' I say. 'It's you who saw all this, now the view has changed, you want to change your style. I'm quite detached. I wait.'

'Listen! "'It's a remarkable piece of apparatus', said the officer to the explorer...." I can't send that, though. There's so much apparatus now, but none of it makes you happy.'

'It's not supposed to,' I say. 'And now almost everyone's an officer.'

'But you're not an explorer, though you might like to be,' she says, laughing. 'You're just one of everyone on the ship, and they're boring holes in the bottom. Will it sink? Will they find gasoline? You know – the waiting is a torment. You half grasp how it's going to end. They've told us too much about all that. The tunnel, the light – and then you don't come back. No one does. All wasted.'

'Everyone uses torture now,' I say. 'You must clench your teeth.'

'Oh, I want to resist,' she says. 'But I don't know the way.'

'I resist all the time,' I say. 'I just don't make a song about it.'

'If there's no song, it doesn't count,' she says. I think it's true. 'You could write cabaret songs,' she says.

'It would be a challenge,' I agree.

'Jack you up from one-liners,' Luisa says. 'Even if there's no way to perform.'

*

Damien says, 'We've become like all the people we once patronised. The guys who've come are just like us, and we are just like them. The aphids have no more juice. The workers – they won't unite – whoever thought they might? It's bosses who are all the same.'

Then Alex brings the news....

'Franz – stuck like a pig. A sight you thought you'd never see.'

'They used to go to India for that – the kings and queens – you must have seen the movie, where the empress Vicky touts a spear and runs into the underbrush after porkers,' says Damien, trying to shield us from the scene. 'The squealing – unforgettable.'

'Franz,' says Luisa, 'was the slowest of us all. He never could conclude, get to the bottom.'

'Well,' says Damien, not trying to resist the quip – 'Someone has got to his!'

We laugh, we smile, if you must die, it's best not be ridiculous. I say, 'The guy – shot on the trolley, streetcar, whatever you guys call a tram – now Franz, the pig....'

'It must be symbolism, or an allegory,' Luisa says, trying to raise a tear. 'My writing's all about that. His was an imperial end,' and so we laugh some more. Poor Franz, his comic turn's a marvel, but he can't enjoy.

'It's all political,' says Damien, 'but it doesn't seem to signify.'

It's embarrassing for sure, to Liesl. 'I hope an end so decadent is not in wait for me,' she says. 'He in his tunic too, the musket... But I'm a good soldier, so I mustn't cry.'

'Of course you can,' says Damien, twirling a long pistol round his thumb. 'We're all behind you....'

'And of course, the idea comes to all of us.... Franz, was a person with few skills,' says Alex. 'Maybe he wasn't stuck. Manoeuvring his arm, maybe he fell from friendly fire....'

'Not friendly – incestuous!' says Damien, brightening. 'Of course – that's why he had what seemed an apple in his mouth! Instead – it was the musket ball.'

'If it's not imperial vendetta,' says Luisa. 'There's a message there....' What might it be? Not she, not we, can tell.

'....all in all,' there's Damien's voice, thin as a spider's lifeline, from deep inside his skull, 'it's better if Franz was murdered. Especially as we won't waste our time, looking for a killer.'

'It's a relief all round,' says Liesl, 'and you promised me another partner – more feminine, a uniform more up-to-date... a weapon with a safety catch.'

This was not the pistol shot we've all been waiting for.

'I've many candidates that run,' says Damien. 'They're my horses. Liesl – she's the one I'd back.'

He hums, from the White Horse Inn. 'To make you feel at home,' he laughs.

'Damien – we're not from—' Liesl begins.

'Not on horse? Nor grass? So I should hope – it's just the music, the hussars, those tight pants, the cavalcades – the little caps remembered from the toffee ads... the polka, the waltz, "um pom pom" – it reassures. It's oldtime schlock, that's true, but my! it pacifies. Krems white – there's nothing like so pure, so candid, white as cream... The Danube, greasy, grey-green – yes, it brings a tear, it twirls. It puts you back on track again.'

'Damien, you're wrong,' says Alex. 'If it all goes down, we're done for; so you needn't plan to blow the dams, bring down the roof....'

'That's sheer bureaucracy,' shouts Damien. 'What I fear is victory followed by decline. That's what they say – don't fear the death, fear the preliminaries. Defeat and retribution. Peace and penury. No leader doesn't think like this.'

*

Later, I say to Luisa, 'This is all too hectic. I should resume my journey. That way, you can think, reflect. I still don't know if you come too. Damien – he's so volatile, so close to one, a skin. He seems to do diplomacy, the rite of passage too. That deathbed – it raises questions I can't answer.'

She says, 'I'm lucky, but with cards and things. Fortune has its limits. The official record – I don't question it, and nor should you. It's better not to make a fuss – and after all, you were there. Just keep things to yourself.'

'This is the happy land, or so we're told,' I say. 'And yet – I need to leave. It's not just fear, an end like Franz....'

'Franz kept diaries,' Luisa says. 'He didn't find his happiness. It was not his happy land. He couldn't understand, how everything was fitted tight together, and quite impenetrable to him. He was ambitious, pretentious too. He never reached first base.'

'Does that mean you'll come with me?' I ask. 'I need the cash. I won't impose on you.'

'I'll bet you won't,' she says.

I don't want to have her with me, yet I find the question, invitation, quite obligatory, pressing.

'Liesl has some unique features,' I say, 'a depth, an irony. Curl of the lip. You'd see her portrait on a stamp—'

'You're quite delirious,' Luisa laughs. 'They don't use stamps any more! They'll fit her out with personality, if she's a winner. If not – back in the drawer.'

She looks at her screen: perhaps she's transcribed Franz's diary. It should sell, if they describe his death.

'What's lacking,' she says, 'is desire. In you, in Franz. That's what Damien has, and it's unsettled you. He wants to win. He wants democracy for everyone. So does Alex, but I'm less sure for him.'

'Are you sure at all?' I ask. 'They don't strike me as you say, though, yes, desire is there. The issue is so wobbly. There's Aristotle....'

'Crap!' she says, 'Though I must say, Franz never got that far into the philosophy. He had his values, that's for sure, but mostly he let others puzzle him. He was all by inference. And, service before everything; he expected it of others, not himself. And my! How he deferred. He let them make an idiot of him. Start to finish.'

Suddenly, it strikes me – 'Perhaps he sacrificed himself for Liesl!'

'Could he have been so foolish'? asks Luisa. 'It's as plausible as someone shooting you in the eye. You seem perplexed. If we had sex – would you know me better, after?'

'Once I would say "yes",' I say. We leave it there.

*

'Hostilities have broken out,' says Damien. 'On a smaller scale, and not where I expected.'

'Leave it to Liesl,' says Luisa crossly.

'It's not her province,' Damien says. 'Besides, she's always with the makeup people.'

'Forget it then,' Luisa says.

'I've done the diplomatic stuff, and sent my guys....' says Damien, seeming uncertain.

'Listen!' says Luisa. 'It's Franz's diary. Not day by day: more intimate.' She reads out:

*'I knew nothing of the country. I was there because of
the architecture. Making my way by train, one day,
when it was very hot – we broke down, in the middle of
wild country. Everybody left the train, and started
singing to guitars, picnicking and such, and even in the
bushes, making love. I thought it was bucolic, but after,
I was told they were afraid another train might come
along the track and crash right into the one stationary
and broken down. A guy I'd never seen before – he must
have seen I was young, a student and a foreigner –
started to tell me what the place was really like. The
arrests, the punishments, the monuments built by
political prisoners... the vendettas from the civil wars..
The spies, complicity, indifference of other powers, the
poverty.... And on he went, with passion. After some
hours, another engine came and hauled us onward.*

*'I never questioned, until recently, if he had other
motives: a provocateur, a propagandist. Even fantasies.
No, I was quite convinced. I have been ever since. I've
always helped in what way I could, the armed
resistance, in whatever strategy they undertook....'*

'Yes,' says Damien, 'I'm sure they'd publish that, if you don't say you wrote it, dear Luisa.'

'There's problems, Damien, says Luisa, 'Liesl, Franz – now me.'

'Face it down, face it down,' shouts Damien. 'We're over there of course, the shooting – I must decide which side we're on.'

Luisa insists. 'I'm pressured by a gang. They say if I don't lend my luck and win them cash, they'll kidnap me, and do me bad!'

'Go, go with them,' says Damien, flustered. 'Where's the harm to you?'

She isn't satisfied. She says to me, 'I have to stop you ending up with Chloe – for both your sakes. I see you think the world is tipping down that way – it's an illusion. The world is round, it's true, but you can float on it as if it's flat.'

I say, 'And then there's Franz – transformed, ambiguous,' and Alex says there'd be a file on him, but no one knows his second name.

The little war goes on.

Luisa lends the gang her luck, and plays the wheel. 'How did it go?' I ask.

'Not well. For them. They understood. They are intentionalists: they said you must intend the good, so if I had misgivings, it was quite involuntary, losing all their stake. I win, when I intend what's good for me. But when it's them.....'

'I understand!' I say. 'They seem sophisticates.'

'Oh yes,' she says, 'But what they intend is not the good. At least – not mine.'

'Oh face it down,' shouts Damien, flustered, and impatient. 'These little wars give me no clue. It's not the big one, but they grow and grow. Liesl would resolve the impasse. No one wants to vote for someone from their minority now. We know our knaves too well. You need a chief that's anodyne. Liesl's from a cartoon town, all day they sing, hotel rooms are taken by the quarter hour. She's safe, she's dull – spun sugar on a sugar stick.'

'Damien, Liesl's not from....' Luisa says.

'I don't care if like Franz she is a terrorist – no one will ask which side she's on. That is for me to puzzle out,' says Damien, pacing.

We are at war again. It is the price we pay. At least we're safe. Everyone has sex again.

'Oh no! Not with Alex! Luisa – you sink beneath yourself,' I say.

'I'll not stop sex because you're squeamish, and besides, Alex has contacts. Helps me place my stuff. Calm down. Jealousy is off the map. It's narcissism. No philosophy!' she says.

'Alex is all sniff and snort,' I say.

'It's so,' she says.

'Jealousy is in our species. Even God was jealous. Territory, our thoughts – we won't give them up. Vendetta, justice – it's all jealousy. It is the bubbling pot of glue that stops the drift. Without our jealousy, we would meld into the trees, the animals. Swans are monogamous, we are not – we're jealous, all our lives. Cry of the wild, the recognition...' And I go on and on.

'Are those your sentences?' she asks. 'That you were paid for? That you now regurgitate? What was the best?'

'Oh, I guess the best – bearing in mind we don't do ads for stuff.... It isn't "buy this auto", it's more plangent, poetry, almost – my best is "All I want from you is you".'

She has no comment. 'This new war. You stir guys up – even the little ones – they'll gnaw your kneecaps. You fall down.'

'That's just my point,' I say.

'Franz had an answer.'

'I could be Liesl's consort. Now the job is vacant, I could fit.'

'No, no, you have to find your destiny,' Luisa says. 'That's what we're working on. If you travel to that island... you're a violent type. They'll cut you up. Machetes – you won't have a chance. And Chloe – the name smells of unwanted sacrifice. More narcissism. As for you – you're marinated in the stuff.'

'You live by making stories, Luisa,' I say. 'Or by passing off. Promoting the good, classifying the bad. What will Damien do next? That's a crux. In you, there is no story.'

'Yes there is,' she says. 'Lots. It's "if you conquer me". It's "who the one-eyed giant was, sitting behind us in the tram". It's "who stuck Franz?" "How will we win this war?" And now – you and Liesl.... Think! – if there's a romance between you two, what a story! Children, abounding, in blue satin. Chloe seeking revenge – another shot is fired: bathos to pathos in a twink.'

'I can see myself in this,' I say. 'But – the guy on the tram, the giant. He looked just an ordinary shortie.'

'You too must grow,' Luisa says. 'If you want to make people's day and ride in the parade. The limousine.'

'Then, there's the war,' I say. 'But that's been done, hashed over.'

*

'There was this beautiful forest,' Luisa says. 'They made a movie – the snails, the lynxes. Bisons, trees venerable, with names and birthdays. Then it all burned down. All, everyone and everything.'

'They build up again,' I say. I'm at a loss.

Being Liesl's partner, morganatic, as they say – to me, it's squalor, supreme.

'No,' Luisa says. 'They built an airport. Then all the things that go around them – hotels and such. They couldn't wait for all those trees! We shouldn't blame them. It's not our place.'

'It's like what Damien says,' I say. '"Those guys, experts – they talk of galaxies and spaces, holes, and endless voyages, where lights don't shine, you meet your likeness coming back from wandering the stars, he's old a thousand years – and... they got us to believe all that! Incredible that we're convinced by the incredible."'

'That's not it at all,' she says. 'Being hunted, a beast, before the forest burns. It feels horrible, although you know you'll turn and gore and peck them. It's things slow and predictable, they rot you. I'm for the incredible.'

'Alex doesn't seem the hunter kind,' I say.

'No,' she says. 'That's the best thing in him.'

'I guess it's good there's things quite unbelievable that we believe, and that we know what they're supposed to be,' I say.

'It takes away the fun,' she says. 'Knowing things come around. As if the murderers were little kids, who didn't know how it has all been done before.'

'That's good and wholesome, Luisa,' I say. 'Not like you at all.'

'Oh,' she says. 'I don't much care, unless it's done to me. But then – it's done to everyone, just sitting in the tram. To get somewhere, that's what you have to do – just sit.'

We've neglected Liesl. There she is, learning her lines, the good cop.

'Have I changed?' she asks. 'There is this other voice I learn – it's not like theatre, this is in your chest at every moment, with sentiments you'd not have dreamed.'

'Have you seen the mafia?' asks Luisa. 'Once, there was a principle, some guy lay in wait, and as your carriage reached the turn, it stopped – the new route... No reversing gear and so – out flashed the history.... But now, it's all done at long range. Almost all the deeds are organised by them, the clan....' She must have read it in a book.

Liesl says, 'Oh, here, people come and go. They have their photos took with me. Damien protects, of course. I've had to learn the countries' names, and other stuff.'

They sit her in a chair, her hair is done in bows. 'She'll never ride the tram again,' Luisa says.

*

Big stories are written many times. Big cities – are often conquered. Maybe I conquered Luisa. It didn't show. We'd drunk the green-wine, took off our brakes....

'The days of humanism are done,' says Damien. 'Trench war, revolutions – firing the first shot. All done with. The question is – a candidate is killed – election for the replacement is assured. But suppose – the candidate's elected, shot ... and then your hand is free. You may proceed. Which way?'

'Posthumanism's tough,' Luisa agrees. 'Before, a death could be explained. God was behind them – almost all. That was a consolation... now, the giant, the militant – they're embalmed. You have to wait. An endless autopsy, what they died for, and from.'

Damien hops up and down:

'It's all been done before. Campaigns that shape and break – there's Liesl, perhaps hers the face that inspired the wooden horse.... Can it be done again? Deciding accidents, managing the chance, the luck. And shall we win? Or will this be the end? Then, where do I go, when it is done?'

We know that crime transforms – confirms the agent, sets adrift the victims to find their landfalls. Is it before us, here and now?

Damien says, 'There are no contracts out. But I do have friends – all have their principles, convictions. Often in conflict. From their diverging passions, Liesl is perhaps.... not entirely guaranteed.'

'Damien, you've taken all her qualities,' Luisa says. 'You've emptied her right out.'

'She's malleable, that's true,' says Damien, flattered. 'That aspect's now reduced in size. The problem is – you fold, you raise, but in the end you lose. And that can't be the end....'

'Goddam it, Damien,' Luisa shouts, 'Then blow the dams, bring down the roof. Show some decision, idiot!'

'Enough,' screams Damien. 'I've burdens! Liesl can't count the dance. And worse – Alex makes trouble. He's stuck into some feisty chick – he crows and preens, he wants to take command from me....'

Luisa whispers to me, 'My last lines, Alex saw my screen: "Nobody could sleep. When morning came, assault craft would be lowered, and a first wave of troops...." Alex identifies. He thinks himself a warrior—'

'Maybe you should rest your literature,' I say. 'It spills.'

'Alex doesn't understand,' says Damien. 'He wants control. You don't direct a war, you place your chips on winning squares. The one who has most chips, most stuff to play, will win. It's mathematics. Alex thinks he has a lucky hand, lurking up his sleeve. This woman, that he thinks he's with. But – it isn't so. He wins who has the most to stake and lose. Or she.'

'I'm sure that must be us,' says Liesl. Her eyes are off in distant lands, her body slumps.

'Codeine. The housewife's friend,' Damien explains. 'Don't quote. It is the truth.'

Liesl smiles. 'Damien,' she says. 'Tell me when it's done.'

He ignores her. 'What concerns me,' he says, 'is the fallout. It reaches all of us, and this is not the big one, this war. War, my dears, is just my metaphor. Everything is that. It's why Liesl doesn't hold a man, she couldn't save that Franz. It's why you—' he points at me '—can't hold a job. One-liners for the President's the most you'll ever do, and not be credited. It's clear, the big one, my revenge, is yet to come, that's why you're here and listening. Everything goes on, until it stops, and then you'll know. Or, rather, not.'

Luisa says, 'This fallout, Damien. Put sleeves, put overcoats, on your munitions. Keep the dust, smoke, from our eyes.'

'Oh, it's not that kind,' he says. 'By fallout – I mean people. They run. They come to where you are. Or try. There's millions. Not so honest, some of them. Some throw stones.'

It's clear. Where shall we run to?

'Liesl can't stay,' says Damien. 'She'll be suborned.'

He holds the briefcase, presidential, ticktock it goes, and flashes red and violet. Destiny all quiet inside, it's just a clock for now...

'I won't stay where Alex is,' Luisa whispers. 'The goddam tram! I'm with the mighty, it appears, and all I wanted was a ride.... A coupla stops. My novels. And now there's Alex, girt with his epic....'

'You Austrians!' Damien says. 'When it all went down – you went on quite a spree! Those bomb shelters – marvellous! An inspiration. The firing from the Engels Hof... and all the rest. Most of it unmentionable – but it's a message for us all. The music stops – you're done for, there's no second chance.... All suffer from the end of empires, it goes on and on, implodes, explodes, like stars that wander....'

'Damien!' shouts Liesl. 'We're not your fantasy. We're people from the street, we have no history, we don't want none....'

Damien looks hurt. 'Doubts, doubts, Liesl, my Liebelei. It's finished over there. Austria. Franz K, Franz Josef, just Franz – poor, martyred. We have to fix the ending over here, is all.'

'"When the end of the world comes, I want to be living in retirement" – there, Damien, there's an Austrian saying for you,' says Luisa, throwing her bright screen to a corner of the room, 'There's one-liners that made up a whole philosophy.'

'You gals,' says Damien, 'Should forget your colour – or make the most of it. When you're in the eye, you must assert yourselves. You're only partly black when you're a candidate. That is the process. Honour it!'

The eye... I feel the glass break, shards of ice... I feel the spear, the musket ball – just at the beginning of its journey. Stopped by the teeth. 'The touch of the unknown' – they say. Terrifying.

Damien grips my arm. 'The storm's demoralised the rest. You are our guide. You are the one, your qualities untouched, unknown. Ferry us to Africa, if you must, to Croatia.

Wherever that may be. Take us to that safe port, with beauties on the sand.'

'Yes, great man!' Luisa chirps. 'You never show your hand, or where you are. Now is your chance. Lead us, take us by our arm, raise your sail, and bring us safe beyond the waves.'

'Franz – you remember him?' asks Damien. 'I have good news. Or bad. We know who killed him. One of ours – I'll bet. Which side was Franz on? I shall have to guess. And why he met his end.... The praise or blame I'll shift to Alex, if I must.... the blame or praise, to me.'

Liesl sobs. 'It seems a mystery....' and Damien says, quite stern:

'It always is, when you try something complicated, and don't explain yourself.'

'Goddam it, Damien,' Liesl shouts. 'Don't be such a fucking statesman. Who killed my love, my lover?'

'I'll be straight with you, Liesl,' Damien says. 'I don't know exactly who. Besides, it doesn't matter. A name....it may be sacred, just as Luisa says, but it won't mean a stuff to you.' We see he's right. 'Now,' he goes on, 'This case, the doomsday case. Alas, I left the key behind. Let's just see how it works....'

'Here, Damien – this rock will smash the lock,' Luisa say. 'I wonder if it works from here. All those airmen, sweating in their cots... released like spores... Maybe a little try....'

'You go right to the highest point, Luisa,' Damien says, impressed. 'No reticence. That's what I most admire. Alex has the key, but – with this rock I'll force the lock! There – it's quite Wagnerian, a couplet.... but we won't, of course, won't explode the world. Not just yet.'

'Luisa,' I say, 'You're drawn to the extremes.'

'Yes,' she says. 'It's the only thing I know. I have the vision – what the guys who wrote those stories didn't have. They are like divers, waiting for their panic to die down, then they drop. You wait, the preparations long, they set the scene, the characters – then plop! It's over. I jump at once, plane down, it seems a lifetime, sometimes more.... Don't you know me?'

'I guess not, Luisa. But the vision – yes! The fear is tedious, so, to see you glide, as if you'll never hit....' I say.

'The air, the sweetness. Can't you feel it?' asks Luisa. 'Just once, that is enough.'

'You people,' Liesl says, still weeping, 'You're the best. So close, so understanding. I'd let you take me anywhere....'

Oh no, I think, not Chloe's island, fighting to make our space. Damien with his terrible weapon that only he can activate....

'If you are interested,' Damien says, holding a shell, or something like, up to his ear, 'The guy who shot the guy, there, on the tram. The story is – he wasn't one of ours. Not one, not t'other. Strangers, a strange guy, is all.'

*

'Well,' says Luisa. 'Here we are, on a freighter. No sails. Looking for an island. A refuge, full of friends. All friends on board, Liesl, me, and you, our questing guide. And Damien, the end of the world, chained to his wrist. The sea goes up and down. Liesls's in charge of the gramophone – she puts on a disc – "Last Man Standing Blues". To eat, there's beans. The mysteries – Franz, the giant guy, my sex life – all revealed, then endlessly discussed.'

'Yes, Luisa,' Damien says. 'That's pretty much the scene. You've left out our philosophies, but I guess that those don't show. You haven't said how most old emperors – they start to let things slip and slide. Then – how it does drag on – the rump, the court retreats, frequents Biarritz. Pretenders. Secession. Movies about Sissi. The last tsarina. Austro-Hungary – the rump. Luisa! You should say we don't want all that.'

We wade ashore. The island is unnamed, or so the captain says. Uncertain its sacrality.

Liesl complains. 'Once, I'd an opinion about everything. Now, there is nothing to be said. How fugitive is fame!' and she sits on a dune to meditate.

There's rust-brown boxes, those containers, on the shore, a line of palms, and stumps behind. A sign says 'Keep out'. There's a pit for 'Parking'. The sun on the containers dances like bees before the hive – I guess there's more activity inside.

Chloe, of course. She says, 'I knew you'd come. But – I've another boyfriend – off hunting in the wood.'

I stroke her neck – 'That's quite alright. It's long, your neck, but you are not a swan. Go forth, and do not multiply....' I say. What a relief.

'Swan?' she asks. 'There's no swans roosting here.' It's true – there's scraps of red and blue that squawk, no swans.

'A little joke,' I say.

'Well, no jokes here. It's serious. The guy that owns us – he has plans. An airport, the stuff that goes around....' She waves at the void.

And there he is, a sun hat on a cube, curved hairy legs. Just as you'd think. Luisa's tycoon.

'Here is Augusto, he's from Rome, just as you'd think,' says Chloe. 'He buys islands, thinks of a way to join them up... an airport archipelago.'

Augusto sums us up. Damien's a puzzle: he conceals the case that one day will launch the thousand rockets, tip the airmen from their cots.

'Aha!' Augusto says. 'It's clear, the guy with the case: an emissary from the Empire. Surely, we can do some deal.'

Damien's unsure. 'What is your plan?' he asks. 'How do you get the cash? The islands...?'

Augusto says, 'Sea empires fail, because the filaments are vulnerable. Land empires fail – access by soldiers of the other sides is all too simple. So – buy lots of islands – there's no centre, and no ships. Each lives by itself. And is as uninviting as all this....' and he waves a hand around.

'I understand all that,' says Damien. 'And about the tourists and your dodgy friends who come to languish on the sand. The cash. That is what interests me.'

'The first one, the first island that you buy, is collateral for the next, which then becomes... and on and on,' Augusto says.

Liesl sits up. 'Collateral Campaign! It said how Austria was not the centre of the world, eternal, proof against all wars. We've come so far, and here it is, reborn and vigorous. Our small campaign!'

Augusto doesn't follow her. Luisa says, 'No, no, Liesl, that was in some ancient book, it's not the same at all,' and Damien keeps the briefcase out of sight. 'It's quite an empire you have here,' he says.

'He gives us passports,' Chloe says. 'But we don't want to leave. We're waiting for our villas to be ready.'

'Where would the airplanes land?' asks Damien.

'Oh,' Augusto says, 'a platform in the sea, of course.'

Chloe's arms – they used to be a feature – now, they're brown and lumpy. 'We had to saw the palms,' she says, 'to get the coconuts.'

'It's not at all like home,' says Liesl, 'with trams and everything.'

'My inventions!' says Luisa. 'I threw away my screen!'

'We shall transmit from here,' says Damien. 'We'll open up the case, and I shall send my planes to win the war. Surprise. That's a prime element. The suspects muster with some guys – and I'll have kept a tab on them. Down comes the unexpected parcel – there's your worst day! In safety here, I'll send them out, rockets, my mosquitoes, dragonflies... see how they hum and sting! And win the war. Alex – he'll be so mad!'

'This here is near the centre of the world,' Augusto says. 'It's near to Africa – most people will be living there by when we're dead. And so, you guys – the hospital's not built here yet, so each of you should sign a sheet that makes you guardian of all the rest, for when the moment comes, you're given up, your friend will sign "ok", we put the sad and moribund wrapped, in a canoe – into the waves. No graveyards here! For they depress, and damage real estate.... Besides, our new religion tells us so....'

There's too much to take in, we sign the form. There's no prison and no court, so we feel free, responsible for what we want to do.

'That about the real estate – that was a joke – you don't need laugh,' Augusto says.

'This here is like where me and Luisa started out,' says Liesl, 'though the accommodation was a step up there....'

*

'What do we do here, Chloe?' I ask. 'We each had reasons for leaving where we were, but movement and arriving cancels it all out.'

'Yes,' she says. 'So does standing still. What we do – we forage. Then, we'll build.'

'Your guy?' I ask, quite delicately.

'Giorgio? I try to make him good. What else is there?' she asks.

'Is that the new religion, then? You're all martyrs?' I say.

'Beware, or you'll be one as well.'

'The animals?' I ask. That's why she's here.

'Nothing to do. What do you expect – they look after themselves. They always have,' she says.

It's true.

'Giorgio,' she goes on, 'He suffers terribly. He used to deal, and now he'd drink. But there's no bar, no alcohol.'

'That's good. It's easy to look after him. I hope....'

'He does the same for me?' asks Chloe. 'If there were cliffs, I'd cast myself down to the wrinkling sea.'

She talks of the bizarre crimes, the only ones they're left with here. Assaults on trees, thieving things and burying them.

We each must choose a partner, a container, those of us who've just arrived.

'I'm with Damien,' Luisa says, scuttling away. 'He has my screen....' and she is gone.

'And I'm with Franz – it is the custom here, living with those defunct,' says Liesl, barring her iron door.

I won't share with a stranger. In the sand, it's cool. I stretch out, the waves sound like an air conditioner. I sleep.

Luisa says she'll help to build casinos. 'We'll just play for chips,' she says. Liesl says she'll lead the opposition, start a collateral campaign, 'frustrating the imperial plans Augusto has outlined'.

Is this my destiny? Is this the end?

Augusto says to me, 'You look a higher kind of guy. The species throws up now and then a higher sample. And I don't trust that Service type – Damien, cuffed to his light-up overnight.... Trust me, though. You mustn't think there is some scam. It's slow, is all.'

He separates me from the rest, pushes me on and on; the sand, the scrub, the parrakeets...

His yacht is long and grey. There's everything – a dolphin pool, some anti-missile masts, chef in a piecrust hat.

'It's a submergible, of course,' he says. 'If you should wish, you can escape....'

'My destiny was here,' I say. 'This awful place, hotter than some hells. But... why should you offer me this way out?'

'Oh well,' he says, 'in every tale there is an innocent, made fun of, secretly; one who seeks justice, even power, despite the obstacles.... And after travails, he or she succeeds, shows mercy, wisdom, lives long, dies pig rich....'

'I never heard all this,' I say. 'It never happened to an innocent. Forget the power and glory, just to escape would be enough....'

'Oh no,' Augusto laughs, 'it doesn't work at all like that. I don't offer you escape. This isn't free-ride time. You're innocent, not stupid or naive. To ride, you need a ticket, just like on the tram. And avoid a seat that's near the window – trust the driver, and the tracks.'

I'm unconvinced. To humour both of us, I say, 'These islands – dotted round, left devastate, until it's time to make an empire of the chain – it all sounds fine. But....' and I tell him about Damien. 'If he loses, he'll blow up everything....'

'I have another plan,' Augusto says. 'If we must survive our end, we humans.... Forget the crap of an escape to distant planetary dominions – I'd take my boat down, down to the deepest trench. And wait. Then, I have in mind – to slip quite gradually, acclimatise.... Into the wine dark, the familiar, amniotic sea. Perhaps grow scales. Start it all over. In a while, crawl up onto the land, when it's cooled down. Hunt lizards. Bond with males. All that.'

'It's for the long term, that is sure,' I say.

'Don't tell the others,' says Augusto. 'Damien holds the end, and we, we two, the new beginning.'

'Morally,' I say, 'I ought to tell Luisa. Who will confide in Liesl. Chloe too—'

'No, no,' Augusto says. 'Luisa lives by fictions. Our idea will end in print. We shall be targeted.'

It's true. It's quite decisive.

Of course, I tell Luisa – who resists being in print?

She says, 'I'm just a writer. You're a reader, that's much greater. You see you're in the epic, and you determine where and how it ends.'

'That's wrong, Luisa,' I say. 'That's too curious. It's not about it ending: epics do that. It's me: it's that I can look away, go to a different place.'

'Then all's just soup,' she says. 'A stew. A gallimaufry, a humble printer's pie. You have to get inside your epic, to concentrate. Then, you know you can survive. I can't – I only make the stuff, set it up. You're the guy with the island now. You've found it. Afterwards, it seems, you're going somewhere else.'

'Only if I go with Augusto, in his submarine,' I say.

I don't fancy it. Millennia in the dark and damp.

'No, it's better to be a revolutionary – that's an easy thing to write,' she says, stretching out her joke like gum.

We think of Franz Josef: who wrote him, who put him in his uniform, and who made the sequels.

*

We play games on the shore – 'Italians', who mostly come from Italy, 'Brazilians', who come from everywhere else. Damien is umpire – gazing at the clouds, strumming on his briefcase. Luisa – we find that she's an athlete, a kind of running back, through the 'Italian' defence, a flying shuttle with a coconut. The Italians are Neapolitans from Caracas. Usually we win.

She has the only suit of football armour, washed up, the Argive helmet too. 'Touchdown!' she shouts. The Neapolitans won't block a lady. 'Well done, you guys,' says Damien vaguely. 'Let's hear it for the flag' – though it's by Canadian rules we play.

She runs, she runs – 'You should see me pitch!' she shouts. 'In the season.' She scores, she slays the offence and the defence, with the nut beneath her arm.

Liesl and Chloe jig up and down, and wring their hands.

When we're exhausted, off we go to look for food Augusto leaves – abundance for the victors. There are fights.

Chloe's Giorgio is our audience. He sleeps, he sleeps – the action buries him in sand. 'Oh no!' says Chloe, 'first drugs, then drink – the remedies all turn against him... Now he's smothered in his sleep. Brush off the sand, and lay him in his last canoe.' This we do, Augusto blesses – off he goes, Giorgio a tribute to the waves, and Neptune too.

'Now we can be together,' Chloe says to me, quite friendly.

'No, no,' I say. 'There's penitence and lamentations to be done. Your religion's quite precise in this,' and Liesl rolls her eyes back in her head, loosens her tongue. 'I see beneath the sand a castle, alabaster steps lead down, fountains of resinated wine... beans on the stove, guys to massage you with virgin oil....'

'She hallucinates,' Luisa says. 'There is no castle here, nothing leads down. Poor Faust! Poor Ulysses! No hell! The only devil here's Augusto, the promise is for four-by-fours and tie rods so we'll build the first hotel,' but Liesl foams and talks of looking for the Ring, maybe it's Wagner's, maybe Vienna's, things she's read in books, like marriage and the mystic bond....

Luisa says, 'Oh yes – I'm into boxing too! The Ring! That's the centre, all the rest is metaphor,' and she's batting football heroes on the nose – 'At last! I'm free of my scenarios,' and she talks of Bears and Bruins, Orioles and Alouettes, we think she's crazier than Liesl, but all is sporting, striving onward.

'Luisa!' I say, 'There is no centre to the ring, to any ring. Even if it ends tomorrow, let's hope something is resolved, something deeper found and sounded – even if we only know how deep....'

*

'STOP,' shouts Damien. 'I have Pandora's legacy, it throbs and flashes on my lap, while you idiots game on and play away your trivial lives! This is the doomsday case, with it, I can explode the world....'

'STOP yourself!' Augusto shouts. 'Respect my plans!'

'Your guys aren't in construction. They're in gangs and fantasy,' says Damien. 'Before too long, Alex'll disconnect my overnight. I have to act decisively.... Besides – I don't want cash. You're in the tourism enterprise, Augusto. That's nothing to me. My empire? Stepping in to distant lands where other strangers failed – that makes no sense. Power's bound to finish – you get some smacks in the mouth. What is the point? Making some bucks? Squalid and unworthy. No, a power that ends, a self-decided crunch – power for its own sake, that self-destroys. It's battled everyone, massacred the weak and then – expired. You've had it all, the power, then it runs out. You're done. Then, you must show that you can engineer your end...and everybody else's,' and on he goes.

'Damien, that way, no one stays alive to see what you have done,' Augusto says. 'Have some vanity! Enjoy the stage! Prance a bit!'

'No,' says Damien. 'That's not it at all. Survival – doesn't thrill me. And besides – there's things, big things, I don't know how to fix. I'm not a wrestler – difficult, insoluble things, they hurt my head.'

'Aha!' Augusto says. 'It isn't power, it's failure that you want to celebrate. You're copping out.'

'Then be it so,' says Damien.

A pistol shot!

Maybe the one we have been waiting for.

But no – it is the lock on Damien's case. At last it yields.

His finger hesitates on apocalypse.

Oh no! Luisa sees the lit-up screen, involuntarily, she flutters to it – 'Slide off!' shouts Damien. 'No crap sporting tales transmitted here. No bathos.' Her hands and feet are dithering, the light's like treacle, spiders' silk. She can't pull out. It's strong as destiny. She types: 'Of all the quarterbacks I've known....' and Damien slams down the lid, he must have broke her pitching arm.

Luisa screams with pain. 'It's the message every writer, every philosopher wants to hear, to send – they all first wanted to run, to score....' she shouts, but Liesl weeps again:

'The old dispensation, so sweet, so cool,' she says. 'And now – they'll never make me run.'

'Nonsense,' says Chloe. 'You snail. Stuck to someone else's leaf.'

Will Alex pull the switch on Damien in time, and save the world?

Augusto whispers to me, 'My offer's valid still. You must have patience, for a thousand years, and then you'll rule, if not the world, at least a sandy knoll.'

The carriage, the limousine, makes the wrong turn. There's the pistol, a-tremble. Like the Archduke....

I'm sure Luisa's right – to run, to score... the narrative proceeds, the hammers and the archdukes fall, the giant's eye is pierced, and so is Franz – but knowledge, truth and justice, these mysteries are ours to puzzle over and elucidate until

the end

2

Of course it's not the end, not the real one. There's always an Alex who disconnects the briefcase and the bombs, sends the airmen back to sleep. See – there's a crane – the bird – studying the flow. There's plants, their leaves like birds' feet, growing on the sill. We're back. The empire didn't fall – and when it does, it breaks; the parts, they carry on.

'What a noise you made!' Luisa says. 'That's why they let us go. We were the Revelation, and the proof that what they'd made up, was true. Or plausible.'

'I don't remember things too well,' I say. 'Tell me, Luisa.'

'You didn't want to live down in the slime, grow little legs and lungs. We left – in the canoe, covering ourselves with palm fronds, hugging close. We were dead, and they believed us so. You screamed, for days. Drugs, they said.'

I remember nothing. It must have been true ecstasy. I say,

'And in between there and here, a plane, maybe? And not drugs: the spirit of the dead, the drunken ecstasy, the guy Giorgio they buried in the sand, got into me. Or maybe remembering a place without a bar or bottle?'

Luisa looks quizzical. 'Yes, there was a plane. They strapped you in, like all of us. We're here to start again.'

She snaps my head right and left, holding my face like a coconut. 'You have the flattest psyche ever,' she says. 'Flat as pewter. The screaming did you credit, though. And you could have found a girl and stayed with her. That would have been a good end. But you dodged that too. Good for you!'

'Here we are, then, back in the empire,' I say. 'What's complicated about that? Besides, what does complexity serve? You should stay with your relatives – that's what they're for, not to be dropped. That's what Greek warriors taught us. And – Franz, Franz K – the freedom fighters? Each a fighter, in his own way. Never figuring in your scenarios,

Luisa! Not a chance. Our old civilisations – that's what they're called. That's where my fossil bones are lodged. Those heroes who record their story – they are always victims. Or watch from the wings, following the action, a step behind. Think of all those Maya – their history long over. They chronicled it all – the wars, the dates, end of the world. Or of the calendar. Victims of themselves, of too much writing all the details. That's an extreme: this empire will drag on. It won't turn out like Austria. Will it?'

'Don't be so sure,' she says, and doesn't follow on. Later, she says,

'The philosopher tells us that objects are unalterable and subsistent. I'd really like to be one of those, not ephemeral. The eye, for instance: a frozen gaze. The doomsday briefcase. Setting a stamp on everything to come. Franz's musket. Our canoe-coffin. It seems I've toyed with all the other fluffy stuff: non-objects. The rooms where I've been me. The guys back there, the island.... My sister too – convinced that we were dead. Were we the objects then? Or they?'

'That's not it at all, Luisa. You don't have the choice. It's not "object or not". You can't jump from object into something else. I think you have to live in indeterminacy,' I say.

'Well,' she says. 'I'm not convinced.'

There's not much to eat here, not much to get it with.

'It's the past me I'm looking at,' Luisa says. 'I'm as successful as I want – more than Liesl, you wouldn't catch me at her game. I could die in a ditch, and still I'd be a success.'

She stares at me. 'Toss the ball back once in a while, you creep,' she says, irritated and amused. 'Just plodding from one thing to the next, expecting it to be written down and shaped. A catalogue of monstrosities – it's bland. You – watching life unfold and pass by, yours as well – you're dross.'

'Don't worry, Luisa,' I say. 'My future lies ahead.'

There is a long silence. I think about us – having a kitten. No sex involved, just a young cat, an orphan, like they mostly are. As an idea, it attracts, you don't need go out in the street and buy milk, not for an idea. Luisa says:

'You know, they'll think that island is a training camp. They could drop something on it, put us on a list to kill.'

'Surely not,' I say. 'We're not religious.'

'Grow up, my love: it isn't what you think, it's what they think,' she says. 'Damien is a rogue. An elephant, they get the must, run off among the trees. Turns on his bosses. He had that case, with all those bombs.... He's unpredictable, he's crazy for conclusions.'

'People didn't foresee the camps,' I say. 'In Europe or anywhere. It was modernity they toyed with. Typewriters and telephones, and places where you made them. That's what scared them then.'

'No one foresaw the camps until they were in them,' Luisa says. 'I don't want to make you paranoid, of course, and we have lived through that. Mostly. The big things – they're under control, they're known about, identified. We'll all go together, in each others' arms, like it or not. It won't be up to Damien.'

'Don't joke about it, Luisa,' I say, 'We've done nothing wrong, that I remember.'

'That stuff doesn't count,' she says.

'This is New York,' I say. 'The only Viennese thing is these trams. All else is different.'

She waves the thought away. 'You know, they're not afraid of secrets being leaked,' she says. 'They think some guy, some renegade, like Damien, will tweak the code and send the death planes back on us, his mates. We who live here.'

Maybe to take a kitten's not auspicious. You think of opera magic, and those plaster figures that they strew around the big stairs rising from the foyer – Kronos, Pandora, Venus the offended.... vengeance is theirs....

68

'You guys don't see it – but us girls, we like a laugh,' Luisa says. 'That's all it is. The secret of the universe, posterity at least. Not hairy bodies – just a quip. Then, we are ready, and compliant. Nine months, and on it goes, the whole, eternity.'

'The literature you touted round,' I say. 'That's mostly about bodies, some are hairy, some are dead. And some in uniform.'

'It's not that,' she says, 'it's passion, that's what sells. Mine, that is, not what's on the page.'

'Well,' I say, 'why should they want to kill us?'

She laughs, and there's a long pause. We're not archdukes, with a number inked on our heads.

'You really don't know?' Luisa asks. 'We know everything. Power, sex, love – everything.'

'Power I'll give you,' I say. 'From both sides, what keeps it up, what'll knock it down.'

'No, no,' says Luisa, 'Anyone can guess that. It's being in it, in the kernel. The slug in the lettuce. Being chosen, on both sides, walking up the steps, sitting at the desk, signing the warrants....'

'For Damien and Alex, and Augusto,' I say, 'and poor Liesl.'

'And poor all the rest of us. If it makes it easier for you to put faces on,' Luisa says.

'OK,' I say. 'Knowing. Love is easy, sex is hard. Much harder.'

'There!' says Luisa, gleefully. 'There – you know all about that too. I told you so. That's why we're targets. I expect that's what the guy in the tram, and Franz too, knew about, though not as much as us.'

'There's religion, and philosophy. We're a bit deficient there,' I say, anxious about my skin, my eye.

'Come on!' says Luisa. 'There's two thickets – one has a beautiful nymph, a tease, made of blue air, giving you a feel. She's philosophy. The other – has a big satyr, made of tar, trying to gloop all over you. That's theology. There – now you know about those.'

'Knowing about it all – what's the benefit?' I ask. 'We run, that's all. The knowing – is knowing it will end. Struggle, bite, spit. No dice. It ends. That's true, that's what no one wants to hear.'

'Of course, telling it – that's part of knowing too,' she says. 'It angers them, it seals our destiny. Besides, we might escape.'

'Maybe it's not Vienna or the pistol shot,' I say. 'It's Rome. Fighting all round, and getting smaller. Damien – he's not crazy. All he wants, is good deaths for everyone. Not a renegade – a third force, one man with a briefcase.'

'Your friend, not mine,' Luisa says.

'I had a waking dream,' I say. 'No, not a prison. A big doss-house. The beds all hugger-mugger, and the smell! Not carbolic, the smell of single men, quite unforgettable, sweetish, dust on the verge of mud. The sleeping sound – like dogs or hibernation. All on the cheap.'

'I've money,' says Luisa. 'Alex. He doles out. You just need sleep with him.'

It's stacked like bricks of green tea.

Luisa and I – we sleep like long marrieds, in the same room.

'We – no, I, was wrong,' I say. 'It's not the pistol shot we're waiting for. I had hold the wrong imperial. We're Romans. Feisty bands prowl round outside, like wolves. They chip away. Roman citizens – they seem ok, but then they aren't. The shows, the circuses – ever bigger, better: it's a bad sign.'

'Luisa! Luisa!' there's a shout: it must be me, the dream is in my sleep.

She's by me – 'Don't shout out like that. 'Luisa!' – you mustn't shout. It's like that guy shouts out – the prisoner: House of the Dead. And you would be my murderer.'

She's quite upset: she says, 'And I'm not Russian either. But – it's the principle. No shouting! I could be Maya,' and she pirouettes.

'You're not dark enough for that, Luisa,' I say.

'Oh, I could be darker than you think,' she says. 'Grand opera, that's me – the grandest that you can. Not silly dreams. Rome was ages going down – and after emperors came popes, then worse and worse. Those big armies, flaking off, not speaking the language like they ought.'

'That's it, then? That's all? Remember, you must die? It sounds like Kleist, or Buchner. They want to kill us for that? It's a grimy kind of paradox....' I say.

'That's it,' says Luisa. She seems dissatisfied. You would.

She says, 'We know that it will end. That's why they want to kill us. That's the paradox. It's saying "it's unavailing". It's being who we are, who say it. It's being them, puffed up like table birds who fear the fork and gravy.'

'Damien would have proved us right,' I say. 'By opening the case when it was armed.'

'No fun for us!' Luisa says: she reflects. 'I should have been a Vandal. Knocking down, then building wondrous palaces.'

'Then there's Wedekind,' I say, remembering vaguely, 'All those Germans – they knew something dirty, round the corner, a pit....'

'Yes,' says Luisa, magisterial, 'But you couldn't call what they had an empire.' I say,

'The guys, that live here, accountants, lawyers – mostly, they are Christians. So, they know about conclusions, and victories no one else can see. They know the answer before the question's asked. It's a justification for what they want, it means we lions go to the arena, dumped out on the sand.'

'I do my reading. Thinking too,' Luisa says. 'There's time, on those new trams. You're right – guys here are on a kind of journey, one that isn't yours. You should have gone to – who was it? – Zoe? No, Chloe. And you were smart, you ducked that. You got your second life. Your bit of luck. Avoiding Ithaca. Good deaths – that's the lesson these guys learned – if not for them, for you.'

'Luisa – we know all that. It's self-defence. Other people plan your end. That's what Franz the bodyguard forgot – he should have watched his back. Franz K., who wrote the books – it wasn't about him, the plot. The guys who blocked him out – they blocked out everyone. That is their principle. And they watched their backs.'

'Well,' she says, 'If you want it littled down like that.... You won't get the commission, to do the massive fresco, write that symphony.'

'How about a soldier?' I ask. 'For protection. There's lots of spares around, some with their arms and legs. He could sleep on the floor here, in his carapace...'

'You mean, his cataphract,' says Luisa. 'Carapace is something else besides. I know a soldier – Cyril. He would do. But that would not avail.'

'A songwriter – that would be more fun,' I say. 'And no more use. My journey, though – it should be without encumbrance.... You can't trust these military types.'

'Oh yes,' Luisa says, 'your fucking journey. Who knows if it's begun. Or if it ends. And we are left here, on our rock, the perilous seas around.'

'Footballers, now soldiers, Luisa,' I say. 'There's too much ideology for you there.'

'Oh,' she says, 'Cyril is empty. Probably an explosion did it. But at least he has his arms and legs. Like a squid. A horny beak, as well.'

'I'm not jealous,' I say, 'but it's well known: those who accompany your journey – they must be chaste.'

'That, I never heard,' she says. 'But you guys....! I don't miss the absent tyrant, who I don't desire. I don't want love. I want to speak and see quite clean, no frosting on the bulbs. But – that leaves sex; and that becomes a bore. Two spoons of sugar – more just makes you sick.'

'Luisa,' I say, 'You don't want love. And sex has less variety than football plays. So – why not give it up?'

'Yes!' she says. 'Genius! I never thought of that. But – you can't play football on your own.'

'You could watch old movies,' I tell her.

Peace and understanding: those we now share.

We can proceed.

*

'I got rid of Cyril,' says Luisa. 'And he took most of our cash.'

'He stole it?' I say.

'I hadn't thought of that,' she says. 'Yes. Maybe he'll give it back to Alex. Or to Damien. Your friends.'

'Maybe he will,' I say. We don't mention that again.

I say, 'I wanted pastrami – instead, there's only plovers' eggs, larks' tongues, and dormice. Cage-fighting. Rome. The end.'

'They tried converting,' Luisa says. 'More trouble. Little profit. Guys up poles, and chastity.'

'If you must laugh at me, Luisa, remember that the laugh runs through humanity,' I say. 'Turns the bones to cheese.'

Luisa says, 'While we're on to questions of conversion – why did God make all those dinosaurs? It's a thing we have to ask. Before us, people didn't have to face that curious stuff, those scaly beasts – life was much easier.'

'It isn't God, it's climate,' I tell her.

'Cyril says, this arguing by analogy – Romans, Greeks, Comanches, empires of all sorts – is medieval.'

'Has he gone? Cyril?' I ask.

'Yes and no,' she says. 'When they exploded him, his organs melted into air. He's a new type of military man. All carapace – that stuff. He says your analysis is crap. If we are Romans, resistance is in vain. The roof comes down on all of us. Sure, the empire will not last, and nor will we. You can't desert, no one will take you in.'

'All right,' I say, 'so – it's tragedy. It all ends in sing-song, gospel, soul and fusion. You lose the battle, they don't send you back to Africa, so you climb up on the stage and entertain. It's cyclical. Empires are just villages writ large. They grow to cities, then implode. That is the world, the way it goes. So, Luisa, what's to do?'

'Cyril backs Liesl,' says Luisa. 'He's on the corner down there. He collects her funds.'

'Liesl's with the renegades,' I say, 'On an island, waiting for the end. Like Sarajevo was.'

'Oh well,' Luisa says, 'if Liesl's rocketed, she'll be hollowed out, like Cyril. They'll all become those new kinds of military. Damien too. He will convert.'

I say, 'I thought he'd no beliefs – not those that you admit to. You must convert from something that you had.'

'He thought a lot about the moon. How when we'd gone, there it would be, just looking down, for centuries, quite undisturbed,' she says.

Luisa – how beautiful she looks....

She says, poking a finger in my chest, 'You see around, how monstrous things occur. You dodge. You see the others suffer – but for you, the thing is just to reach an end, unscathed. There is no end – you're just a tale. I'm off. Away. You might decide to start a massacre right here. I'm not in your fable. No longer, not any more.'

'Ah, Luisa, Luisa!' I can't think of other things to say.

'Don't say that!' says Luisa, picking up what's left of all our cash.

Then, there they are, Luisa and Cyril, side by side, squatting on the sidewalk, begging, the bricks of cash behind them.

I go down. 'Luisa! I did you no harm....' I say.

'No whining, brave adventurer,' she says, sharply. 'I've got protection now, and when they come to get you, I'm not there.'

'And – my love for you?' I ask.

'Too late, you slippery soul. I've got protection: my immortal warrior,' says Luisa, and she raps at Cyril's ribcage. It gives a distant sound.

'Go away,' says Luisa, waving me away. 'You snoop. I'm not your destiny. Work it out, something original. Not Chloe, you parked her on the island, with that crummy dee-fence. Not being stuck, like Franz, not shut out, like that Franz K.'

'Maybe on your screen, dear Luisa, there's the key?' I wheedle.

'Whatever it is,' she says, 'it's not been written, nor been thought.'

Cyril's armour's opened, and I see – ribs, brown ribs, all the way down. A sting, that stirs. More ribs, a potent tail. A roach, that lasts out palaces, lives for ever in the cracks in temple floors.

'Tell me, at least, Luisa – where are you from?' I ask.

'Not so fast!' says Cyril. 'I'm the watchman. I come out in the light to show there's lots more of us, legions, that wait until the dark to swarm. Remember the Comanches – terrible things they did, and then were done to them. It's waves. There's one! – it comes to break your boat, it swells up from the grey. And you cling on – your mates go overboard, the sea is full of floating parts, of arms and knees and elbows, flick flick, they break an instant the grey skin of the sea, and then.... They're swept away – see, their faces, hovering above their death, how they implore.... But you are hanging on, you shout "farewell". In less dire times – that could be a taunt. But it's for serious. Then your soggy ship, listless with all the sea it's taken on – it struggles up, it's on a crest – and down it bears! It sinks, and all go with it. Vengeance is yours, and justice too, and righting all the wrongs. Down go the captains and their mates, down the great helmsman, marines – two

75

stripers and three pippers – the commodores, one gold ring or two or more, down, down to the guardians in the deep. All those gold rings, glistering in the mud! And how those guys all sing! It's operetta time, it's Wiener Frauen, Land of Smiles.... Luisa? Where is she, in all this ocean, borne up and crashing down? Good Croat? Bad German? None of that? Or something else again?'

'I'm something else again, dear Cyril,' says Luisa, quite storm-wracked.

'Look,' says Cyril, tensing up his length, pointing some stubby fingers at me, 'I had to splat some guys for you, guys maybe better, so's you could be free and condescending. Maybe you need some teaching, now. If they're after you, maybe I should get there first. Not for a prize, a medal: just because you're there, guilty, condemned. Besides, that would maybe save this lovely girl,' and he squeezes dear Luisa. 'You know, a big heavy guy like me – if I just lay on you, covered your face, your thin chest, it would come apart, your sticklike legs and twiggy arms – a tremor, and it's gone. Your bird, your soul; I'd ease myself upon an elbow – out it flies, it circles round the room, it sings its song, a tweet, a sickly sparrow thing, your precious gift.... You're gone. I take a trophy. Maybe I'd carve out an eye, and put it in my tin.'

'Poor Cyril,' says Luisa, giving him a kiss, caress. 'How you have suffered.'

'It's not just him,' says Cyril squinting at me. 'It's who he represents.'

'Luisa,' I say, 'if they're after both of us, and you're the one who has it written down – you said it's what we know. And that is you, for ever, too.'

'Oh no,' she says, 'I don't remember. Anything. You're a blank sheet – how can I do a deal with you, or know what you think you know?'

'That wasn't what you said,' I say, quite anxious now.

'It wasn't written down. Besides, the good thing here, is we can change our minds. Our stories too, and what is good and bad. It's probable that what you are is worse than what you aren't, or what you were,' she says. It's true.

She goes on, 'If Cyril does for you, it's one threat less for me. Your journey – who knows where it leads, who are your friends? Damien – surely that was threat enough for you? You chummed with him, and took his story in. And now you're on your own, condemned, exposed, and on the run. What is the charge, where is the judge? What is the sentence, why are you so keen to find it out? Oh no, my friend, you wanted to be a hero, cutting necks – your long sword tricked out with seaweed, vengeance would be yours, new empires and new laws. All that....' And she shakes her head. 'No, no, you've muddled it all up. I see no hope for you.'

'This will help,' says Cyril. 'My father – he was just like me. And in his time – they were already here – the parasites, the insects. Longhairs. That's how you knew. It was our cash they wanted. And to mount their shows. The music...'

'It sounds like a good time,' I say. 'And good to know your father was like you. And – Luisa, I guess your father too resembled...?' She doesn't respond.

Her history stays closed.

'It's all irrelevant,' she says. 'There's always guys... and when they're beat, there's other guys. You're sometimes with one lot, then you aren't.'

'That's pathetic, Luisa,' I say.

'I have qualities, I do,' she says. 'But not enthusiasm.'

'That's chicken,' I say. 'Those trolleys – it's not to make us think of Prague, Vienna, Sarajevo. They come from Memphis. It's for the music – it brings in the tourists.'

'There was a shot in Memphis too,' she says. 'Shots there were all over.'

'Come on, Luisa,' I say, to warm her up. 'Passion! There were guys here, Lincoln Brigaders, fought in Spain. Here was supposed to be the promised land. I read your stuff, that's all I know. Experience at its best. It's tough, the struggle: perhaps sometimes they let you win.'

She brushes off her memory with a hand. The hand circles, rests on Cyril's stubby head. 'That was quite different,' she says. 'That was earlier. Now, they'll get us, even if we sing. I know how it turns out.'

'I won't sing,' says Cyril, abruptly. 'Not in public. But then, I'm the only boy who never dreamed of being president. Most people, make a story of their future, and slide into it.'

'Yes, yes,' says Luisa. 'That's what Damien did; and Liesl – she's so dumb, she was grateful someone told her she'd a future. That's why she's candidate. There's millions of them. And thousands are presidents.'

'Take this pill,' says Cyril. 'Let it melt in your soft sweet mouth, Luisa.'

She does so. 'It's ash,' she says.

'It's for combat,' Cyril says. 'And in a while, they come for you – the farmers from Bunker Hill, then all the rest. They fill the spaces in your brain. You can't wait to obliterate a face. Know your enemy, that's what they tell you.'

'It's true,' Luisa says. 'They're all over me, into me. There's hardly room. My head teems with them.'

'They don't come to your room any more, not to get you,' Cyril says. 'They're already there.'

'It's terribly banal,' Luisa says. 'The pill, it doesn't lift a bit. Do you want cash for that? I should begrudge!'

Cyril shoots out a feeler, takes a slice of notes from the bundles behind them. Luisa pulls a face. She says, 'I want rid of these guys, all of them. They're ants, all over me. I see them in my mirror' – and there it is, it's metal, it must be how she brings them out, communicates, the swarms inside, however painful – 'The past. All dressed up, mothers and fathers. Terrible. In photos. I never had them, parents, in the real... Did you?'

She chatters on. Dealing with all these strange guys, the souls wafted on her pill, they're like spirits waving, in bits of uniform, it makes her wince, you see she's hurt, would like to shrug them off.

I say, 'Are you sure, that when you ran your plays, under your arm it was a coconut? It might have been a head, your head.'

We laugh: she says, 'Damien and Alex – they're the new species, that's for sure. Not so delicate about survival. Shit on the species, that is what they say: if it's strong, it'll go on, notwithstanding. If not – you've seen the way. The killing's the experiment.'

It's quite upsetting. 'Luisa, I don't know where to go,' I say.

'Oh, you're ok,' she says. 'They wouldn't strike this sidewalk – it's one of theirs. Or would they, Cyril?'

He's noncommittal, he has no other look. I say, 'Protection? Cyril doesn't even have his arm.'

'Oh yes he does,' Luisa says, 'Lots of arms. And legs.' We laugh, but not so loud.

Cyril says, 'You see, intention, experience, reasoning. They're tough to read. What happens – doesn't mean a thing. It's like the Poles and Jews. You meet a Pole, she's quite delightful, and you scratch her, and she says, a little voice, a bit of blood, as if it's secret to her "... and yet, the Jews, they have the money".'

I say, 'No wonder those Poles didn't take to communism.'

Luisa doesn't follow: she says, 'We've so much money, you and I, we don't need even think about it.'

'How they hate us, people here, Luisa,' I say.

'We've no country, and no faith,' says Luisa, 'It's not worth targeting a pair like us.'

'Problems of today, that's what Cyril should address,' I say, to cheer the mood.

'Cyril is all problem,' Luisa says.

'The past,' says Cyril. 'That's where it all started for me. You guys say you've never been there – but your mouths are full of it.'

'Right now, it's just guys on horses, riding round. "Promised land", "Slough of Despond" – that kind of thing,' Luisa says, and to me, 'One-liners. Like you did. "Never trouble. Life goes. Rome wasn't built." Made your fortune, I bet.'

She's made hers, her fortune. 'Bandits, riding round,' she says. 'Then tribes, then nations. Circling round, raiding, trading. If there's a centre, they'll go for it. But not yet.'

There's a crackle, as Cyril bends this way and that, lies on the sidewalk curled round like a query, brown and green. 'You guys,' he says, 'are quite confused. The only certain thing's your fear. To keep you safe, you'd need a thousand of my mates – and we're available, but even then, it doesn't change a thing. You're still exposed, out here in the street.'

'I'll try another way,' Luisa says. 'Memoirs. They sell. And they reveal. "When the time comes, the King of Poland will mount his horse and ride up from below the earth and drive them all away. All of them. You as well." There go the Germans – that's your Polish theme.'

Cyril sighs in disappointment. 'You're further away. Leave it be.'

He can't protect us. Better that we go on with my journey.

Cyril says, 'Combat. It changes a guy.'

'But Cyril, you're so sleek and flexible, what more could you want?' Luisa asks.

Maybe he knows something about Franz. We think of Franz, though not so much…. Or the one-eyed guy, the tram.

We look down, from our room. Cyril's still there – and then – he's gone! I ask, 'Did you bring the cash, Luisa?'

Of course, that's gone as well.

'You always need a soldier,' Luisa says.

It may be her philosophy – to me, it's superficial.

3

' "Liberty or death!" cried the anarchist. "Now we'll execute the prisoner!" '

' "No, you cretin, liberty or death is for you. The prisoner will go to prison," said the officer.'

'You've got it wrong, Luisa,' I tell her. 'It's "said the socialist". It's a kind of history joke.'

'Well,' she says, 'I guess you change it round as time goes by.'

'We'd tried most things,' I say. 'Then Cyril was an interlude, removing all our cash. Puffing up our fear. Set to watch us.'

She says, 'Cyril wanted to change himself. That's what the people want who read my literature, my lines – they all want that. Cyril was a great success. He changed, absolutely.'

I think of Luisa, her last scenarios – Toller, the writer who 'used to be a German', and the President who wanted to be German, a Berliner. She's outside all that. Nothing to do with Germany – quite the contrary, she says.

I say, 'I guess we're Roman citizens for ever. It's our fate.'

'Oh no,' Luisa says, 'we have the passports, and our death certificates. Augusto gave them. We can leave, and you – you can avoid the destiny of lording it: that scrubby island, then the submarine, those exploits undersea, and after infinities of time, rise up and entertain new species of hominids – with your adventures, and your princely blood.'

'Luisa, you're quite the reactionary,' I say – it's not a new discovery.

'Oh no,' she says, 'I'm just a feather. Everyone likes those – a tickle, a drifting. I'm the trivial – "culminating in the fourfold swing of an axe, a revolver-shot, and the tightening of a soaped noose". Now! That's the way to start a book, to get attention. The beginnings are trivial, it says – an abduction, a runaway. I'm trivial, I push the pebble from the summit, it rushes down, recruiting more imposing rocks, buries the town.'

'I feel uneasy,' I tell her. Really, I feel disoriented.

'You wake,' Luisa says. 'In your mind, there's mountains. You remember an epic – the first two thousand lines, twenty thousand still to go. You're Kirghiz. That is definite.'

'Luck,' I say. 'Remembering – it's just luck. It's easy to come by.' I must avoid that island, Chloe, her embroidery. The container. The massacre: the briefcase that brings an end to everything, no one can open it, not just yet.

'Alex will settle it,' Luisa says. 'That's the point of empire. When you're in it, you're yourself alone, whatever you want, wherever you came from. Then you go out in the street – you're part of everyone else. It's a foul trick. Descartes, I guess. Narcissism, and then – outside and on the bus, everyone's a narcissist.'

'That leaves no space for love,' I say. 'But lots for murder. Yes, it's Descartes – he must have known all about ends.'

Luisa laughs, 'Well, you are a chocolate bun! Such sentiment! The guy who killed the real Luisa – he was a convict, hard labour for life, no remission, no eagles flapping off. It's not you,' and she pauses, 'Or maybe it will be.'

'This is deep and heavy stuff,' I say. 'Let's play football.'

There's no coconut, but we do it all the same. We crouch, we shout out numbers. Then we lock.

My, she's strong. 'My, you're weak,' Luisa says, panting. We stay, locked there, crouched, a long long time. We don't advance, we don't retreat. It's victory. We're straining, close as close.

At last, we hug, like football heroes do. 'Where shall we go?' Luisa asks. 'The empire's out to get us, but outside, beyond its spirals....'

'The island is impossible,' I say. 'That's not my destiny. If you go some place there's stones or waters that they want –

it isn't safe. Or if they feel they must make friends.... And if there's nothing anybody else would covet, well – we can't sing the songs or do the dance.'

'We'll think about it – maybe watch some docs, or get some leaflets,' says Luisa, but she's desperate.

'It's all like long ago – there were those Greeks – wanted to make the Trojans democrats. A great mistake, recruiting gods and goddesses – there they were, upon the sand, their shields of cobwebs, swords of green and gold – just lights that cut your liver out.... And all for vengeance, what they say was honour. That flighty girl....' I chatter on. We did it all when I was very young.

'The story's good,' Luisa says. 'It could become an opera. But "flighty girl" is just the cover. And I'd bet – you wouldn't go and fight.'

'If you are clever, no, you wouldn't go. The logic of the situation pushes it along....' I say.

'Oh, it's philosophy,' she says. 'That doesn't sell. It's inconclusive. You should sex things up....'

'If they abducted you, Luisa, or if it were just the mood to run off somewhere – you'd still be one of them. Them here. The football. And the pizzas.... They'd come after you, for sure.'

'I wouldn't want the fuss,' she says, 'and doing what I'd want to do.... it's sacrosanct.'

'No, no,' I say, 'it's history. You can't just duck the causal chain when it comes snaking round.'

'By the way,' says Luisa, 'this is Vera, she replaces Cyril. She's our snoop.'

'Hi guys!' says Vera. She seems a solid tackle, like a marble block, she's painted so's to stand beneath the brightest lights, she's tall, so tall you hardly see where she ends up, her tan a little blurred, the curls electrum.

Luisa is much taken with her.

Vera says, 'You two don't exchange a word that's meaningful to overhear, and so you get the spying personal.

I'm your good angel, your surveillance. I listen and repeat: I get my orders, I've a boss. But I – I always tell the truth.'

'Of course you do, of course,' says Luisa, holding Vera's arm, and feeling up and down, as if it were a lamppost. 'But tell us – what have we done?'

Vera says, 'You guys – you know it all will end, and so it's useless going out to war, negotiating truce, avenging the abducted, all that stuff. And worse – you think to run away, escape. If all did that – some place would overload, all would sing identical songs, dance the same round – then there'd be famine, people would spill out.... And it would start all over. Empires are made by winning wars – beating guys down, then guesting them back in as slaves. And what would be the point of that?'

'Knowing there's an end, is just my job,' Luisa says, waving a paperback, that clearly says 'The End'. 'But if we're treacherous – at least you'll come with us, and settle, when we find our paradise?'

'Dear Luisa,' Vera says, 'of course. Who'd be so stupid they'd refuse? The problem is – our destinies are jumbled up. This guy here,' and she towers over me, her eyes bright white – 'He has a home, and he won't go. He has no qualities. He's stubborn, that is all. You, Luisa, if you escape your murder scene – will be a queen of literature. And I – must always tell the truth, and yet come out on top. It's complex, as you see.'

'Of course,' Luisa says. 'We all must win. It is that kind of game.'

'It's your defeatism, my dears,' says Vera. 'It stops you playing well. You'll have your nemesis, for sure.'

'And is it you, my sweet,' Luisa asks, hugging Vera's leg, 'Who'll call the bolt on us?'

'Oh no!' says Vera, 'I don't have that capacity. The bolt's unleashed – or so we call the operation – by someone else. I am its guide, no more.'

Luisa whispers to me, 'This Vera – what a patsy! She always tells the truth, so we'll get round her easily, if that time should come....' Aloud, she says, 'Those books. Even the sombre ones – the message is that though they end, you pass on to the next. The human pen – indomitable.'

'Or so you say,' says Vera. 'Maybe you should have stuck to song – that's maybe more equivocal.'

'That doesn't work,' I say. 'Remember – "*Wie sind wir wandermüde / ist dies etwa der Tod?* We're so tired with wandering – is this perhaps... death?"'

'This is crap,' shouts Luisa, thinking fast and unavailingly. 'It's not about books and songs – it's messages, exchange! In general! That's the human spirit, surging forth.'

'Oh,' says Vera, disappointed. 'Trade? Commerce? I'm not a fan of that.'

Luisa takes me aside. 'Vera's structurally odd. Her poundage! It's not there! She's tall, but only slightly heavier than air. She'd never make the squad. If she's so ephemeral, perhaps she'll come to love us, care for us. Deflect the bolt, the blow....'

'It's only Vera says she always tells the truth,' I say. 'And you don't know if she's ephemeral: maybe she's only insubstantial. Must we believe that all of what she says is true?'

'Yes, for now – it's the best way,' Luisa says. 'And we don't need to tell the truth – no one believes us anyway.'

'You guys, you whisper, but I hear,' says Vera, not put out at all. 'It seems to me you fear a move because you think you will be poor. It isn't so: here, you can be poor as anywhere – the problem is, your talents... You are not gifted. Seeing the future isn't smart for you, it's a disaster. Only the very special ones, the nobler species that one day must come – seek, and even make, a future they can calmly contemplate.'

'I bet it'll be capitalism,' Luisa laughs.

'Oh well,' says Vera, laughing back, 'this capitalism you talk so much about. It's a default setting. It's what you get when you can't think of something more attractive, causing guys less hurt and waste. Or when you're busy treading other paths....'

'That sounds mysterious,' I say, 'you ought to be as loyal as can be, to the things that are, given your job, your watching brief.'

'I tell the truth,' Vera says, 'that doesn't mean I'm stupid – and besides, the truth is neither good nor bad. It doesn't mean we love the boss, although – the boss is boss.'

None of this helps our case, our minds: Vera repeats, 'If you believe in truth, you must believe in me.'

'If what we know is true, why are you tasked with our destruction, then?' Luisa asks.

'My, how you jump around an argument,' says Vera. 'The answer is – I've been instructed to. Now, let's talk of love – that is my specialty – and why you two don't feel it for each other.'

'My suspicion is,' Luisa says, 'since you know everything – you'll want to sell our story, if we can't ourselves....'

'It's our job,' says Vera, 'to know more about you than you do. Besides, if you'd won with Liesl, you could believe any goddam thing you like, and take it out on others too. You should have loved your sister more, Luisa,' and she frowns, knocking Luisa's hands away.

'She's my sister like I'm Croatian,' Luisa says, and shows her teeth. Then, on her little screen, she sends a message to me, hiding it from Vera – 'Hey, love may get us out of this! If Vera's really into love – then let's pretend, and if she has a heart up there, perhaps she'll let us off the wrath....'

'I can take you anywhere you want,' says Vera cutting in. 'I'll be coming too, of course, but I shan't pry. In the empire – or beyond, in what they call "the next", "periphery". What you guys call the everywhere, the world. I'll bring your change of clothes, some soothing paints for if you must strip completely off and prance.'

'We must avoid the island, where they're held as if in dreams or under spells. On the beach, they while away their ignorance,' I say. 'They're vulnerable. Vera'll know about the giant... and Franz, who got stuck.... so, should we give them Damien? Alex will have had his money back – what he gave for orgies, and for patching Cyril up. But Damien – the doomsday case – that must be worth a bit. I seem to have in mind – that he'd some part in seeing off the former boss. For us, a pardon, even, if we say that we'll forget all that.'

'Forget's the word,' Luisa says. 'Forget, and don't blackmail. These top guys meet exotic ends – or else they don't. They change their shapes, they've lookalikes, they're showers of gold, of plumes...Be very careful – maybe you shouldn't turn Damien in—'

'Oh no,' says Vera, bending down to hear. 'Damien's an umpire. They need him where he is.. Even if it's sandcastles that they build. Beach volley, too. And he's a powerful guy. We'll keep him in reserve.'

'There's no alternative,' Luisa whispers to me. 'We must love one another, so as not to die.'

She grasps my neck, and shakes my head – a teasel on its stalk. This embrace is hot as pitch, she murmurs something – 'What?' I ask.

'Play up, and play the fucking game,' she says. Dear Luisa, brazen love. What pain!

Of course, they want to keep a hold on her, Luisa: desirable, an athlete. But me? The outcast?

Bourgeois supreme? 'No!' says Luisa. 'Not you at all. The journey! That's what people want to hear – how they might get away, and also come back home.... Escape the war, and carry out the massacre! And home for dinner, with respect! Forget your slogans: – it's the adventure counts, where there's a tingling menace, freaks and thunderstorms, but no threat.'

'That's right, I'm sure,' I say. 'For us, though, it's not at all like that.'

'Oh Vera,' says Luisa, turning sharply away from me. 'How I'd love to feel passionate, quite fluid – for this guy here,' and she points towards me.

'Look, Luisa,' Vera says, 'I'm an obedient servant, but I watch, I don't glue. I don't cast spells. You white guys, stuck on your Europe and its transport – you have a problem letting go. Don't turn to me – if it's managed love you want, go to those witches, Damien, or Alex. They'll uncork your bottle.'

Vera has a warrior's phrase. I wonder if she is a true believer. You must obey all orders, no credit in the execution; you need to be alert all day and night.

Luisa says, 'That wasn't the answer in the register I sought.'

'I spot your purpose, dear,' says Vera. 'But – if I switch sides, it'll be for fun, and not for you.'

'Don't waste your fine writing on her, Luisa,' I tell her. 'We're family, she's not.'

'I see us all in Turkey,' Vera says, surprising us. 'There's lots of almost everything that's there, or has been.'

'Those are odd planes,' Luisa says, when we're at the airfield.

Some are light blue, with an eagle painted underneath. Others are dark dark blue, with a star.

'The light ones are for day,' says Vera. 'The guys look up and see the bird. Someone on board will snap them, from their faces you see if they are innocent. Same with the dark ones.'

'What if, in the dusk, the night comes on, the bird becomes invisible?' I ask.

'Oh,' Vera says, 'I expect they'll work on it. Some paint....'

We land, and there's a rocky place. 'Are those your sheep?' Luisa asks, and Vera says, 'Oh yes, they could be mine. Do be a dear – milk some of them,' and she is chivvying off some peasants who've been lounging round. She settles down, and soon is knitting rugs.

Luisa and Vera – they both seem at home. 'I bought this scrub on spec,' says Vera. 'You could bring up children here.'

I guess you could, they do.

We could be stricken here, no one would tell the difference. I wander off. Maybe there's some cave, without a monster or a plaited snake. Instead, there is a dog.

It chews at me, my arms and legs, it starts upon my face as if it wants to change it, and in a while Vera comes up. 'Shoo, shoo!' she says, kicking at the beast. 'I should have told you not to stroll around. You ought to go to hospital, but then again, maybe you won't. That venerable hound – it seems to recognise you. Maybe it has bad memories.'

'This foot looks rather dire,' Luisa says. I have a sharp idea:

'Don't fuss,' I say. 'Things that aren't congenital, they grow back on.'

There would be one strike, that would do for both of us. If Luisa's far away, I have a chance. There is the sea, outstretched, that sucks you down... but if I run off to the beach, and find a boat – I'm safe!

'That foot,' says Vera, 'you won't run far with that. There's guard dogs all around – they don't forget a face, especially one that's chewed.'

She and Luisa whisper together. I hear Vera say, 'If your guy isn't up to it, there's locals here who are – there's one who has a Merc, an indoor toilet... you could do far worse. Besides, if the worst comes from above, you won't have had time to get bored.'

We hear from far away, 'God is great....' and then lots more: Vera says, 'This monotheism – you'd think it was fresh egg! The old time stuff – it lingers on, but "one" is all guys think of. You'd imagine that they couldn't count. "God is great" – there's a one-liner that you should have thought of. It would have got you off some hooks,' Vera says, and laughs towards me. I hold my foot in place.

Luisa says, 'This here is fairly bleak. The company is scarce. Since to the island we won't go – maybe a plane would bring our playmates over here....'

It's quite a joke, but Vera says, 'I'll see. I'll ask. We welcome sheep – the goats are better left behind.'

Liesl's the sheep. That leaves only the goats, Damien, Augusto. And the Italians.

'Of course.' Vera leans down close to Luisa. 'It's all a story, and an epic one.'

'I know all that,' Luisa says. 'That's how I made big money selling things, and then I read a book that showed the few shapes that stories take. That's how I became a writer's writer. I don't get the credits, but Holly- and Bolly-woods, they're full of me. People think it's complicated, art, but it's really simple. The songs are simpler still. The painting – well, lots of it is scribble, and the rest, you take a photo, pin it up, you take a brush.... People like a dance, if they have muscles left after they have dug and threshed. That's pretty easy too. Then, off they go and start again.'

'Yes, my dear,' says Vera. 'People will work hard. The next thing is – they must fight as hard. For whatever they may want to get or keep. Even the monotheists – you wouldn't think they'd quarrel – but it never ends! Now, look at him!' and she points at me: 'The limping wounded, carried off the field on that big shield of his!'

Luisa whispers to me – 'I have to speak to her like that – quite superficial. This is her mode of thought. She's armed, and unpredictable. I might even find a cause, some others I can save from vengeance, point in the right direction....'

'No, no,' I shout. 'Think of our danger, not of battles just or not, you might provoke.'

'Well,' Luisa says, drawing away from me. 'I am a statesman, so I think. At least as much as Alex, or as Damien. Every president – there's Alex, right behind them. Damien – sharpening his shiv. It's no big deal.'

My foot is settled back, snug in its sock of flesh, as sound as it has ever been.

'This house has no roof,' I say.

'I wanted it this way,' says Vera. 'So if anything should fall on it, the walls would be blown out, but easily stood up again.'

'It's so that anyone above can see us,' Luisa says.

'I should be starting from here,' I say. 'My journey. But I could be ending it.'

They look at me as if I've just discovered that.

'I want to see the wrestlers, oiling up,' Luisa says. 'I'd love to join in, but I don't see where they are.'

'Oh, they're a long way off, my dear,' says Vera. 'Down on the beach. You hear the music, very faint.'

If we could deal with her – one of the monsters on our path – we might be free. But we've no cash, no crew.... Vera tells Luisa, 'And stay clear of glistening bodies on the beach. They shine like armour, from high up, or swords and javelins. When you look down, the urge comes on – to be a part of it....'

'I know, I know,' Luisa says. 'I feel the same. If there's a stab, right on my head – a blade of hydrogen – I'd want it should be part of some grand war.'

I say, 'It's not like that, and grand, it's not the word... even the biggest wars round here – it's love, or contracts. Spite or status – that's the best you get. The rest is wanting goats and olive oil, or slaves and virgins – whatever suits you best.'

'Oh no,' says Vera, 'It's "lord it up". You humans can't all be Egyptians, so – you're Nubians, with pyramids that's sharper, redder, close together. If you're not up to being protected by the father of the gods – well, a son, or even feisty daughters, do as well.'

Love or obedience? The bride abducted, or the broken word? Those were the pretexts that caused the biggest fight round here. Luisa and I – we're not involved in either, bride or word. 'And that's why you're in this trouble,' Vera says. 'You could have known. The pretexts change, but you insult the boss, say he's not for ever…. That's enough. It is the same for well-regarded guys like me. Step out of line – down comes the sword. Of course, it may be Damien, fiddling with the case we don't know if it's armed or not. Open it up – that way you will find out.'

'Damien is special,' Luisa says. 'It's up to him if we all play on, or not.'

'He's my friend,' I say. 'And he's a pig. I hope he ends as one – a stuck pig.'

'Hey!' says Luisa. 'You have to be on a side. There's nothing else we can be.'

'It's true, Luisa. Many sides have been attractive. Africa, for example. Great guys, built interesting things,' I say.

'That's not exactly what I mean,' Luisa says. 'You know, there's no way we can end in jail. What we are, is serious. It wouldn't matter if you murdered me, like it could happen when we were in Russia, in the deadhouse. It wouldn't count. We're in something stickier, much bigger.'

I say. 'For me, there's nothing but the voyage. Not you, and not the witches, not the crew I said they'd all deserted, but there they were, drowning, calling on me with love in their eyes. No fine writing. Maybe start a gang... and take Vera, all that crowd, take them out. That cloud they sit on!'

'I hate you,' Luisa says. 'And Vera too, maybe more. I love being on a team, being the fastest. Not this waiting for the punishment, this nebulous stuff. Hate your riffs, your slogans; her sneak bullying.'

'You two,' says Vera sharply, 'you take up the gun – you're dead! No waiting for the order – that is it! Over. Applause. Curtain.'

'We're not contesting anything,' Luisa says. 'It would be useless anyway….'

'Then what is it you guys want?' shouts Vera. 'Eternity? Or paradise?'

'No, absolutely not,' we say. 'A change of scene, maybe.'

Vera's silent for a while, then. 'Look! There's Liesl! Crawling up the beach.' And there she is, exhausted, like an iguana, turtle, she squirms her limbs, and lifts her head, the hair like plaited snakes, to see the dangers that await. An ocean swum – or dropped off.... Augusto's boat!

We run down. The beach is full of beefy Turkish guys, their tight black wrestlers' pants aglow with vegetable oil. Luisa tries a hold or two, and slithers off.

'Liesl!' she cries. 'You had no qualities at all, but now I see you're stubborn, fixed to life like frescoes on a wall. To swim so far... and leave your friends—'

'No, no,' says Liesl, 'Not at all like that. I had a falling out. Disputed umpires' calls. Our frolics ended bad. Augusto said I'd start again to weave the evolutionary chain – he'd dump me in a trough, a slough... I'd swim and swim, my arms and legs would turn to fins, and in the end, I'd find a shore and start the human trip again.... I should become a hominid, with special powers, like breathing underwater, laying eggs upon a shell, not bothering with guys and all that sexual stuff to procreate.... Instead – I see it was a scam. For here you are, and on the cliff, those towers, the pikemen and the trumpeters. It seems a war zone.... Here's Luisa, with her lizard's tongue, mocking my lack of qualities, and here you are—' she points at me, her fingers, if she has them still, in gloves of weed '—trying to avoid the fight and steal a boat, and on to somewhere else....'

'Dear Liesl,' says Luisa, 'you are a perfect candidate – for marriage, or for other things. Your modest wants, desire to please, to say the normal things that all expect.... In your imperfect way, you are the perfect specimen. Maybe Augusto saw in you a species type that lives together happily, exchanging commonplace, and when the sun's too hot – finding ice caves, drinking salty broth, or living upside down like bats when there's no room to stand....'

'Luisa, dear,' says Liesl, at her end. 'I need a drink. Perhaps I imagine it – I see a pitcher, frosted, Margheritas are they? Or Manhattans? Augusto was abstemious, it drove us mad, the football, the beach volley, hot containers... it was hell, although it made us fit and strong.'

'Find her a basket,' Vera says, taking control. 'With rushes. Maybe she's about to change.'

Luisa lays a saucer of raki beside Liesl. 'It was the drink,' Luisa says, 'When she was engaged in Prague, her boyfriend thought they argued over his impotence – but really, it was drink. The krugels, and the rest.'

Liesl perks up, 'Ah, Prague,' she says. 'The drink. Pivo, I think they called it there.'

I wonder, 'Suppose Chloe follows her. Could she be the new human kind, the child of hope?'

'Oh no,' says Liesl, drinking, 'Chloe's turned old. She sits, she tats, embroiders on a frame. And she waits, maybe for someone who will listen to her tales. Her mouth's a cave, the teeth have fallen in. Fat as a sow. A temper, too. Science is a magic thing, of course – all those undersea monsters we had never seen – the giant squid, those tiny whales...but no, you'd need a miracle to lift poor Chloe up and launch her.'

That's a relief. Meanwhile, the wrestling on the beach proceeds: more boats, and screaming. Smoke from fires, sounds like the banging armourers make.

'I feel my grip is loosening,' Vera says. 'If all free spirits cast themselves up here, it makes surveillance doubly hard.'

That's true. Augusto has untrammelled energy. He ships guys in, he drops them overboard. He moves everywhere, his grey boat, sleek as a shark. 'Screw all this,' says Vera. 'Don't think I haven't wanted to call the bolt down on me, even on myself! We, my lot, had history, tradition, we were an institution. But people – they invent! First it was one big God, then it was peace, and now free trade. We smaller potentates – maybe our story's over. Maybe Damien is right – best go out with showers of sparks, than linger on in beige decline. And there's another thing, you guys. The white-coats, the magi of the blackboard and the new-coined words: they say the sun will last for centuries, and give them time to solve the other stuff – no air, no water, and no food, all that. Well, it's not so. They've lied, the science guys. I've contacts in the mountain tops – they say the sun is looking rickety, the dawn is later every month, the sunset earlier. Don't take bets! The heat is running down, it's turning off, the chicks don't have the time to learn the mating songs, nor trees to think up fruit.'

Vera keens. We are all desperate.

'Let's keep it straight,' says Vera. 'There's much confusion – there's wrestling on the beach. There's fighting somewhere else. You're not involved. You're simply waiting.'

'We're not in jail,' I say.

'No,' Vera says. 'You can't leave, though. You are in range.'

Liesl laughs, happy in her creel. 'Since you are dead,' she says, 'I must be dead myself, and there's the proof – an angel, tall as a candlestick,' and she points at Vera. 'Franz should be somewhere here – a death so terrible, a life so mysterious. He'd be a puff of spirit, not like you two, such rosy corpses.'

'No, not at all,' Luisa says. 'We have our death certificates, but passports too. We cannot move, at least we are alive. But – Liesl, you are silent; white and silver, every moment more fishlike – we could float you far away, lower you down, in the Scamander....' Liesl hears 'salamander', and says, 'Yes, yes – I feel the cold and wet. Put me in the fire, and I'll come back to my full life....' and Luisa says, 'The fire is what we hope we can escape.'

'Chloe,' Liesl says, 'she has no passport. She will die alone, still waiting, still embroidering....'

'That's nonsense, Liesl,' says Luisa. 'If she had a passport, there's nowhere she could go, no one to take her, no one to keep her company.'

'It's true,' says Liesl, settling back. Her teeth are neat, sharp as a pike's – she grins. 'Augusto only wants the finest specimens, to try us out. Where he comes from, the Eternal City – he says they're nearly perfect, all of them, they're specimens. Like him. They pray all day, he says. Except – they die. There is some flaw....'

'Ain't that the truth,' laughs Vera, lying back on her chaise longue, showing her gums.

This is not the time to speak of Alex, his politics, his sexual habits, but we do.

'He has no fantasy,' says Vera. 'Where others smoke cheroots, imagine orgies delicate as dreams of gossamer – he must pay to watch and prance around. They all wear masks of former presidents – it makes deep gloom. He thinks it fun.'

Luisa looks uncomfortable: she says, 'The money all goes back to him. He has no use for it.'

'And isn't that the way,' says Vera comfortably. Down on the shore, we see small lightning strikes. Or – it could be gleams from bodies, trying to lift each other up.

'Let me go down, and try a hold or two,' Luisa begs.

'If you are trying to escape, or put a distance with this guy,' says Vera, sitting up, 'you risk a lot. Of course, I could change sides. Or just nod off, have a blank page.'

Liesl lies gasping on her reeds: her sister says, 'She could have been.... She's so....' Luisa stumbles.

'Yes,' Vera says, 'quite nondescript. A princess or a *pute*. Freedom fighter, bandit queen – it's all the same to her. I may seem cynical. She is another one who has no qualities, but she doesn't have them, if you follow me, in such a perfect, a luxuriant way – she fits in anywhere. A universal screw. For engineer, or for handyman. Not that it's pejorative, you understand – we all, we sheep and goats – must strive for perfection, on our backs or on our fronts, with taser in our hand, apology on our lips....'

'Just a few throws,' Luisa begs again. 'It seems a trivial thing....'

'It is, it is,' says Vera.

She won't let Luisa go.

Vera says, 'I fear you two haven't had much from each other.'

'No, she hasn't,' I say. 'Though it was travelling together that brought us here, all bound up, inseparable. Making a target we wouldn't otherwise have been. Leading our lives to whatever you might decide for us.'

'Oh,' Vera says, 'that's too portentous. I could keep you here – and then again, you might go away unscathed! Nothing happening, except time. No love, no hurt.'

'Speaking of that – I feel I don't know her, Luisa's beauty, not at all,' I say.

'Oh yes you do,' Luisa says. 'It's all there, all there is, all my quotes, there's nothing more. Knowing more – what good would that do? Just knowing what we do has brought us to this bad bad state.'

To help us out – here's Damien. 'I'm off Augusto's boat,' he says, 'but not as one of his hopes of better species. I've always been the higher type.'

He's struggled through the marshy river, swapped an insult with the wrestlers. He has the briefcase still. He says, 'I shan't open it. I have a deal with Alex. Neither of us is too sure just how it works – if you open it, and that's the end, or just the start of something electric that you have to learn.'

I see no resolution for us through his presence.

I say, 'Whatever are your motives, Damien, maybe you're right. Do deals – and then, make up your mind. Finish it, all of it, before the worst. Don't fumble on with Croats and Austrians, what they did and had done to them. Or all the rest, guys in the middle; the Emperors... the past. The distant and the recent past, the yesterday. We'll draw a line. Let's say that something was the worst that could be done, even if it's not the case... you look a little, round about you, and—'

'Oh, all that's been discussed,' Luisa says. 'The praise and blame – all on the table, in the protocol. There's nothing more to say about it. It's what is happening to us that counts.'

'Such moralism,' says Vera. 'What falls from the skies – doesn't depend on guys like you.'

'You must believe your side's the best,' says Damien. 'Maybe it is. That's the moralism, Vera, as you know. And you...' he points at Luisa and myself. 'What do you know of the design? Who is to win, who disappear?'

He waves the doomsday case. 'This is one answer. Honour above everything. Out, everyone, with clangs of gongs.'

'You guys want to wait, until the world falls in the sun?' asks Vera, looking bored.

'Those wrestlers,' Luisa says, tugging at Vera's drapes. 'They're not like Neapolitans, if there's a gal who wants to play – they let you, and they take her on, on equal terms. Just let me try....'

'Look, Luisa,' Vera says. 'We don't do research. A strike's a strike. If you're in the midst, you're hit – too bad for everyone. Accept your destiny.'

'Suppose it's love, then,' says Luisa. 'Suppose I want to save this guy,' and she pinches my cheek.

'No, no,' says Vera, 'I respect, I contemplate. But why should what you guys do interest me? I'm an expert in love, not a mechanic. You – I cannot fix.'

'Look at the tracks,' I say. 'Up to the citadel, down to the beach where constantly the boats pull in. Wrestlers carried down to be embarked. Waiting for triage or the funeral pyre. Like there's a timetable, the distant sound, as the lady with the breasts strides round the ring, strikes the steel bar – new round....'

'That's crap,' shouts Vera. 'It's not circular, not up and down – this moment is unique. Open the fucking case, Damien. Open it, have done with it. Apocalypse. Or nothing. Quick.'

Damien makes a face, as if he's toiling with the locks, he squats with effort – then falls back. The case springs open, and we turn away, cover our eyes, our ears. Will there be a smell, a flash, cordite or phosphorus – something we shan't ever tell our grandchildren about – our brains, receptive, analytic to the end, our memories alert, cut short....

'Why, it's a bird,' says Liesl, who can't cover eyes, and maybe has no ears.

'It'll be an eagle, that's for sure. Maybe with two heads. A sign, a portent,' and Luisa tries to follow it. It rockets up, trailing its golden shower.

'No, it's a swan,' I say. 'Hear how it whistles, creaks. That is the chosen bird of love – away it flies. From which of us, I wonder?'

'There!' Damien says. 'You will be satisfied. That was a wonder, shut up in there so long, and you had thought it must be bombs and poison, leaflets saying to "watch out". Instead – a creature, pleased to be off, and ignorant of all around.'

'A sign!' Luisa says. 'From Alex. Nothing will end. Nature will soldier on. The air is thick enough for wings to grip. They don't ignite as they bear eagles to the citadel... the city with the gates – so many, seven, seventy – each with its renegade, ready with the key to open up and let us good guys in....'

'That's enough, Luisa,' Damien shouts. 'No quotes, no fevered thoughts. Throughout the world there's cases, of all kinds. I brought the one that had inside – a kind of swan. It signifies monogamy, if that could interest you guys...' and he looks round at our disappointed faces.

'Hoho,' laughs Vera, 'that's the best one we have heard today! A bird! The answer is – a swan! The world ends – not with a bang.... A whoop! Now, that is genius!'

'Dead scenes are hard to do,' says Damien. 'The plaintive ones are naff. The ones that seek to draw some meaning out, as if it adds, detracts – so what? You–' and he points again at Luisa and me. 'The threat above. You know exactly what and why, exactly what it signifies for you. You're lucky gladiators. Here's the blood, and we're the public – you'll be dragged off, someone will rake the sand.'

'And as for you,' he says to me. 'You're spared the journey. Not that you've anywhere to go, except the terminus. But Luisa.... come on, Vera – let her have some sport. You can keep her in your sights. Lightning can always strike twice, in the same place too.... She won't escape, if that's not her destiny.'

'And me?' asks Liesl from her basket.

'Ah yes,' says Damien. 'You're the little girl in the photo. Do you get killed, or are you the survivor, the "sweet little Viennese maiden"? Here's a puzzle for you – does it matter if your destiny comes from someone depraved? Like Alex. Or someone like me? A man with a mission? Or might Vera and I have nice Liesl steaks off you, when the shouting's done?'

'Oh no,' Liesl snivels. 'I'm bony, through and through.'

'It's all in Luisa's books, I'm sure,' says Vera, who's not read them, that's quite certain. 'The photos, and the lives as well.'

'What I think of, is about poor people, what's to happen to them,' Damien says. 'Poor people don't figure largely in Luisa's books.'

'They're dull,' says Luisa, 'What you call poor people, that's supposed to rise and rule the world. But you see their faces, pressed against the panes. Some sell tickets on the trams, and others dodge the fares.'

Damien says it's intricate – he wouldn't put a number on it – who is all right, solvent, and who is not. Luisa says he's statesmanlike, and then she whispers to me, 'We two – we might make a pact for suicide. Finish it off, take the initiative.'

'Luisa, Luisa,' I sing to her, like in the Deadhouse: in the story, it is she who's killed, and I go in the penitentiary. That won't happen here. 'Luisa, we are blocked – there is a future, we're not part of it.'

'We're not heroic,' says Luisa. 'That's the trouble. That's why no one helps.'

It's hot. Damien and Vera finish off the pitcher. I sleep. I dream of me and Luisa: it's pretty good....

Down on the beach, the guys hop to and fro – dodging the lightning strikes, being cast down, and being carried off. 'That's all a part of it,' Luisa says. 'That's athletics. Taking your chance. Oh – let me go down, and dance between the thunderbolts!'

It's an idea. With Luisa on the beach, I have a chance up here – to parley, run away, or stay so close to Vera she can't get her clear shot at me....

Damien says to Vera. 'Love and assassination. All around. Vera – that's your slogan too – love and murder. Some say it's a paradox....'

'Well, it's not,' says Vera. 'It's the way I am. I don't criticise you, Damien, you and your doomsday case, although my future's maybe tied up in there too....'

They argue on. Luisa is skipping down – I see her through the stands of reed, she strips off well, the guys down there – they greet her, there's a line to see who'll try first hold on her. She's happy. They are happy too.

Vera sees her: my, she's angry. She takes the briefcase, tries to open it – 'No, no,' shouts Damien, 'not yet. Today is not the day.'

'You smart guy,' Vera shouts at me. 'You think you'll sacrifice Luisa, and stand a better chance with me up here. It isn't so. Experience means nothing to you – that's why you journey – someone more intelligent would see the peril can't be dodged for long....'

The lightning dances on the beach, like swords of light or glass. Guys tumble down – and there's Luisa – outlined in fire, a flaming angel, or a torch. She's struck. And then – she's charred, she's gone. Taken up, quite disappeared. Another end bizarre, like Franz, or like the giant. All ends are maybe so, not needing explanation or analysis....

'I think it wasn't even one of mine, that strike,' says Vera, angrier still. 'She muddled into contests that weren't even hers. Now, she's escaped, gone into oblivion. No medal, and no funeral march.'

'It's the oil. It fries them up. They put it on to make themselves slippery,' says Damien. 'They'll never make it to the citadel.'

'If that is what they want:' says Vera, putting a thong round my wrist and tying an end to her chaise longue. 'There is a scheme. The winner runs up the hill, then back, and everyone to their boats and off back home.'

'We should mourn for Luisa,' I say. I have the time, I've a life sentence.

'Give it your spin, then,' Damien says, settling a briefcase under his head as he lies back. 'We'll tell Liesl everything, when she wakes.'

That won't be soon.

'I need time, lots of time,' I say. 'I'll sum it up. About her literature... "Luisa skipped, straight to the end she went." That sounds quite wrong. Her running? "She departed, she was... a streak... greased lightning...." No, absolutely, that won't do. I can't coin it clean. She must have been my muse, my muse is dead with her. Poor Luisa... I could never hurt you.'

'Well?' asks Damien. 'You haven't got an epitaph?'

'Not really, Damien,' I say.

'You must try harder,' Vera says. 'Until you get it right, there'll be no travelling for you. And there's still your punishment to come.'

I don't believe she's any plan to let me go. I have no destination anyway. I say, I sigh,

'Dear Luisa.'

Broken Chords

'Remember that Kazakh boy? Dressed as a soldier. Well, he was a soldier, a Soviet soldier. Got up on the stage in the park, and did a woman's dance – with verve. Don't you remember, the scarf? The undulation? Boys, they do the women's part: sometimes they sell them, now. To do a private dance. Catamites, they've become. Don't you remember, the applause, everyone for it, the artistry, the confidence? Was it Tbilisi? Or Baku? It should have been Baku, but it seems that it was Tbilisi.' The father strains for a response, some sharing.

'No, I was a baby then,' says his son. 'You took me as your cover. You spied, all over.'

'I spied, but only for me. I was curious, not a pro. It's all done long-distance now,' the father says. 'The park... the violinist, that they said did not exist. The guy who made up verses for you, mocking your foes. Remember those red ten-rouble notes they pushed into his hands?'

'No! I wasn't there,' the son says, irritated. 'I was a baby. In the basket, in the park.'

'It was around the time your mother fucked off,' says the father, pressing on. 'We two could do another spy trip. The shopping's better now. Sell our memories. If we get back safe.'

'You have to be careful who you are. Too many lines you shouldn't cross.'

'Well,' the father says, 'you were born in Africa, so you're black. Your French is bad, that means in France you speak funny, so you're black twice over, from their Africa. In the States, that English accent – they think you're gay. So, there you are. A sort of changeling. It's always my point. My irony – "serene irony" – that's what the poet called it. Irony has no colour and no faith.'

'They don't understand you,' says the son, 'And that's not irony – it's ridiculing the pretension, pretending that people aren't bigots, or that they're treated equal. Or that they're different only by what you can't see – what's in their heads.'

'It seemed kinder, long ago. Perhaps they hid the bodies better. When I think – yes, there were mountains of bodies then, but not in colour. Anyway, my mission's passed to you. It's yours.'

'What mission's that?' asks the son. 'Making yourself comfortable?'

'It's not so easy either,' says the father, 'As you'll find out. You're soft.'

*

'I'm concentrating,' I say. 'The wax is running out my ears, into my hair.'

'That's not wax, it's bad thoughts,' says the guy.

'I can do the upside-down pose,' I say. 'But it does stress.'

'You have to think,' he says. 'The very small, the very large. There's no big difference. Try not to get lost in either, but they should look substantially alike. There's no affect, that's the first thing. Neither the krill, nor the black hole – they're both unfathomable. Nothing to do with you, that you can change, or eat, or surf in. Or grow in pots on windowsills. That's how you should encounter everything, that's how you are yourself. Immense, and universal, tiny but basic, huge, but an infinity of end.'

'I see. I understand,' I say.

That's all it is, that all it takes. Seeing, grasping. From other generations, after my father's, come creations of a different size, but all the parts the same; extinct in their huge distance. They have always been – but only we identified them, with our telescope. Don't need worry about them, their impinging. Things, though, my father never knew. I am the universe. He wasn't.

The teacher, the doctor, priest, philosopher – his face is round. He smiles, although it seems a smirk. 'You're my best subject, ever,' he says.

'Thanks, Omar,' I say. It's what he wants, his treat. I've trained him, to come to heel.

'I have this dream,' I say. 'I'm falling down this black hole, smaller and denser I become, sucked in and eaten out, like a winkle from its shell.'

'Don't worry,' Omar says. 'It won't happen. And there's no white rabbit out there in the void, when you wake up, the story ends. Watch the red dwarves don't get you, though.'

'You put things in perspective, Omar,' I say.

'Yes,' he says. 'And you want my perspective? Well, I don't give a fuck for you, your woman you don't mention, your dead mother, father – I don't care for you, and you don't care for me. I tell you people stories, and you pay me, or you make excuses, and anyway – I don't care for you. Even the law – it does not insist. Free not to care. I'd go on the streets and shout for that.'

'Yes, that's good,' I say. 'I need to hear that.'

'Work it out. Fight it out among yourselves. No moral weep, no "Do what I say, and you'll have what I've got, some day." Imagine I'm a foreigner, stuck in the country that you don't know where it is. I don't want to live up close to you,' Omar goes on.

'Don't exaggerate, Omar. Your case is made,' I say.

My agency. 'Prop. myself' – advises people what they have to do. What they can. Might. So, I have to keep myself informed. I'm interviewing Sylvia. It seems I need an accomplice.

'If I had a little sister,' I say, 'she'd be about your age.'

No, it's not seduction, nor even incest that I have in mind.

She's very cautious. 'Your agency – you liberate people? You train them? You exploit their powers?'

'Oh no,' I say. 'What you really mean is – do I ask a lot of cash? The answer's yes – as much as I can, and as much as they are able to think a thing, any thing at all, is worth. But – no freedom: just another weight – more knowledge, more uncertainties. No training – what a bore that is! It can take years, and what for? Bright ones do it naturally. Their powers? – it's clear they're not so evident. That's why they come to me. No – it's showing other paths.'

'Rich guys, without a clue?' she asks. 'That's it?'

'I could call you Sylvie,' I say. 'That's woody, pagan.'

'Have you others to interview?' she asks.

'I could have, of course. Hundreds. But I'm doing nicely with you. My father had a mission, understanding the world, preliminary to changing it, if he'd lived long enough, and had the firepower. He travelled when that was still worthwhile, with differences all around. I don't have any of this. It's like the philosopher said – "Philosophy should be the theory of what we do, not of what is." What is, is quite uncertain. Taken as it is, I'm not sure it's interesting, or digestible. Of course, if you lose me money, that path ends.'

'You'd take a risk with me,' says Sylvie.

'I didn't say I'd pay you,' I say. 'There's no risk.'

'You're like a hundred years ago,' she says. 'Like we would go to Africa, shoot rare animals and get a fever.'

'Concentrate on yourself,' I say. 'Don't consider the others – they're thinking about themselves, what it is they lack. One person can't do much, make much noise – two, even less.'

'I've had battles,' Sylvie says. It doesn't show, I can't believe she won them all, and that it wasn't others had already been on her battlefields.

I have no clients now, since she worked here. She has lots. She says. 'I tell them what they've done is their philosophy. They're thrilled. They're keen to do some more.'

'I always wondered how guys went off each day to work, and do the same goddam thing, with no respite,' I say. 'But – careful, Sylvie! Don't take it all too literally. And don't let's make it a religion.'

'Literally's the only way to take it, when it's written down,' she says: I guess it's sex, accounting for how she's so popular.

'I love those Mexican trains,' I say. 'Long; real heavy metal, that's what it truly means. Yellow, and wetbacks on the top, like candied fruit on cakes. I knew a guy, worked on Canadian trains. It's military. In the caboose – you can sleep, but you can't read. That way, prophecy in your country, or anyone else's – it's not on.'

'That's what it takes,' asks Sylvie, 'to be a prophet? Reading? And they can't be wetbacks, if they're on a train.'

'I'm speaking loosely, Sylvie,' I say. 'And to be a prophet, you need space, and common sense. The only thing guys plan for in general, in the world – is manoeuvres. Exercises. Spying on the deadly stuff they say they'll never use. All the rest's defaults. They improvise, and call it science. Hypothesis. But what works – is army. Everything else is finite.'

'I've heard all that,' says Sylvie. 'Just let my genius run its course, and then I'll think of what I've done.'

'A prophet hectors, Sylvie. Prophets are bigots, and the future doesn't interest them too much. They don't foretell – the future's what everybody knows. Women can be prophets – that could make us rivals. My father thought it was in my grasp, prophesying – but the real stuff lay beyond. He used to say, "Democracy is of the Right; and don't expect benevolence. What matters is, you execute the comrades who screw up, you cut the throats of all the sons who haven't had the sense to join you. No meandering, do what you must, to the end, no musing about humanism. The rest is cups of froth, it's strut. If you're not up to this – then strum on fantasy, find your slot, your business. Crawl into it. You're just a writer on the shelves, inventing, beside the elves," and he'd laugh. Sylvie, that's what your genius is. Froth. Fantasy.'

'Your father was an eloquent man,' says Sylvie, much impressed.

'Well, you don't do all that being hard and realist on your own,' I say. 'It's mostly travelling, then getting old. You need a team. Then, all he had left was disappointment with his son, with me.'

*

Even if you've seen one before, a naked body – someone else's – is a shock. You're so used to the clothes. Used to the talk about it all, the organic – and then it's there, in front of you, with demands that clothes don't make. A thing, a body, it seems unmodifiable – the things it can become – old, crippled, a cadaver the next step – seem so far away. It's not aesthetics. The cow in the field – who thinks of it, reduced to steak? Tough, the life fights back, clings in your trachea. A body, naked: it's for admiration, or for sex. The opposites. Sylvie's to be admired. Sex is mostly about you first. She's out there, beckoning. Then she's disappeared, and you're a monster, all reason gone. Scrabbling on some skin, dribbling, too. It's a puzzle – she'd see it in the same way – I guess Omar would too.... It's all philosophy.

'This is a reward,' says Sylvie, as if she's always known beneath the clothes there was all this speculation, 'because you're so poor at philosophy.'

'Well, that's done,' she says, when it is. 'It's something you'll remember, probably.'

'It's very biological, all this,' I say. 'I remember people by their clothes. Or by their names. Omar – if he was Portuguese, that means "the sea". *O mar*. Quite inconclusive. Like having fathers.'

'Two guys came yesterday,' she says.

'You told them they were doing right? Were they tax, or cops, or mafia? They should leave happy that they're doing good.'

'Oh, they did. Said they'd be back.'

'Of course,' I say. 'It used to be empires. Now we're back to countries. I don't like them either. A country has small mountains, rivers, grass, and geese. This one has holes in the ground and firing ranges. Empires send platoons, countries send two guys.'

'It's not that you go out,' says Sylvie, 'and see.'

'We should leave,' I say, 'immediately.'

'You're thinking wrong,' she says. 'Digging your father's archaeology.'

'Before we go, we must scream,' I say. 'It's all there's left.'

'That sounds a different therapy,' says Sylvie. 'I talk. Even if they don't understand. There's all these languages. It's all quite Balkan. You reach a compromise, a few words, defining you as separate.'

'No, Sylvie – it's not the Balkans, not India, or China, or the Arab lands. It's right here – see – down in the canyon....' Electric buses, guys parading up and down, like they were in marching bands. New York. It could be Buffalo.

We scream. There's nothing left.

We don't try to be in tune – she has a good vibrato, I'm in the roots, where snakes breed and the ants reorganise.

The guys below – they think we're sirens. Air raids, not death on the rocks. They run – you can run from rockets, not from rocks. They're safe. They know they aren't. America – they ran here to be safe, they armed themselves. Their fear has followed them, it waits on every block. Now from the skies, it falls, a flaming Godzilla. They pulled it with them, behind them, tugging on a leash. 'Oh, repent, repent,' shouts Sylvie, entering the spirit.

'There's no need, Sylvie,' I say. 'It's no use. They'll be punished, without knowing the why or even when. It's history, it catches you. What the movies showed – all that will come and sit upon your shoulders.'

We scamper down the stairs. Out in the street, Sylvie screams – 'It's come! At last – it's payback day – all the good and all the bad, you'll pay for what you've done, like all the rest, and all you did it to. You're not immune – it happens to us all, to all of them....' We skitter down the street. Guys stand aside, some try a punch, a trip. They've heard it all before – the air that suffocates, the thirsts unquenchable – but never shouted out, never screamed – two beardless prophets, gorged with the words. Bonded and seduced by sex. At least, that's where Sylvie's raptus starts. With me, it's all philosophy.

The cops can't decide – to shoot us, or send us with the other mad people.

'We need protection,' Sylvie says: she grabs some pie from off a stand. 'Oh, I'd die / For pecan pie,' she sings. Guys assume we're a street act.

'No, Sylvie,' I say, 'I don't want to attract a swarm of weird people, with their twisted hopes. We've been into therapy. That's been done too.'

It's not snowing, so it must be spring or fall. You can't tell from the fruit – in the stores, it's never seasonal.

I say, as we slow to a saunter, 'My father knew – social revolution would from now be made by bourgeois guys. The bourgeoisie knew all about it, revolution, and they cared. So, not the workers, not an underclass: the bourgeoisie. Behind the ignorant enthusiasts, in whose name... there always was the bourgeois guy, who knew what it was all about. The bourgeois knows the consequences, he invented them. That's what "serve the people" means. He hated them real bad, despised them. Doing the tough work – that would be the simple soldiery, the marines – and that left him to steer the ship, find the ports, ride the storms.'

'Tell me something I don't know,' said Sylvie. 'Did he think that things would happen here? If we were in Warsaw, or in Rome – all round we'd see dictatorships and war, occupations, massacres, urban guerrillas, and the rest... laid down in people's heads, neat strata, the foundations. In time, there's bits of peace, the solidarity breaks down, and everyone's in therapy. Then something decisive starts over....'

'Here, it's all bubbling,' I say, 'shapeless. There's forerunners, survivors – it's all a broken vase that's been repaired, all improvised – the angel on the handle pasted in the base, nymphs in the reeds all upside down and randy....'

Sylvie stares at me. 'Yes, it comes to me,' she says. 'The broken vase. America. It's not the salad, not the melting pot. It's like a stew. We're farro. In the stew. That sylvan scene – where I am principal – it's all mashed up. The vase... once it was worth a lot, not now.... Now, the image is a stew, monkeys and dogs stirred in together. And elks. We're the farro, you and me, floating on the top, then sinking down. Mmmm – I love farro. Soft and malleable – it floats, sinks too.'

'Well, Sylvie, sort it out, these broken images. Now, we must run,' I say.

She glides along beside me, unstressed, keeping the air within: she says. 'Of course – there is a flaw. If here's a broken vase, you could smash it into shards again, make it like it should have been. But a stew... it's that or nothing.'

'That's sort of what my father said,' I say, to cut her short. It's not. He wanted something different: – but not a salad, not a stew. Not something old, restored. Not liberty. He didn't believe that made much sense. Equality – he didn't think he had an equal. Fraternity? Maybe, but not with brothers, not with family. No, really, not at all. None of those.

'Freedom was a negative thing,' I say, quite out of breath. 'Not having it provoked change. Not having it was a good, an accelerator.'

'There's lots I don't grasp, and there's not the time or the person to ask why I don't,' Sylvie says. 'There's that sign, *La*

111

coca es vida. Maybe it's like freedom, like your father said. And is it drugs or drink?'

'Just run, Sylvie,' I say. 'Those signs are meaningless.'

We stop. There's no one following. There's a waiting, a recurrence. Just two guys, going to call again on me.

'What can they want?' I ask. 'My father left me nothing, nothing useful. I don't pay tax because what I get, I spend at once.'

'That's not how it works,' says Sylvie. 'You're too generous.'

'The mafia uses telephones. The cops – they'd want my father, but he's dead. Maybe we can't foresee a good future. The past – most of it's indifferent, and lots we'd rather that it hadn't been. Are we in some way degenerate? Is it that we aren't of use? Don't make stuff?' I ask.

'Of course not, it can't be,' Sylvie says. 'That's the beauty of it here – there's millions round like us, and busy busy too. We are the grease, we help it all go round and round.'

'To get elected here,' I say, 'you must believe in God. You must be pretty theological – and on the other side, it seems there's preachers, with their books. Is it my misbelief?'

'Oh no,' says Sylvie, 'that doesn't matter squit. You don't want election, and you wouldn't be.' She ponders. 'You never studied, did you? Not anything.'

'No, nothing,' I tell her. 'Not me, nor my father. It's all experience, all made up. And you, Sylvie?'

'No! I've no qualifications, nothing like that. Quite different experiences from yours, too,' she says. 'Experience – it's all you and I know.'

She sees a place where they sell – 'Oh, pies!' she says; 'Come on.'

There's two guys sitting there. They're waiting for company. 'Why!' Sylvie says, 'That's the guy who does my tattoos.'

He might be. The other – what might he do? You pick up suspicion, it's a family thing. My father started as a Jacobin. Then it was the vanguard party. Then himself, the critical critic. Sylvie had said, 'Your father – he didn't much go for the masses.'

'No,' I'd said. 'Some places, pretty large ones, he wasn't welcomed.'

She's gone in, kisses the tattoo guy on the head. Imagining how it feels, the sensation, the hair, the gel – not pleasant. She thinks I've followed her, but I've hung back. The guys jump up, run after me. Sylvie stands stupid at the door.

Oh shit! I think – these guys – they learn to run in all the places where the president has made his moral gestures, given history his twist. Chile and Guatemala, Grenada and Iraq – the places where he hopes for love, comes up with basketfuls of snakes. It's just about all over, everywhere, his Midas touch, turns all to dross and strass. Good cop, bad cop, flattening countries, after, giving them gifts.

And all those guys – maybe they cut each others' hair, so they can recognise their pals – how they can run. They're gaining on me.

A refuge? Up the steps here – seeking a small utopia, even with a secretary. My body, my system, is breaking now, sucking in the air – no longer works. The brain steps partly into a nirvana: no narcotic like the present, all the guys here are selling dope, no instructions on the packet, you make it up.... It's like Marseilles, the old quarter still resisting, nearly eighty years of it.

The Indians have taken refuge here, the last massacre, in the Mato Grosso, just a few survivors, cut in half with those machetes, but still soldiering ahead, a coupla jobs to keep each half a-struggling on. There's Omar – *O mar* – you have to travel on him, on the sea, gruff and disgruntled though it is, would suck you down. Your bones are worth a dime.

Oh no! The guys have caught me. The tattooer holds me down. These urban 'scapes, escapes or escapades, it's quite a situational, and the layout doesn't help you get away – the two guys kneel on me. The one without the gel says, 'Sins of the sons... are visited upon the fathers and the grandfathers, even unto....'

It takes a while: they tattoo me, where I can't see. I guess the word, although I'll never read it. 'Soft'. They know all about me.

Later, I say, 'Sylvie, you betrayed me. You brought me to them. We didn't run from them, we ran towards.'

'I know, I know,' she says, pretending tears. 'It's the tattoo. It does no harm. I'm covered in them. It shows that you've been caught. We almost all of us are tagged – there's butterflies and swallows, that show we have escaped and now been caught. There's warrior signs to show aggression, and there's names of people you've let down, and crosses that show disbelief. They catch you, everyone gets marked, and everyone's aware of what they haven't done, or what they crave, and all of that is known, recorded somewhere.... You could falsify yours, if you wish, add words to it – "soft gold". That's for the Mato Grosso, and the mines. Or "Softer the sun, on your last morning lifts...." Wealth and art. There!'

'Nonsense, Sylvie,' I say. 'People were tattooed before God told them it was a sacrilege on all the skin he wove. Now, it's a police operation, for sure. They have it written down. It's evidence against.'

'Don't worry about it,' Sylvie says. 'It's nothing. It's just – a man opens me, then I close myself, and I'm alone inside again. That's all I need to know. Inside, I'm Guy Debord, though much less fun. And you?'

I go along with this. Really, I'm interested in the history, not in knowing about me, or her. Things finish, then they go on again, like a big animal that eats itself, gets ever stronger, ever smaller. They're not good or bad, trundling along and eating, that's all they can do.

'What do I know?' I say. 'Inside, I'm full of blood. We all are. There's no need to be a moralist, Sylvie, or unload things on to famous people. Blood – it's our food, our fuel, ours or other people's. Remember Spartacus – his profession, killing his brothers, then the revolutionary struggle, then the crosses. And, Sylvie, you snitched. That's not original.'

She wriggles, rolls herself up, and giggles. '"The totality for kids" – that's my inspiration. You remember, they had Lenin saying, "I couldn't give a fuck about 'Revolutionary young communists' either." Genius – those guys had it. Your father? He was a passenger. I'm afraid that you are too.'

'He told me how they used to bomb the jungle, the Americans. Our brothers. Poisoned air and fire,' I say.

'Oh, you must see how it's all different now,' she says. 'Even if you don't, and it isn't.'

'The new guys – they're tough,' I say. 'It's true – the men no longer sing the women's parts in Chinese opera. That's something softening too, I guess.'

She doesn't seem convinced. Maybe she doesn't understand. 'Libs, cons, and rads – how you play on with those old games,' she says. 'It didn't ever work like that. There's a task for you – what do we think next? – while I'll go on, telling people what they are.'

The new guys, everywhere – they're not just tough, they're hard. They fight for what they've got and haven't got.

Sylvie – she wears power suits – clown suits – baggy, and ready for the wind to lift her off, a kite to snag in trees where Jung's skeleton is perched and happy, singing to the spotted birds. Her face is docile, though, letting the clothes do all the work, whether they're on, or on the floor.

I wear my skates, and join with all the other suited guys, swooping along, pretend to get to some employment before our brothers on the trains.

Sylvie says, 'You failed your job interview. I'm proud.'

'You leering in, and your red cartwheels in the lot outside,' I say. 'They broke the seriousness' – although I'm proud too, and relieved.

'That was the sign of "now",' she says. 'Bear it in mind, it cancels out regrets. Those guys – one with a tiny head, the other all grey tufts, gummed up with snuff – if you had sought out freaks...! Stick them together, you would make one monster. Two's a hatch. The hairy one, the Tufty – he tried to make out with me.'

'"We need a guy who's delicate," one said. "The old regime, this dispensation's tailing off, its sweetness draining from the hive. The new guys, in those countries we don't know where they are, that once were far away and now are not, they jostle you aside. They bring harsh news. You may regret the bangs and blusters that we brought. We're ordinary now. We are awake, the brain is clean. We'll sell our stuff, for sure. But – from the guys that we employ, we need an afterword. That maybe starts it all again, another journey, just a few of us, steered by the stars...."

'So, I told them, "If you want to know the future – it's civil war, city states, secessions. Invasion, occupation. Deserts, the flow of people up and down, masses like the buffaloes, the Indios, the passenger pigeons. Roaming between the mines and wells. Camping on the shale, sleeping on the broad-leafed grass, with an eye on space, where maybe they will find a home, a homestead, a square of dust to hoe." They didn't want to hear. Said I wasn't on the team. Fantasy, they said. I told them, it was just the things most people already knew, them too. They'd shut it out.'

'It's what you're father said, but without the songs,' says Sylvie.

'We can't believe in nature,' I say, thinking of what I might become. 'Nor sites, nor seasons, not old things, nor portable things like books and parures. Not the spirit, not the structure. So – not France, not China. Not all the terrible lessons the Americans have handed out. Where do we go, Sylvie?'

She wanders off.

'Omar must be right,' I think. 'Yourself. No one else, not neighbours – what a noise they make.... You must make yourself the sea, *o mar*. Swallows and regurgitates, but not a mouth, a stomach, not an anus, not a gut. That's full of everything you could imagine – all invisible, unfindable. An envelope that hums to itself, atonal: moods, colours, signifying nothing. Not silence, not beauty – just an undertow of splash and sift, a conversation about nothing, with yourself. The sea. That's what I must be, a sea that needs no place to be itself.'

Sylvie's back. 'They're, you're done,' she says. 'You found your answer, like I knew you would. Not good at much, but – wow – that's what you're good at, the answer.'

'That Kazakh boy – my father said – he was from the world's umbilical. Not a conclusion, but the point where all beginnings start. A fairly useless place, desert and mountain, where all the contradictions meet. That is the answer, Sylvie, to all the questions. Powerless, it's at the confluence of all the powers....' I say.

'Maybe you should tell those guys, and get the job,' she laughs.

'They want to know what's profitable tomorrow. I don't know,' I say.

'You appreciate Omar more than you do me,' says Sylvie. 'And you steal my money.'

'No, Sylvie, I've freed Omar from being just a human, but I've seen – I must be nature. The other nature, with a capital letter – that's gone. It was trial and mostly error, and it's buried. So, as they say, you must invent it yourself. Invent yourself as it. It's like your money – theft is property, and then more theft. And so on. It's only chance that Omar's name is "sea". I'm not becoming Omar – I'm becoming sea.'

She's quite angry. 'Then you don't need money,' she says. 'And I might go, seek love. Seek another person to do it with, definitely not you.'

'Oh Sylvie,' I say, to needle her, 'don't give yourself up so easy. You'd think of me, when those armoured junks sail up the river and Kozinga takes New York.'

'It won't happen,' Sylvie says.

'Not real Chinese, of course,' I say. 'Just the metaphor.'

'I have a new partner,' Sylvie says. 'He's for the emotions – he doesn't do philosophy.'

Her new guy – sits relaxed, and twitches to her Kraftwerk discs. Sylvie moves around him nervously.

I'd guess he's seventy kilos. His casual clothes cost money I could spend instead.

'My father tried to save the world,' I say. 'It can't be done. I guess it was a stupid thing.'

'Oh, I wouldn't say so,' he – Chip – says, quite vaguely.

'I'm not trying to reassure you, Chip,' I say.

'We could dance,' says Sylvie. 'Just us three – but it might seem ridiculous.' I think it would. She says, 'Chip is a Chipewa. His parents – they were Indians, but he's had the nature stripped right out.'

Chip says to me, 'You should go to India. That's where they thought we came from. If you're at a loose end – there's lots of Buddhism there, just waiting.'

'It was an honest mistake,' I say. 'Those airports all look the same.'

'Oh, that line again!' says Chip, turning away.

I say, 'Maybe what my father believed – it wouldn't work. We wouldn't want it to, if we'd survived. In the world, all that fervour died away. Left boats crammed with people looking for a beach where there weren't cops. My dad stayed true to himself, false to everyone and everything outside,' and as I say this, I wish I hadn't. It's just excuses for him. He didn't want to make us happy, just hard and tested, and then thrown aside.

'We?' Chip asks sharply. 'We? None of us, here in this room, or anywhere, survives. Nor your father, nor mine. You have to start from there. Sylvie and me – is our end happiness? Some gets the club and some the needle. The rest is all ideas. We love them,' and he walks Sylvie into the other room.

I say, 'My father – he spoke figuratively, of course. Those who did what he proposed, like cutting throats – you can be sure, he had a sour analysis.'

There's no one left to hear.

*

I hear Sylvie, she's shouting, with a new voice, acid. 'Do you all need be gay, you guys? Is it the fashion?'

Chip comes running out. He sits, troubled, deep in a chair: 'That guy – the brain masseur, Omar – he has all the clients here that count. You're the only guy that I know, avoids the action, sits in the corner like a spider, spinning weak nets.'

'It's not like a hundred years ago, everyone had conversation and a character. Now we've just the walk-on roles that's left,' I say.

I'm intrigued: Chip says, 'Oh, I know most things too. The people that do them. My outfit's one of those that takes in money, churns it, out comes more, spreads like butter, makes you fat, die early....'

'And Sylvie?' I ask, thinking of writing all this down. I don't know why.

'She was twelve. There was the soldier – they say she had him sent away. Gunned down, of course. A victim for those ascetic guys, they say we are at war with them. They keep the score, and don't expect we heed what it is they want.'

'I'm amazed,' I say. 'It's medieval. It seems that I'm the monk, deflowered. Lady Macbeth with her aria, in the next suite. Other people's lives – books with unwritten chapters.'

'Well,' says Chip, 'It's not paedophilia, of course, though she was very young, our Sylvie. Those circus families, you know. At six you're eating fire, and seven – out of the muzzle. Then, it's human pyramids, and catch-me in the roof.'

'Her muscle-tone, it's true ... exceptional,' I say. 'But she just does philosophy.'

'She's never read a book,' Chip says. 'That's why she's good. Your trouble is,' he peers at me, 'you don't ask questions. You just juggle with the scraps you know.'

'Come back in here,' shouts Sylvie, 'you renegade!' Chip grins wrily at me, and shuffles back.

I hear him squeal, 'Oh no, rape, rape!' and Sylvie shouts,

'I'll eat your eyes, and fill the sockets with your tiny testicles.' I guess it's all in fun, it wasn't like this between us two; muted and casual rather.

It's all a mystery. 'How should we behave?' 'Do we have a nature?' 'Time shuffles the pack – what are these new cards slipped in, the old pips cancelled, not a squeak?' Are these questions right? – and see! – the answers have already changed....

'Don't touch that, you creep!' shouts Sylvie, and there's Chips shouting, 'Anything but that, anything at all,' and then he's back with me, in his suit, without his shoes.

'We'll never see her like again,' he says, and Sylvie joins us, looking exactly as she did before.

She says, quite cold, 'Chip here – he recognises all that stuff you said, about the occupation, massacres, the entrepots, all that. He says he's had it all, it's in his genes. His people didn't make it. Well, he's still here. The only trace is, that he likes a smoke. We get it off the Kazakhs.'

'I can't believe it, what you said, about tattoos,' I say.

'Chip's soft as well, although he has rich deals,' she says. 'He has the mark, like you. Soft. When I'm done with him, we'll look for your tattoo.'

This is not the essence.

'No, it's not,' Sylvie agrees. 'What's to be done?'

'Short lives,' says Chip. 'Get accustomed to them. Impermanence, not leaving stuff behind. Live as a fugitive, a warrior – everyone must be used to that, like it or not. Women – live longer, but in more pain. They make things, and these flake away. Tough kids – the ones that last the least. Plagues – think of avoiding them, not that you will. It means – walking with your nose held high, so's not to breathe them in.'

'Well, Chip,' laughs Sylvie, 'you may be right – but that's the story of your folk, and where's it got you? Immunity?'

*

We three – it's a domestic scene. All three, sat in a row. No poems, and no travelling. The past is bones, our bones. Now, here's the breeze before the hurricane.

'My father's friends,' I say. 'One, chased out of Chile. One – walked across the desert in Ethiopia. I hear how in Moscow, there's gold leaf on everything, three kinds of caviar. It's vulgar. Not just bread and sausages, like when we were there, and there was socialism. That taste! Never surpassed. It was all a puzzle, in the end... victims and victors, tramping round. It's like the physicists say, a thing explodes when it's too big, and all the little pieces start off again, in miniature.'

'No, no, there are black holes,' says Sylvie. 'Americans – they don't make good refugees. The Spanish ones do best. Male bonding and the shooting – those are a help, but almost all the other skills are useless.'

121

'You guys,' says Chip, 'have seen so much, it hasn't left a mark. It's all just this and that, a "maybe and on the other hand". The experience has all burned off.'

'Chip,' I say, air-boxing, 'I quite like you, notwithstanding – but if you want love, you'll have to pay lots more.'

'I don't disburse without some service,' Chip says, haughtily.

'Why – I could break you like a chocolate stick...' I say, puffing up.

'Come on, you turkey cocks,' laughs Sylvie. 'That tufty guy, who interviewed – he has an island, it's used for fiscal fraud. He'd pay a trip. We'd meet the sourest of the *crème*, write a report, unmask the powerful, drink from crystal spigots....'

'Oh no!' I say. 'I see it all. The bar. The maraschino – so sweet, there's grey sugar crusts around the bottleneck. Sicking in the bidet, all us three. Excess, it's not our generation's thing.... Then – these desert islands, besides the pools and bars, they're always full of sand, that grinds like glass in your best orifice.'

Chip perks up. 'If you want a hobnob with some criminals, I'd truck some in. You needn't leave the room.'

'You must know the President, Chip,' I say.

'Of course,' he says, 'everyone knows him. If you guys had TV, you could get to know him too – send him a dollar bill and get a parchment back. He doesn't stand on ceremony, ceremony's his lymph.'

'This is dangerous ground,' says Sylvie. 'We could research an occupation of the States. I'd set the terms. No armed resistance, all those bangs and stiffs. A character study, how guys would get on...'

'Why wouldn't they resist?' I ask. 'All those grunts.'

She shrugs, Chip says, 'Maybe they didn't feel up to it. Maybe they thought they'd lose. Maybe they were glad at last it happened.'

'There's talk there is a million Trots somewhere – perhaps they had a hand,' I say, not quite convinced.

'It was Ginsberg said that,' Sylvie says. 'My grandfather saw him spouting, once.'

If we got cash for such a project – better not mention Ginsberg. Nor Burroughs – except for the cash registers.

'If we were occupied,' says Sylvie. 'Who'd collaborate? And who'd resist, and why?'

'The Feds would do the work,' says Chip. 'There would be shootings, but that's only fair, and expected.'

'A different colour on school buses,' Sylvie says, fantasy taking flight. 'That would show that things were not the same.'

'There'd be a civil war,' I say. 'That's always part of it. The newborns versus all the rest, perhaps. Then, there'd be militias, Swedish drill for kids.'

'New clients for my loans: – maybe they would build some stuff, and make new movies too,' says Chip. 'Changing the aesthetic makes more friends than fiddling with ethics. That's what they'd change. No House. Marimbas and cembalons. Small breasts on the screen.'

We pause, contemplating. 'They'd split it up, the place. Have some new capitals, and flags. Maybe take God off the coins,' says Sylvie.

'I think you're crazy, both of you,' says Chip. 'That isn't how it's done. They put their new guy in, fix the elections. Don't even need to visit here.'

'My father said it was like that anyway,' I say.

'That's a cheap shot,' says Sylvie, laughing.

'My grandfather said the same,' says Chip.

'And there's another cheap one. Besides,' Sylvie says. 'Without fire and water, air and hurricanes – the change would not exist.'

'The best thing,' says Chip sagely, 'to be in, is autoparts. In bad times – a necessity. In good times – much the same.'

'My grandfather went to readings,' Sylvie said. 'Ginsberg, those two Italians, and the Frenchie too. When things are really tough, the poetry takes off.'

*

I tell Omar about the project. He says, 'Asking people what they'd do when there's an invasion? They'll kill you quick as shit. You carry the plague. You add another to their fears. Just make it all up, like they do in science – that way you'll make the news, and get asked back. Now – about this mind and body problem....'

'No, Omar, I don't have that,' I say.

'Everybody does,' he says. 'It's like this. Of course they're different. Your body falls to rubbish. Then your mind goes, but after. Your old self is unrecognisable to your young self – but your mind connects. See, that brain up there, it's like a hank of wool: it lies supine, like spaghetti. Then, when you've knitted it – it's a sweater, a potholder. See? That's your mind.'

I tell Sylvie: she says, 'I didn't have the problem. Anyway, it's not knowledge Tufty's after – it's me.'

Chip says, 'All these theories, the discussions – it just lets you compete to do the cruellest things to cruel people.'

'Well,' says Omar, squaring up, 'what's wrong with cruelty? If there wasn't that, there'd be no way to be kind. Besides – all what we call civilisations, they're a mix of both: – like in your head, I dare say, Chip.... There's the two impulses, side by side. You know the consequences of each – but you insist there'd be a battle, then a beautiful cohabitation You roast your enemies, we pour phosphorus down their throats. You whittle, we do *repoussé*. That's how the work is done, that's how we trudge along, better and brighter every day.'

'No, not me,' says Chip. 'I want no therapy. "No God, no tsar, and no heroes", like the song says. I've had all the history I want. I sit here in my suit and shoes, and don't await the call.'

Omar waves him off: he turns to me, 'Your father – he'd some trouble with those bodies too – all left lying mindless, stacked, despite the theorising,' and he laughs.

'My father disavowed what he couldn't find excuses for, or at the least explain. It kept him on the hop, being on right sides all the time,' I say. 'This invasion thing – everyone's already seen the movie. If we start asking, they will want more soldiers.'

'They're supposed to think they ought not do it to the others,' Sylvie says. 'Imagining it done to them. Playing the role of bleeding heart.'

'You freak,' laughs Omar. 'They do it to the others so it doesn't happen here.'

'You're all obsessed with bodies, that's the easy part,' says Chip. 'Just think – if you believed in spirits, you'd need investigate those too. Enough! Your project, your research – already it's done quite adequately. Sylvie makes her sacrifice, she takes the cash from Tufty – and that's the end of it.'

'That's not the end of anything,' shouts Omar – 'You're all Cartesians, your naughty bodies cured by muscular minds. All of you here – you're all bipolar – depressed, you shoot, manic, you vote and feed the poor. Set yourselves right....' and on he talks, his body and his mind in two-four rhythm, words formed like pearls, a necklace dripping from his mouth.

'Well,' I say, 'I need no pills and phials. Mine is the condition of the sea, thought and action one and indivisible.'

'You've got things well in hand,' says Omar. 'Most of the knowledge – it's already yours. Chip, Sylvie, me – we could start up another country, run it with our skills. This guy here–' he points to me '–he is the sea. Make it an island, surrounded by this guy. The three of us could do as well as all the rest. No risk, and no attraction there; just a rock, a skimpy beach – no one would try to conquer such a place.'

'Relax!' says Chip. 'Of course, you could run the world. If done well, someone would invade you. If not – you bleed out on the sand. Forget the maraschino. Your citizens back the criminals, they envy them. They have no grand design, none of them. They palaver round their secret table, within their locked walls. Why bother? Govern them? Feed them? Fill their eyes with molten gold, parade your generals with pheasant feathers on their backs? It's a delusion. Remember – "he carries the child who takes him down the lonely path". That's what keeps it going. Generating generations. Bread in the bin, that guarantees tomorrow. It is enough.'

'The freaks all come to me,' says Omar. 'It's heaven and hell. The angels come to me, say it can all be saved. No heating up, no grubbing up the food and stuff it down. If only – the devils would stop stoking up and laying out the tables, killing the tasty chicks. It's civil war. All at school together, then into white coats. Now – they fight it out, with prayers and oaths. I tell them – stand on your heads, dear angels, it'll calm you down. It works.'

'Well,' says Sylvie, 'I'm the happy one. No kids for me. And I can brush old Tufty off.'

'For me,' Chip says. 'The money is a means. It opens up to choice – but doesn't tell you any of them.'

'My father – I didn't bury him. He did it all himself, sent himself laughing up in smoke,' I say.

'At least – he had the last laugh on you,' says Chip.

'I knew the talk was all of breaking chains and having new ones hammered on,' says Omar. 'I prefer to live without.'

'There's talk in the street about the chains, being born in them, and losing them: I believe in protest,' Sylvie says. 'I believe in all of them. It's just – standing in a crowd, waiting for some guy that I've paid his wage to come and billy me. I really can't give up the time.'

'My friends,' says Chip, 'since you've no time, and battles now are all with nature – a long slog, uncertain end, nothing much you guys can do... I nudge it this way, and then that – it's mostly unproductive, I admit. But – you go in the street, it's lots of work for profit small. Big change comes trickling down, it's soup on plates, not songs and flags.... My group owns a plantation, over the hill – maybe you'd like to look it over....'

And of course, we would.

'Here,' says Chip, 'Here's a machete each. In the heart of every bush, there lies a fruit. Just try your skill, and gut a row or two.'

'Really,' says Sylvie, 'we'd in mind a day of rest and feeling sorry for the hands, and deprecate their lot.'

'Well, you're in luck,' says Chip, 'and so are they. The hands are gone – we couldn't pay enough. A favour's done to everyone. They're out, you're in, and life goes on.'

'What wondrous fruit are these,' asks Omar. 'They're like pineapples, but the taste is – pastrami, or a jerky, llama strips hung in the sun....'

'They're crosses, naturally,' says Chip. 'The taste's irrelevant. It's pretty much whatever you remember.'

We toil all day, and Chip says the experience is one we'd not have had before or since.

It's dark, 'The fruits are luminous,' says Chip. 'That way we're not stuck with nine to five,' and we slash on and stack.

We roast, we peel, our sweat smells like salami or a pemmican. There's beetles too – 'Help them!' shouts Chip, and so we do.

'I hope his group owns no deep mines,' pants Omar – 'Yes, we do,' says Chip, 'Hot mines, and pickaxing on your back.'

'It's time to leave,' says Sylvie, deeply stressed; but none of us recalls the route we took, or how to quit the fields.

'We overdid the songs and jokes,' says Sylvie. 'Coming here in Chip's old truck. We didn't see a thing... was there an aeroplane...?'

There may have been.

'My group owns so much stuff, it means I don't need be anywhere,' says Chip. 'Not anywhere special, at one time. No one checks. Where we come, we dig and chop, we drill and juice, we strip and trawl. So – you don't become attached to any place before you start to make it work for you. One virgin site looks like another. The stars – we haven't penetrated, but we peek, we watch them die and dwindle, we part their curtains, and with our binocle, we assess their treasures. We weigh their moons, we sniff their vapours, price their mounds and fissures. You should come with me....' and he stops, he's reached the incongruity. 'I mean, I'd let you sneak a prying glance.'

'I might like that,' says Sylvie. 'That's what friends are for.'

'You friends – you didn't pick as much as hired hands do,' says Chip, holding up a paper. 'That tells you all you need to know about economics – history too.'

We're exhausted: Chip goes on, 'All anthropology is there – your shanks that wilt, libidos slack as empty sacks.'

'And tomorrow?' Omar asks.

'Is another line of work,' says Chip. 'If you're agreeable, of course.'

'This has been a profound experience,' Omar says. 'Chip knows nothing like it. Since his father hung his feathers in the closet, Chip has lived in the ghostly world of not quite having, not quite being, not ever knowing... where his feet are.'

'I'm sure you know,' I say. 'I'm sure money gives you a handle on some certainty.'

'Oh, that's not it,' says Omar. 'Sure, he's in transit, like us all. But we've invested blood, not calculation. If we'd calculated, we'd not be here in all these vegetables. We've lived a bit of life. Look at Sylvie – she's cooked herself beyond the boiling point....'

Indeed she has. She's purple, with yellow spurs, like on a gourd. We sluice her down.

'That grey tongue!' says Omar. 'Try her with tequila.' That we do, and she revives, still red and purple; her dessicated breasts stick out like carrots.

'I'll skip the mining, please,' she says.

Omar and I – we do a dance, shuffling at first, then stamping. 'That's the spirit,' Chip says, settling down to watch. Then Sylvie's off. She bounds, over the heartless shrubs, through the bamboos, a joyous hare. 'Oh no,' says Chip: 'I hope she didn't eat my fruit.'

'We didn't, but she did,' I say.

'That stuff's for energy. That's why the hands ran off. Not wages nor the unions. Just vital juice,' says Chip. We don't believe him – but... there goes Sylvie, up and over trees and mounds, her legs seem longer, stilts, she buzzes like cicadas do. 'Oh no,' says Chip. 'I hope she isn't going to mate.'

'Chip, my old friend,' says Omar. 'You may be a tinge misogynist. Sylvie, a woman. Weak, greedy, randy too, prostrated by the sun: – maybe she's only taken on too much fuel, instead....'

'It's good stuff. It burns you out, quicker than the booze,' says Chip. 'That's why they die so young, the hands. But they are strong, inventing rituals, and toiling in the sun. Those fruits – they make you glow, like working in a cobalt mine....'

'...no mines,' comes from Sylvie, a glister of a sound.

'Does it tell the good and evil too?' I ask.

'Cheeky!' says Chip. 'The gatherers, they're like potatoes in a sack, identical, as we are told. Good and evil – they are much the same when your are hoeing rows. We don't grow potatoes any more, it's got too hot.'

'The pineapple,' Omar says, shrugging off the banalities, 'Gave its name to the pineal, the eye of God that's hidden in our bone. If you believe such stuff. A blind eye – that's what we all need. Sorts out the evil problem, and the good. It isn't in my therapy.'

'Well, Omar,' says Chip. 'We all do therapy, and we all are in it. It prepares us for the end. Something accomplished... maybe climbing trees, like Sylvie here.'

'What else you've got to show us, Chip?' asks Omar. 'Mines, rockets, lustrous paints?'

Next day, Omar and I go down the mine: there's a ladder. 'Slide me in,' says Omar. The roof's a finger from the floor. Omar can't slide in. He does. 'I didn't eat the fruit,' he says. 'You have to soften up your bones. You're back to liquid cells and stuff they use to make your brains.'

'Can you reach the jewels?' I ask.

'Of course not,' Omar says. 'This is a shaman's trick, for spaces that aren't possible, and full of secrets too. You mustn't touch the jewels, or else you're stuck.' He lies, a huge polyp underneath the earth. I hear him slowly breathe.

I say, 'Chip is hard on his friends.'

Omar doesn't move, he's a jelly slice between two breads of rock: he says, 'It's right he is. He makes us show what we can do. Besides – it's too late for him, to do propaganda by the deed. What's he to do? Make a bomb? He's a money pro.... He's won, as much as you can. Others are more reflective. You knew Ojibwe – they are different up there. They plant potatoes still.'

'Anyway,' I say, 'you and Sylvie – you're two remarkable individuals. You could start something off, quite new, if individuals can do that any more. Like – found a people, a past.'

Omar finds this funny. He can't laugh too hard.

I say, 'My father is my past. It doesn't give me much to go on.'

Chip says to Omar, 'Time's up, old friend. Should we grease you out?'

'A little thought will do,' says Omar, slithering. To me he says, 'Too bad your father wasn't into electropop, or drugged up, winning medals for the DDR. That way would have been best, more dignified than what you are.'

'I see myself carried on by some woman's dream, maybe to Africa,' I say. 'Romanticism – that'll be enough, will finish me. Then renouncing everything, her too, being miserable, and living on in disillusion. All self-made, home-made.'

'Your time will come,' says Omar, not kindly.

Sylvie has recovered. 'You're a rose garden, Sylvie,' Omar says. 'Patches of red and white.'

'It was fantastic,' Sylvie says. 'Except – the sun, that once gave us to eat, and worship it – as it dies, and swells, it burns you up.'

Chip says to me, 'I've some special work for you,' and I say, 'You have no workers, Chip.'

He says, 'It's all crap jobs. Technology has freed them all, those worthy hands and feet. You see how hard I have to graft, instead. The mine – no longer do we hammer to extract the jewels. We suck: and put them into sacks.'

'I guess my task involves those lustrous paints,' I say. 'I bet you suck them into cans.'

'Imperial green, bordeaux, and Chinese white. Alhambra, mauve, and cadmium – scorched earth and violet ecstasy...' He reels them off. 'Colour is made by light,' he says. 'The Mediterranean – that's full of light. Go – find me that fresh colour, capture it. Do what you must – the competition's there, it's stacked up into armies, and there's bombs and rockets used. They say it's for a future, but it's not. It's all for light – the colour that it hides, creates. The only worthwhile future – is light, and colour. Like it's always been. Find it for me. Then, you can share my luck.'

Sylvie has overheard. 'No, Chip,' she says, 'those voyages are old chapeau. There's satellites now, that peer in your top drawer and count your socks. This sailing round and meeting tarts, and wrastling snakes, and fighting guys in bars – it's all been done. The light has been, and gone. The colour's exactly what you have in stock – "scorched earth". Don't try to fool this innocent, this patsy here. What you really want is no doubt quite nefarious....'

131

'I want the light, the colour,' says Chip. 'Must be the Med. China, India, over here as well – it's all obscured by smog.'

'He wants the paint so's to contemplate, not put on someone's house,' says Omar.

'It's life,' says Chip. 'That's why you put it on your face. Death too, sometimes.'

'Always back to this,' I say. 'My father said we're all too bright to have relationships. And as for families – look at the *troia* Helen, she was an early warning. Expect nothing from the dumb. Death, sometimes.'

'Your father was perverse,' says Sylvie. 'Dump him. He fell in love with stuff, made excuses for its faults and his enthusiasm, then cooled off. No lesson there.'

'It's true he was perverse,' I say. 'Without the perversity, there was nothing left. But I – I have to start from somewhere, before I end.'

'Start looking for my colour then,' says Chip, laughing.

'He can't carry it back,' says Sylvie. 'How would you? You can't paint a paint, either.'

'That's for him to figure out,' says Chip, and Omar nods.

'I don't mind the Mediterranean. It's good the way they let the old things just fall down. Then other things are built, they fall, and tumble in on them. Now, the churches and the mosques – falling down, blowing up. That's how it should be, making space,' I say. 'And Chip, if it's trucking dodgy stuff around you want – I'll take a suitcase.'

'You should bring us back a story,' Sylvie says. 'Someone must make stories that people can remember. Not fine writing. Your father....'

'He was always waiting for it to start. Then he realised that it wouldn't, and he stopped talking. No story there.'

'I prefer to live,' says Sylvie. 'Things shape around me. You're quite passive, you could spin.'

'There's no stories now. Not that you remember. Guys aren't naive, they suspect a yarn, and if you tell a tale, they think you're conning them, or above yourself,' I say.

'And they're right,' says Chip. 'You have to act, or else you contemplate in silence. Campfires, foundation epics – we've had all that. It's life and death, just when you thought you could be comfortable.'

*

'Of course, I shan't go,' I tell Sylvie, when Chip can't hear.

'He's paid you,' she says.

'Money's good anywhere,' I say. 'Go or don't go. And I don't know which colour he might want.'

'It's not colour he wants. You're to set up a network, that can do anything,' Sylvie says.

'No, it's not only that,' says Omar, listening in. 'You are the scapegoat. You're the one who's sent away, to bear the blame for all deeds done past and future. Chip pays you, you take on all his sins and peccadilloes, and you wander. Do you have protection over there?'

'There was a Turkish woman, Aliye,' I say. 'Long ago. She did pictures in coloured inks. She had a shotgun. Maybe they ended her in jail.'

'It's not enough,' says Omar. 'Chip trusts you, he doesn't like you. Sylvie and me, we do gymnastics, is all. You alone, you are to bear the sins that's in all the books, and make Chip friends all over. The colour he wants is gold, but not to spend. To eat off, and throw in the bin. He wants fuel, to carry him far and high.'

'It's what we all want, more or less. It's banal,' I say.

'That's why he trusts you. You're stupid, you don't know the first thing!' says Sylvie. 'You don't recognise his happiness, what he wants. That was your father's problem – he was a stone, he just rolled. He thought happiness was on a distant star. It's not, it's in the trough before you.'

'You get that from a magazine, Sylvie?' I ask.

I'd like to see Aliye, I think, shooting off her gun at the outside, careful not to hit anything.

'Forget her,' says Omar. 'People you know are owls' pellets, full of stories. You don't want those. You want guys who represent big simple stuff: benevolence, weapons, scholarship, pills, dope, insurance, computing fantasies, guys who calculate the damage you make from landing, digging, in a sad place, and from not. No showbiz types. Chip can't do that, bring the guys, the single-minded animals together, load them on his ship.'

'That way, you bury your father, again,' says Sylvie.

'Why should I want to do that?' I ask. 'He's dust in the wind.'

*

Here's Aliye, splashing inks around. 'You don't want to mess with those guys,' she says, hearing of Chip's plan. 'And all known colours – they're here, on my shelf.'

Her apartment's full of stuff, 'to keep the fucking neighbours out,' she says. I pick up a bent spear. 'That's for fish, when there was so many, they sacrificed themselves,' she says. She's withered into a black grapeskin, two suspicious eyes loping round, borrowed from a self-regarding crab. 'Water refracts, you see,' she says, 'and seems to bend. This bent spear ends up straight when you plunge it in.'

'I see,' I say.

'As for Chip,' she says, 'remember, "Never work for anyone." That's what the good book says, that your father and I read aloud to you, in your basket. You can't start too young: learn Capital when you're six, it's yours for life.'

'How'd you get your money, Aliye?' I ask.

'My sister was a better artist than me. Then she died. So, I sell my stuff under her name,' she says. 'That's what family is for.'

After a while, I say, 'I need a story. One that people can remember.'

'Fine,' Aliye says. 'But I'll take half of what you make, when you retell.'

She sits on a goatskin, and we drink some storytelling booze. 'There came the day, as must it will,' she says, 'when acid were the seas, and parched the Earth. The last crumb eaten, the drops from last night's raki drunk... "Have no fear," the big chief says. "We'll activate the plan." They're all prepared, the people of the Earth. With push and scratch they all stack in – the hugest rocket you have seen, prepared to voyage up and down, until they find another earth, and there to start it all again. The last guy present is the one to start the motor, jump inside – and off they'd go. Inside it's dark, and smelly too. "Hurry, hurry up," the people shout. But there's no fuel. They've used it up.

'The last guy there, he swings the handle round and round – to no avail. And there they're stuck. It's not an end with dignity, lying one atop of other, and no sacred writings there to help, and those who pray, they do just that, and likewise those that swear. And so the chapter ends. That's it, there is no more, no one survives.

'You ask – "How do I know?" Well, there were three guys, too busy to pile in and maybe sceptics too – about the rocket trip. Hungry and thirsty, there they sat or stood, and talked and argued, thought of making love or doing exercise, or looking at the sky.... Perhaps they spoke about the Kurds, who knows.'

'Aliye, they could be Omar, Sylvie and me!' I say, entering the spirit.

'Well, yes they could, but they weren't, I dare say,' she says. 'You can always hope.'

'Come on, Aliye, the end!' I say. 'No story without the end!'

'These three guys – how lucky they were literate!' she says, eking out. 'They looked up, saw the cosmos silent, as it always is. No rocket. No new earth. They guessed the enterprise was ended. And they wrote it down. A story in its essence quite similar to mine....'

She looks triumphant. I say, 'It's a con, Aliye.'

'It gripped you, though,' she says. 'It roused your sense of smell. It promised you the structure. That is what matters. People will remember it.'

'But Aliye,' I say, 'it's common coin. Everyone knows that tale. It's not like faith, or principles, that differ one to one. It's told a hundred times, in slightly different ways.'

'Exactly so,' she says, triumphant.

'It's banal,' I say. 'Capital was better, it had footnotes, and jumped about.'

'Listen,' says Aliye, 'there is no con: I've told you what you want, the story that makes your reputation. Alas, you'll be known as "anonymous". You can't have everything, fame and truth don't go together.... The point is – a network like the one Chip wants – it subverts everything. It contains all contradictions. It puts conformity into the resistance, and radicalises reaction. You think you're anticolonial? Your cash comes from the empires. You want to rule for ever? Here come your rebels, some with priests and some with jurists. They'll make you hop, and then they too will have to hop. You have to take a side – that's what you want. Which way do you jump? You find you have to jump, is all. Jump, and more jump. And so it goes. There's no state interest, nothing behind the chain of guys, no latching on to history. The network always does the opposite of what each upfront protagonist desires. It's quiet subversion. Every principle is hollowed out and voided; each dirty trick becomes a principle. There's resolution – but it's a stasis. No one wins, all think they've lost but can't see why or where. They think they should have won – instead, they're sad.'

With an effort, she tilts her neck, her eyes point upwards. The mouldings on the ceiling drip, like icing not quite set.

The inky pictures seep and creep like sea-floors swept by swells.

'It sounds right, what you say. But – I don't quite understand.' I say. 'It's all quite new to me. I don't know where I stand.'

'Your father knew,' says Aliye.

She's smug. I can't say 'Fuck my father, what he knew.' It doesn't help.

'There is no stasis,' I say. 'There is a quest. New forms of power. I'm attracted. Even if Chip doesn't know what he's at.'

'You don't know what will happen,' Aliye says. 'All you think, is how you hope you won't get hurt.'

'That's the attraction, Aliye,' I say.

'It's too big for you,' she says. 'Stick to colour charts.'

All around, there is a swirl. 'This Chip,' she says. 'An American. An Indian. About as un-American as you can get. He brings us chaos as a project, not what we already know, the chaos quite fortuitous.'

'Isn't chaos good?' I ask.

'It doesn't last, my dear,' she says. 'And while it does, it isn't fun, and then when order comes – that's not fun too.'

'It's good you talk of fun,' I say. 'Chip promises a prize, to those I weave into his net. A trophy hunt – with bows. It seems in Africa, the lions are breeding fast. They're mostly in a park – and so, the little ones grow up... And then get shipped, and you can shoot them, for a price. The surplus goes to make another surplus – more and more lions, and heads to tack up on your wall.'

It surprises me, it seems, not Aliye. She nods.

I say, 'Chip has no workers, so there's here no metaphor. The lions – they do no work. They simply grow, they're hunted, and the chain of being gains and loses other links.'

'Well, what do you expect?' asks Aliye. 'They run, that is their fun. If you refuse a bow or gun – the logic of the cull – is inescapable.'

'Yes,' I say. 'You can't escape from logic.'

'These networks,' says Aliye. 'They're new. Everyone has them now. Collecting, trawling. Contacting your people in the structures, and milking them, like ants with aphids.'

'It's the way, it's how it's done, all over. It's like disciples. Anyone, any origin, and any faith, any colour, any tastes,' I say.

'Me, I know no one,' says Aliye. 'Knowing people's dangerous. Every decade you come to me, with extravagant tales, and say how the world has moved. You seem to know the strangest guys, and yet – you're on terms with all of them. You think you know me, maybe. But do you buy a picture? Even look at them? Your father – he knew no one. He didn't like them, other people, and they didn't see him. That was how it worked. He knew he was tinier than the smallest of his thoughts. He didn't need some guys to puff him up.'

There's nothing to say. She says, 'I knew about the lions.'

I say, 'I didn't.' She gets angry. 'You wouldn't recognise a revolution if it dragged you in the long grass, and ate you.'

She gives me a small paper, torn, blobbed with various inks. It could have been a trial. 'Take this. Maybe your boss's colour is among them,' she says.

'And take these figs!' – and here's a basket, heavy with them. The branches of the figtree come in the windows. A fat log lies on the carpet, sugary with life. 'They want to cut it down,' Aliye says. 'It fills the courtyard. Below is dark, real dark. The foliage blocks the gas they use to keep the young guys down. It doesn't get up here, but now it will.'

The street is empty.

I take a cab, the driver says, 'Those figs will do. Consider yourself as having paid.'

They say they should have built the city on the other side, in Asia, where the water's fresh. Now, it's spilled over anyway.

I give Aliye's inks to Chip: I say, 'Your project isn't good. I shan't be part of it.'

'It's the new power,' he says. 'The network. Makes the structures work – for me, and everyone. But – if you want to be a loser, go ahead.'

'Turkish politics, I bet she told you,' Sylvie says.

'No, we talked about her tree. And lions. No metaphors there,' I say.

'Ah,' says Chip, wistfully. 'Meeting in Istanbul, where everything meets.'

'Chip,' says Sylvie, 'You're nowhere into power. You're second level. The tops is presidents and popes. Or banks. Depends on what you want to take away. You'd be behind the scenes. Those guys make the treetops move. You're just boring in the bark.'

'Besides,' says Omar, 'Once it was to get a class in power. Now – the game is just to heave you up, on to some sticky throne. The best thing's for everyone to have their power...'

'No, no,' says Chip. 'Everyone should have no power. That's freedom. Sow it all around – it's war of each on all.'

I sit and watch them argue: I feel I'm aging. My belly loses flesh, I'm like those wooden virgins, carved from olive-wood, stomachs flat and empty, like small acorns above their legs, a smile beatified with dope, hands clasped tight to hide where there's no sex.... The meat drops off, the bones stand proud, the gristles tauten, snap and blacken. The tongue swells up, then disappears, the rictus spreads from ear to ear, the teeth are dribbled down to where the nipples, hard as garnets, brighten up from pink to purple. Inside, the tale is different, it's pap and offal, the liver with its yellow pustules, seams of blubber white....

'....' Chip's been saying, then, 'As you know, I have an island, like that play where there's the storm, a bunch of guys are wrecked, they talk, and then they leave. Life in a frame – that's what I want, it's theatre—'

'Plays are like that, Chip,' says Sylvie. 'There is a bunch, they talk and mime, then you go home.'

'Don't patronise me,' Chip is furious. 'You creaking acrobat. I know quite well what's life, and getting on the island, and then leave. In real life, you cry a lot and eat each other. On my island – maybe you would bond, you three, and I could learn the human tricks – the ties beyond the clan, the family – ties I never had, but now are central to my plan....'

Chip talks on and on. An island, with us three, to teach humanity... no bar, no games. Omar lying like a polyp on the sand, and Sylvie up a palm.

'Tattoos are changing,' Omar says, changing the topic too. 'Talking of islands. I saw on someone's backside – "My treasure is within." Then a monster. "Cast me not out Lest I enter into you." The cops will have to read the bards. Me – I'm clean. No one writes on me.'

'Fashion's not the trouble,' says Chip. 'I want to find how humans work. I'd bring to visit you – the President of here and there, top committees too. You see, with countries, decline and rise take longer than you've patience for. It's watching tides. Conclusions – they can rarely come, and least from where you think they will. Countries and continents – they go on, much moiling, with foaming waters, flights of populations.... But when it seems resolved, you're scattered into air, gone, and missed your chance.'

'I got no tattoos,' says Omar, 'because I didn't go where Sylvie went....'

'This is interesting,' Chip says. 'The kind of thing I need to hear.'

'OK,' says Sylvie. 'It was prison. It's the best place to catch up with literature. That's why they let me out. I passed the test. But – you come back covered in quotations.'

'You must have done bad things,' says Chip, as if he can't imagine anything like that.

'Oh yes,' says Sylvie, offhand, 'you start by meeting people – a guy who slept in other's automobiles. He went to India to preserve his legs. Because he drank. He sought out the ascetic life. Another, his girlfriend was a fireater. But she was young, fourteen, they say. She cheated on him, for her it ended, bad. Being with them, hearing their tales – you don't have time to earn and do dull jobs.... Prison is like war – rational and grotesque, all at once. You want to get rid of people. But – what you want is not to lock them up, the guys, or kill them. What you want is something else. That's the grotesque part, the contradict.'

'Oh I'm not sure,' says Omar. 'I might want to kill guys, or to lock them up. Just that. Then prison, war – those would be reasonable.'

We try to think of good answers. 'I find this subject everlasting, fascinating,' Chip says. 'To have great power on people – even if it is the kind that has no guns or handcuffs, that you feel the effect of, but not the means or the intent.... to have that power, you need to know some people, better than I do right now. It's not the arguments I want, or justifying or apologising.... It's stories. Lives. That's what I need to know about.'

'It's the wrong start,' says Sylvie. 'Talking of two different things. People in the one place, they've nothing to do with those in the other.'

'People need protecting from people, I guess,' says Chip. 'Including me. It's pretty simple.'

'I protect myself from both,' says Omar. 'Jail and armies.'

'It takes you away from experience,' Sylvie says. 'Just for a clean skin.'

'I lived in a place,' says Omar. 'All my neighbours were criminals. They spied on me, the scum. If you do exercises, you do it alone, no one can help you.'

'I got put away for helping people I knew,' says Sylvie. 'It was a girl thing to do.'

Everyone says that.

Chip says, 'Well, with you on the island, I could observe you. That's an enlightened thing to do. This guy here,' he pulls me in the ring, 'he's the sea already. I lend my island.'

141

'It's true we do a kind of therapy,' says Sylvie, 'but only on people who are well. We tell them how to live, and that is what they do. For us, the good thing's getting paid. The other stuff – we improvise.'

'Exactly what I need,' says Chip. 'The human touch.'

'What's in it for you, Chip?' asks Sylvie. 'Why isn't second level good enough?'

Chip mostly ignores her, then, 'First level is reaching the top and then you must come down, by fall or scramble, or they unhorse you. I fancy something more permanent, not where your army's already gathered on the plain, with guys in braid and rules. "Supreme leader". That would do. Beyond argument, above the fog.'

Where is this island? Halfway to Africa?

'I had it towed,' says Chip. 'Here in the river.'

It's red and gold and reeds. You could raise a stall, sell eels in molasses on it, blue plums battered in eggy crusts. That's an illusion. It's a flat, a stage, a platform. It's a pier's end, wrecked, deserted, amputated. I'm carried out, floated on Omar's back.

Chip comes on waterski, Sylvie on his shoulders, a winged victory. I recognise her chant – and the name she's bawling out, Siddhartha. The island is more raft than rock. 'It's minimal,' I say. 'It's unimpressive.'

'That's how it's meant to be,' says Chip, and Sylvie and Omar nod. 'I could turf it or cement it. It'd still be flat.'

'Yes,' I say, 'it's you, Chip. Unpainted boards: elsewhere, pure colours.'

'They're not pure, silly boy,' laughs Chip. The three are at home. They lie on thin foam squares. 'I've brought no grand ideas,' says Chip. 'Since here, all ideas are grand.'

It's so, I guess. We stretch out on our backs. We are four, are all creation.... no, we are four separated ones. We could be made of steel or jelly.

It's dull, looking up at the sky, interrupted by a gull, a plane. 'It should be empty, that sky,' I say. 'It's not one thing or another.'

'Then it's both,' grunts Omar. 'Fuck you, grow up!'

Sylvie says, dreaming, 'Supreme Leader – it's still first level, nothing more. Everything still goes through channels.'

'Second level, though,' Omar says. 'Who wants to be a Krupp? It's grovel.'

'Chip, tell us how you started on the money trail,' says Sylvie.

'Oh, I sold the lands,' says Chip.

'Break the taboo!' shouts Omar.

'I sprinkled it around, the cash,' says Chip. 'The President, other tall poppies too. They do experiments, when they find the bones. It's not all from massacres – drink and the devil too,' and he hums a line or two. 'The president comes out here – he practises his swing.'

'That's the best thing I had heard,' says Sylvie, 'That he's in a band.'

'Oh no,' says Chip. 'He hits his balls to where that guy is waving.' Far off, there's a black man in a coracle. A floating hole. I see there's scoops smacked in the planks here. The guy leaps up and down.

I ask, 'Why'd you want a network, then? It seems you already have the best....'

'Oh no,' says Chip, 'that's over here. You must think global. Remember – it is not to spend, but to accumulate. In fact, the less you spend, the better,' and we're sure he knows it's true.

'See!' says Chip. 'The isle rotates. It can take off. Or be a dance floor.'

It's a spinning disc. Omar and Sylvie raise their arms, their heads glow like candle-flames.

'It spouts!' says Chip. The water, pink and green, shoots up and turns to spray. All four of us, we're pink and green and gold. You could pray to us. We can't respond, the platform turns too fast. It makes you nauseous.

'This is living!' Chip shouts. 'I love plain things, and see how they come grandiose, and lift you up.' We're sufis standing still, the world whirls round, the water plumes. We see some secret things – there's the lady, Liberty herself, curved like a boomerang, the buildings leave their vertical, and turn to hooks and hunches.

'Faster, faster!' Sylvie shouts, and she is airborne, her little slippered feet do *fouettés* in air. Omar spreads out, sticks to the boards, a treacle-smear with eyes.

'See, you idiots!' Chip shouts, 'this is what you get if you have lots of cash! Experience quite unparalleled....' And we would stay for ever, us and the rest transformed. It slows. 'Enough!' says Chip. 'Sometimes it makes you speak with tongues—'

'Oh, I am sure I was,' says Omar, quite entranced, 'You couldn't hear me for the spume, and the machinery.'

'Hey! Hey, you guys with seawrack in your hair!' It's the guy from the floating hole. 'The President is on his way!'

'He's always calm,' says Chip, 'so we don't spin him up.'

Are those the dragon boats? The galleys from republics of the sea? No.

'He loves that paddle-steamer,' Chip shouts out, and now he hugs the guy.... His office makes the President tall enough, gives him a jaw. He smacks the balls away. The guy in the coracle waves his arms – 'A hole in one, each shot,' he lies. It's over. 'He's so keen on ritual,' says Chip. 'He doesn't say a word. I'm sure he saw you lurking there.'

'Chip!' says Sylvie. 'No one can party like you can. It's all been most extravagant – the company baroque, the twirling killed the thirst and hunger dead. Now we could sleep, our questions quite unanswered.... The guy was clearly level one. Nothing to say, he made no observation sharp or dull. What a pain, to end like that!'

'My father said Stalin was always very cordial,' I tell them. 'But he can't ever have met him. His daughter liked to dance.'

We go back to the shore. The guy in the coracle lies there, coiled sleeping like an asp. Does he live without resentments?

Sylvie says, 'Chip – the President, he doesn't know a thing. Nor all those guys who visit ... they're emptied out as walnut shells.'

Chip makes some mild complaint. Then Sylvie screams at him, 'We don't know what's going to happen next. Don't you grasp? We're terrified.'

'It's been like that since they fitted us with brains, and made them so's they pointed backwards,' Chip says, trying to calm her.

'This time, it's different,' Sylvie says. 'That's why we cling so to our bodies – how they torment us! – write on them ... so's to do what? To recognise ourselves when we are lost? To show more difference? We see the others driven to the edge, and then beyond, we see them lying there, as flat and calm as Omar. Into the pit they go. Some have numbers, so you can tell them. We have writing and designs. It's our insurance. What will happen? We don't know – we have the fear, as if we knew.'

*

'You can have clients,' Sylvie says to me, when I am settled in, 'but not when I have mine. I'll give them some Jung today – he's dry. Take their minds off their minds.'

'I'll only stay a day or so,' I say. 'Your clients seem so complicated – their problems!'

'Oh, they burrow into those,' she says. 'If only they'd admit how scared they are – all the rest would scud away. Imagine if they had a pantheon – those spirits to placate... they'd have no time for therapy.'

All this – it's not the work I want to do.

Sylvie says, 'Another week, and I'll be cured. There's nothing wrong with me, of course, but in a week, I'll give it up. It was good I had the chance from you. First, it was college boys, then rich deadheads, thinking of something else – then you, looking for a sugarplum. After – there was Chip – so much more interesting.'

'It's useful to know all this,' I say, put out.

'There is no mystery,' she says. 'Those guys who started off by studying the ants, the bees – that was genius pure!' She's quite delighted. 'It's about stability, the durability of the realm, the death of the leader, or their idea, and their regeneration. There's a condiment of divinities. Beautiful people, mostly, but capricious. There's a judge, at the end.... And temples. Stone or paper.'

'Don't tell me there's a trial,' I say.

'Oh, there's trials, but they don't matter much,' says Sylvie. 'It's the judge with a garrotte who counts.'

'Did watching the golf put this in you, Sylvie? Or did you just read it somewhere and forget, and now it pops up back?' I ask.

'No, not the golfer. The guy in the coracle. He's always there,' she says. 'Ready to catch and lie.' She laughs. 'The balls they shoot at him....'

'Once you know this, Sylvie,' I tell her. 'There's only to stand aside.'

'That's what you do,' she says. 'Spying's in your blood, your father's blood. That's it – you stand aside. You don't join any of it – the dance before the hive, guarding the queen, transporting the larvae. You pry, you tell, you know, but you don't do. Neither support, nor yet subvert.'

'Neither way seems to have much point,' I say.

'That's because you are an ant,' she says, 'who'd like to be a bee.'

'You're hitching up with Chip, I guess,' I say. 'You can do that because you're a beauty. The details... the stories, the parades, the rhetoric that comes in many shades – they just adorn the plan. It's not your plan, you're not the architect, but a builder – yes. The great design's to make the state that won't endure, seem everlasting. The detail doesn't matter. You're all chrism, Sylvie. You're an enchantment. There you sit, upon the empty throne beside the emperor. Rising with him, instructing what to do.'

'It's not the upward curve,' she says. 'It's that the fall should be magnificent, part of the trip. You should believe in tumbling down with all the passion, the delight, you feel in soaring up.'

There's nothing great in being beautiful. There is anxiety you'll get more spots. Yet – after all, it must be great, that 'being beautiful', just like the poet says.

'It's not I'm beautiful,' says Sylvie, 'Just the proportion's right. I'm not the beauty – it's my skeleton. To butterflies, we're quite a sight – the little heads, the stumbling feet, the colour uniform and bland. No flight, no metamorphosis. Tiny eyes.'

'You're with Chip full time?' I ask.

She evades. 'There's trouble in the palace,' she says. 'It takes two to pull the President from his bed. It's absurd, his depression – when he took the job, he knew he had to kill people that he didn't know. There's his two helps, one wants the succession, the other sees he has the power to put an end to everything, and can't decide: to spare or to exterminate. They get him dressed. I'm not surprised Chip keeps his distance.'

I say, 'Omar says they feed the President jokes, like – "This guy – they came in to arrest him, though he thought he was clean. They took guys off for being in the wrong tribe, having wrong passports, thoughts or friends... so, the guy thought he was covered. But no – they caught him for being left-handed... it seems that someone with a knife...."'

'The ones who laugh at that – it shows they're friends. That is the test,' says Sylvie.

'Chip must be clean,' I say.

'He's depilated thoroughly,' Sylvie says. 'I wear black so you can't see what's written on me.'

'That's not work, Sylvie,' I say. 'What you're trying to do now, with Chip. His schemes – they come across to you as fantasies, like you've been sniffing smoke....'

'Work?' she shouts. 'You call it work? I fed them Schopenhauer. It comforted. But I could tear their flesh – it'd be consistent. Everyone should bear their burden, like I do, and Omar too.'

'But – Chip?' I ask.

'He has the marvels – you have seen them. They're made to be ephemeral. It takes so little to transform – a pistol shot, it brings the forest down. Remember Yugoslavia – the shot led straight to Hitler. Then – to everything thereafter. So it is with Chip – a small report... a supernatural push or prod. The voyage starts, the launch....'

*

Sylvie calls. I'm invited. 'Yes, it's a launch. Maybe of my face. We're having a reception, not a party – so, that means you don't do sex upstairs.'

There are no mariners there, so it's not a proper launch: it's mostly guys in suits, exchanging tips.

'My,' says a woman, 'You look out of place. You come in off the street to look for eats?'

Her name's Roxanne, on her badge: she's maybe got tattoos that show the guys she's been with, and I peer...

'No, no,' she says, 'It's just a chest, there are no trophies there – you needn't stare.'

'I do her music,' says Roxanne. 'It's up this loud so guys can't overhear. But for a fee, I'll rent you a device that let's you listen in....' And she does, though it's not worth the sum.

'There he is,' Roxanne says, 'Chip. The man without the qualities, that means he must have all of them. Who knows what plan they have, those two? To conquer heights – that is for sure, but who's to push, and who's to pull, Sylvie or him?'

'Well,' I say, 'I'm really curious. Were I to find the cash, maybe you'd find what Sylvie does, or wants to do?'

'Oh yes,' she says. 'I love to spy.'

I insist – don't work for someone else. It makes living in any kind of way quite difficult. 'You mustn't think you work for me....' I say to Roxanne, and she says, 'Oh no, of course not. I love prying into other people. That's how you live, and feel alive.'

The guys stand round, in little clumps of two and three. The music covers them. My father would have felt superior, to all their secrets. Objectively, I guess he was on their side. He wasn't one for purity, for an idea that chases people to the fields and starves them as they dig and plant. He didn't want to start things off again, taking the better, arid path. 'Behind the drive for altruism, there's always some self-indulgent boss,' he said. He liked guys small, impure, he felt at home with them, looking down.

'You know,' says Roxanne, 'Chip doesn't plan a thing. His cash sweeps him along. Myself, I think those terrible experiments – if you don't share something of them, you've really lost all hope.'

'What can you mean, Roxanne?' I ask. 'It's quite incongruous here, I'm sure. What experiments?'

'Oh well,' she says, 'some of the Chinese things. Pol Pot. Where you're happy that it didn't happen to you, but—'

'Is Sylvie into that?' I ask. 'She's quite farouche. She didn't get it from me.'

'Oh,' says Roxanne, 'with you she got to study the philosophy. Peasants, cities – all that stuff – it doesn't bother her. It's the parabola, the gesture, the ambition – that's what matters. And your father. Like me, she's keen on spying – that cop who said he didn't know what side he's on, but on the whole.... and ended as director of the Cheka, for the Bolshies.... He fascinates.'

'It's all new to me,' I say.

'That's what it's supposed to be,' says Roxanne.

The straight guys have all left, there's only us two, and Chip and Sylvie, left. Roxanne goes on, 'The music scene's all over. Movies are miniature. Good looks and tits – we've seen them all. The politics is guys in suits. Now, it's our turn: it's what you said. Farouche. It's voodoo in our heads, without the fooling with those animals. It's climbing up to fall straight down. It's digging up the dead and burying them again. Apocalypse as farce.'

Sylvie joins us: she says, 'It's worshipping the deities... you know they don't exist, and watching as they bring the lightning strikes and plagues.'

'I thought Chip was involved with cash?' I say.

'Of course, that's needed,' Sylvie says. 'But it flows in and out, just like the sea. Just like you say you are. You gave me some ideas – ideas you hadn't got, you as the sea, digesting everything, always renewed, more acid, saltier, lifeless too.... Just depth and motion. Me, skimming, never making land...'

Chip stands and nods, his polished head waves slightly to and fro, like an old-time radio valve.

'It sounds all symbols,' I say. 'Beautiful satanists, all that.'

'You soft guys – to you it's enough things come up as art and heritage,' says Sylvie. 'Never the real thing. All this intent – reason, belief, calculation – the results, you understand, are quite arbitrary. Justice finishes as revenge, guys in iron boxes savaged by pitbulls.'

'Begin from the other end,' says Roxanne, trying to help out, 'You might reach the grand things you started with.' She doesn't sound sure. I think she doesn't care too much.

'What deities have you and Sylvie had enshrined?' I ask.

'We get them from a book, and try them out on vacant lots,' says Roxanne. 'Picking out the beauties – then quick sex in animal disguise. Lightning displays, of course. Sometimes we have to goad them on.'

Maybe Roxanne's spoofing me. She's soft and sugary, Turkish delight, your eyes run over her like hands. 'It's true,' she says. 'I'm not proportional. But the material is there, stacked up by clumsy fingers.'

It's true, she's like the blobs of dough a baker leaves and bakes when he's laid out a tray of perfect biscuits, each one as beautiful as Sylvie – yet, it's so, the material is the same.

'Good looks is coming back. It's been unmentionable for years, though fortunes were still made on it,' Roxanne says, and wriggles noncommittally.

I say, 'I recommend an expert – he will change your shape, brain patterns too, – an oriental cast as well, if you will buy the book,' and so by puffing him I've been a friend to Omar, and his trade.

'We'll see how far Chip goes,' says Sylvie. 'Will he run, or will he fall? It's an experiment, but one he wants, perhaps. Another fall: there's been so many ends, another one will scarcely rock the room.'

'Besides,' says Roxanne, 'some of us – we never had ancestral lands. He has an enviable past, that only he has access to.'

*

Omar tells Chip, 'Beware your women. There's a game in play. They waft you up, to see if you will fly, and if you fall – it's just more fun.'

'Who told you that?' asks Chip. 'Of course – there's always been quite other Indians. Even the wrong sort – building those pyramids and torturing their equals on the top. Say "Indian" – we're the fall guy. I thought all that was past. You people – you all came from caves, not washing, eating grubs – but that's been put behind you – I dare say you never think of it. Besides – where'd you hear all that?'

'Oh, well,' says Omar, 'that's what politics is.' He gestures at me, as I'm listening at the door. 'The secrets are the ones that you don't tell, or even think.'

He limbers up. 'I'll show you guys! Wrestling. The deal is – keep your weight low, full of gravity. That's what politics is – *gravitas*. Say, do, what you like. If you don't have *gravitas*, it's all smoke and crackle.'

He crouches, flat and dry as a cowpat on the mat. The other guy – looks stretched, as if he's down from his cross, starting his second sporty life. He's long. He doesn't need to bend. He flips Omar over, as if he were a leaf. They try again. He spins Omar like a frisbie.

'Yes!' says Omar, feigning triumph. 'That's the lesson! Even when you do things right, there is some freak who makes a fool of you.'

He strongarms the victorious crucified wrestler out the door. 'Great demo, Fritz,' he shouts, when the guy has left. 'You see, Chip – it isn't just you Indian guys. Maybe you should avoid to be a group. The groups – they end up bad. Neanderthals, Armenians, those Carthaginians, Hereros, Jews and communists – the dark wing settles over you. There is no count, no trials, no fancy explanation. Apocalypse that follows on the one that's gone before.'

'Omar,' says Chip, 'we know all that. Now – it's not the groups. It's everyone.'

'We all go on, living as if we're immortal – but only the richest ones are going to make it,' Omar says. 'Chip, you're one of them. Don't you feel like taking some of us with you, ever upward, like they say?'

'No,' says Chip. 'I don't even know if I'm going anywhere. Some have castles, some have islands. I have an island. You guys – there's not much work for you. You've all the time you need to have your brain pick out some scheme – just think, if you were hoeing maize, you wouldn't even know the questions.'

'It's true, Roxanne,' says Sylvie. 'I screw men so's I can criticise them. More intimately. Am I sick, Roxanne?'

'It's your forte, Sylvie,' says Roxanne. 'Don't give up on it. It's a victory.'

'If you say,' says Sylvie, 'but now, there's Chip. It's time to launch him too. We are the horse, we know the way. He just sits atop and whoops. People get tired of everything, even of pretending. He's the new. There was paternalism, then markets, then the intimate. It's waves, Roxanne. Sit higher up the beach, they won't reach you, not today. The worst thing you can imagine – it's already happened. Or it's still happening. Chip: stripped and hairless. Expect no good of him – but differences. Extremes. Those you've not considered. They won't do you good. But – he's the great change....'

'Yes, yes,' says Roxanne, 'the change while we wait.' She sees me lingering round the door. 'Hey,' she shouts at me, 'write to your boss that we're all gay. Or indifferent. That way, they'll get no blackmail money from us.'

'I don't have a boss. Everything I do, I do for love.'

'Sure, you have a boss,' says Roxanne, 'A boss is your fetish. You pinch it, try to pull its head right off.'

'I'm sure that's what Jung said,' says Sylvie, trying to calm a storm. 'This guy's quite innocent. He spies and lurks because he doesn't know a thing.'

'I'm stifling in here,' Roxanne says, taking off her top. 'This city! Chip – doesn't he have a space somewhere? We could do sport. Here – it's the words, written on the walls, guys in the automobiles – they shout them, don't mean a thing....'

'Don't be precious, Roxanne,' Sylvie says. 'They're insults. That's not so hard to grasp. What pisses me right off – it's all the art they do – they say it's valueless, ephemeral, or else it's up to you to make it mean, look harder, the gesture, yes but no! – the artist is the work? oh no it's you! And on it goes.... The fucking venue's just the same, and so are you, and so's the guy beside who tries to press your thigh. Roxanne!' she screams. 'It's all the same! But dull! Repetitive and obvious....'

On she goes, till Roxanne says, 'I know, dear Sylvie. That's why we both want something new.'

'And that won't be the same, the same parabola, those goddam words?' shouts Sylvie. 'And put your top back on, Roxanne – we're not equipped for fondling here.'

Roxanne is blushing, but I don't think it's shame. Sylvie calms, she says, 'Once, Aphrodite intervened in this. Now, all is up to us. Why were we left to fix this shabby scene without a help, a prompt?'

We have no answer, and I think she doesn't wait for one.

'I'm hot, Sylvie,' Roxanne says. 'I wish I was like Omar, living in his body all the time. Where does Chip live? In the grasslands? Hot, Sylvie – it's not about the universe, or brotherhood. It's too much power, we use it up, it goes nowhere but in our skin, it makes us sick....' She weeps.

'Come, Roxanne,' says Sylvie, cuddling her. 'It all will pass. There is a law that says, that everything runs down, there's less and less. It is the only law we have, no good it does to us.' She brightens. 'Maybe Chip could rent an iceberg – it is all the rage. We're towed to see the animals. We're cool, so cool. They take us off when it is time.'

I say, 'Chip exploits his environment; once he was a wolf, now it is offices. Until the fox comes – with better technology. Humans fear the fox, who kills more than he can eat. He's a rival, so they hunt him down with dogs.'

'You don't mean "technology",' Sylvie says.

'Yes, why not?' I ask.

Later, Roxanne says to me, 'There's nothing to spy on, in Sylvie.'

'I don't pay you in trust, Roxanne,' I say. 'It's only cash. Just tell me anything at all.'

'Innocence,' she says. 'Lots of people seek it. It's not recognising evil.'

'You're thinking of the fox?' I ask.

'We're good guys, as we are,' she says, 'but if you say our lives are at risk, there's someone out to get us – each one will resist in their own way. Without appetite, or with it.'

'We're good guys,' I repeat. 'You can hardly tell each one of us apart.'

'You spies,' says Roxanne, 'you have more rules than most of us. I see you – making the rules that ship the people off. Omar – won't risk his body – but I can see him sign a warrant. And as for Chip.... Sylvie too.... No limit.'

'There, Roxanne,' I say, 'that's some secret you've just told. You're worth your pay.'

*

'I don't believe in renting,' Chip says. 'There's always someone waiting, somewhere. So I bought.'

We're sitting on this iceberg.

'Are you bored, Chip?' Omar asks.

'Never,' says Chip. 'I just look this way. They'll snap us. Then we're done.'

'No, Chip,' says Roxanne. 'We've to see the animals, before they all die out. But I don't see them – there's just birds, and dark things in the sea.'

'You have to wait, Roxanne,' says Sylvie. 'They come in ones, they're not like us, a pack.'

'Our pics – they'll be on all the little screens,' says Omar. 'We're a story without words, in just one line. But – I've lain here, made a shape. That, I'll leave – and join them on the boat that's towing us,' and so he does. His outline disappears, quite fast, and Roxanne says, 'We're not melting – all else is.'

'That's not the point,' says Chip. 'You don't need believe in what we do. How we are solid, and the ice – it's all ephemeral. But – it's a step, obligatory, like in beauty and the beast. A look, a glance, of love, that must intrude, reveal.'

'It's right,' Sylvie says. 'The ice isn't just to chill Roxanne. It's being a family, loving the beasts. You have to show it, lots of loving, so you can be good at something else.'

It comes into my mind – the Moscow store, the GUM. My father said to me, small boy trotting after, smelling strangenesses and pickles, until I was just a nose with legs – 'This here is set out like the *grands magasins*. You might see Proust, coming up the stairs. Making his purchases of biscuits.' Perhaps you might.

I saw a lump of ice, bigger than this iceberg – since I was smaller then – 'It's to cool the caviar', he says. Then came the thaw, the melt, right down.

'It's all for our campaign,' says Chip, 'whatever that's about. Don't take it serious. There's no bears to punish you, however hard you look.'

The ice is disappearing, and we jump on the boat, leaving the sets of eskimo boots behind. They were included in the price. They bob away – 'I had a wastebasket one time,' Roxanne says, 'made of an elephant's foot. Those boots – they bring it back.'

'Well,' says Omar, 'there's our extreme. The cold. Then the warming.'

There's nothing much to add. How are those animals, the ones we didn't see – how are they doing? Maybe they were there, we didn't know enough to recognise them. Probably, it was reciprocal, the ignorance, and they stayed well away from us.

I feel Roxanne slide her hand into mine. 'It wasn't real,' she says, quietly. 'The foot.'

'I didn't think it was,' I say. The hand seems boneless, quite indeterminate. A toad. It squeezes – oneTWO, oneTWO....

Then Omar rises up. 'Not now, Roxanne,' he says. 'I've pondered this one, over time. You two can hear it first.' Of course, she's fascinated, so am I. Roxanne lets me go.

'The thing is drugs,' says Omar, in a voice that's rich with minerals. 'The history of the world. The sports is all about it – guys who play and guys who watch. Football! There's guys who couldn't read a paragraph, they watch for hours. And what? Is this drama, like you're overseeing ants knit shawls? Of course, there's lots of criminals involved – you see the hammer? That's a convict's ball and chain, it's canting talk, for thieves. Throw it away, your manacle, far as you can. And see them, crazy in the park, with their jumps and spears and sticks. That game they call pelote? It's a giveaway: you spell it p-e-y-oh-t-e. That's the sense....

'And all the stuff the feds have seized – they don't flush it, you can bet. It's for the army, so's they can do the things they do. Politicos – the calm! Unnatural. They're sending out those flying bombs, and yet they're on TV, with jokes and what their kids have learned at school, and sorry for the blood and stuff, and doing little dances....'

'That's all well known,' I say. 'What's new, Omar?'

'The pyramids,' he says. 'They never found a spoon or pan. Those guys – they didn't eat. Each hefted up a six-ton block and made a shape – for what?.... a tomb? A boat? A plane? It's like religion: – those lists of names, not heard before or since. Hazor? Ziking? Names for your kids? I'll bet! The walking dead, speaking with tongues, the flying here and there, bilocation and the word of God – "just wait, I'll take it down, I've got some gold plates somewhere here...."'

'We've heard it all before, Omar. So what?' I say, and Roxanne says she's clean – 'I wouldn't do the dirty stuff,' she says, and here's her hand come creeping back....

'Indians – they drink,' says Omar. 'But don't do dope. Chip's maybe the first who wants to do his thing without a fantasy, as realistic as they come. Just think – those cow boys they were up against. Forget their feminine side!

157

Transmogrified, they were. Not lady into fox – boy into cow...!

'I don't see what's your point,' I say. 'Old Marx – he said it all. It's opium. Or something else you've stashed there in your shoe. It is the human race, it's how it's fuelled; that is its history, Omar. Get reconciled!'

He's quite deflated. Roxanne says, 'No, Omar's right. It is a thing to be explored. I'll spy it out. I'm clean, and so's you two. I'll spy out Sylvie too. Maybe all the things she does, and Chip as well, is all because they're clean? Is that the plan – to see things as they really are? No mirror, and no telescope?'

I feel it's kids' talk, this, but I've got free of Roxanne's hand at last.

'Dammit,' says Omar, quite disconsolate. 'I thought I'd got it – the mystery of everything.'

'Maybe you have,' says Roxanne, sliding a podgy hand in his. 'It's just it's all irrelevant to everything.'

'I'll try the vertical,' says Omar, rising up. He takes a pair of shining stilts, with springs, and bounces up and down.

'Do you always bring those, on a boat?' Sylvie asks Omar. She's standing beside Chip – the two of them, tall, frantic, on the bridge... like Rimbaud's king and would-be queen.

'Well,' Omar says, 'it strikes at any time, the hand of destiny. There's some in charge that want to end it all and quick, and others castled in their offices, settled for the long haul. Sometimes a circumstance will bring them both together. It's called a window of opportunity. The pistol shot – and then, the army that's only to parade, not fight, is dashing to the front. The dream you're emperor, everywhere – it gets a nudge: there go your warriors, whittling their darts, fulfilling every wish of yours....'

'There's the ideas,' says Chip. 'The saving people, doing noble things...'

'I thought I'd covered that,' says Omar huffily.

'Intentions ought to get some points,' says Sylvie, making peace. 'Hey guys – how's my getup look? We won't ask votes for our campaign, or set down op-ed stuff. Just be important, meaning grandiose things – by being here, upfront and mostly silent.'

She wears a plastic apron, not much more. It looks like fur. '"Lounge leopard" is its name,' she says. 'We'll put them on the grasslands. Real ones, leopards, pecaries. No lectures on the authenticity, please – we've heard it all before. You give a hand to evolution – no one thanks, nor should they blame.'

'Ah yes, the grasslands,' Chip romances, as if they weren't there always, just behind his eyes. 'We'll stock them. Stockyards – maybe that's the word?'

'No, Chip, no!' screams Sylvie. 'Fuck it, fuck you! This won't change the world, nor any thing! I could be Sissi – this time, it's me that pulls the trigger. I live on, become the empress, building plywood cities. No Franz Ferdinand – just my interminable old age, fucked by black horses. As the whiteys' star goes down – the Spaniards will invade, of course. Some life into the dance... Flamenco on the Pink House lawn. Open the silver mines – oh no! the Indians have a low-grade guerrilla going on, where there's no maps.... What's to come next? – junks up the Hudson, your Ambassador limo won't run on this new toxic oil.... And none of it,' she screams still louder, 'none of this is mine. It will all happen, even if I'm lying on a sheet and having Borodino red-tattooed upon my bum!'

We're all on guard. Chip hears he's to be victim of his suicide, Sissi will spin some tale, convince the cops, take the top spot. America won't need to change its name, but all the rest will change. No more fried egg sandwiches – Madrileno eggs in rancid olive oil, paella full of grit, you pay in silver oblongs, look like they been sucked and stamped with cleats.... We see it all, the future. There is nothing new. It's all different, but you've imagined it this way and that. That's

159

why you spy. That is the point. The future is a country known, that you have helped to make... it doesn't frighten any more....

'What did your father want to find?' asks Roxanne. 'Or did he just pass on?'

'Not finding things,' I say. 'Just watching. No one to pass on to....'

*

'Hey, guys,' shouts Chip, white and frayed. 'Guess what – I've lost all my money... I had it banked, and now it's gone, without a word!'

It was our money too. It was our upholstery. He may not have realised.

Desperate, he says, 'They say the iceberg broke the bank. You pay by weight, it seems. It's on the futures – wow! Each kilo is like gold. The guys must know it's getting hot, and ice is on the outs...'

'No, Chip,' says Sylvie. 'It's all your companies. They circulated stuff, they didn't do a lot. And if the leopards eat the cows – the price of cows goes up, and you can't pay to compensate. You see, my dear, nature is all a to and fro.'

'They should have said,' says Chip.

'You looked so beautiful, the two of you,' says Roxanne. 'Declaiming French upon the ice.'

'At least it wasn't Mallarmé; sequins and trollops,' Omar says. 'Sex below zero – you can't even notch it up.'

I remember the book that ends, with satisfaction, disappointment. Your lover going out the door to join her friends, routines: how she didn't care for anything "but the mouth-organ and the pistol". Pretty sexy too, that end.... Chip's lost his cash... what's there to say?

'Imagine,' Sylvie says. 'It's been blown up by inflation, and then there's Hitler. Or Sarajevo, and they gave you a shoebox full of dinars when you changed ten bucks.... Then came the massacres. Your cash has just been stolen, Chip. Goes on someone else's pile. Making the country strong....' She laughs.

'At least,' says Chip, 'they're thieves that know how valuable the cash can be. It's not some sleazy guy who sells your stolen medals in the pub.'

'I never knew!' Roxanne says. 'Chip – what you get your medals for?' To me, she whispers, 'Sylvie took her share. I hope she didn't bank it all....'

'Disaster for you guys, not for me,' says Omar, limbering up. 'School should tell you what to do when you are poor – not when you've made it. My clients see me as a relative. When things are bad, I'll go and stay with them. That's what they're for, the families.'

'Omar,' Roxanne shouts, 'things are worse than looking for free loads. They say there's fighting everywhere. The Guatemalan army's moving west to join up with the gangs. The Mexicans have made a bridgehead north of Juarez. There's rebels everywhere. It's not the million Trots – it's everybody else, with guns and principles....'

'Roxanne!' says Sylvie. 'You listen in to all those spoofing radio stations – it isn't happening....' but Roxanne says, 'I'll send my little girl away – maybe to Italy, someplace like that, and she can work and send me cash.'

'You have a child, Roxanne?' asks Omar, quite amazed. 'How old?'

'Oh, three or four. She doesn't live with me. I can't stand kids. But once abroad, she'll work – they set them to it, over there,' she says.

'I'm not fighting anyone,' says Chip, 'I want my money back, is all. Horseriding, painting faces – it's no answer, when you search for cash. Besides, the President will sort it out. He seems a docile guy. He's trained for football coaching, I believe.'

'No, no,' says Roxanne. 'He believes those hostile guys are terrorists and foreigners. He's ordered up atomic shells....'

'They'll never bomb the property,' says Chip. 'They're there to see it stands.'

'When there was that Easter thing in Ireland, Chip,' I say. 'They said the Brits would never use artillery against the buildings – but they did. Learn the lesson! – that's what my father said.'

'You two are shadows,' Roxanne says to me. 'You and your lurking parent. Unless you take a side, how can we like you both?'

'That doesn't prove a thing,' says Sylvie. 'It doesn't seem there was a pistol shot, nor anything, not like the European wars. It must be spoof, and we won't need to pick a side.'

Chip says, 'If I had cash again, I'd hire a landau – you could recreate the scene. Turn on the bridge – and then this guy....'

'No, Chip,' says Roxanne, anchored into spoof. 'We're not that interested in your histories. At least we ought to check it out: these civil wars – they're pretty serious things.'

'Maybe you guys should form a pact,' says Omar. 'Look for the truth. The guys round here – they say they all can carry guns. So, unless they simply like the weight, they'll use them too. Seek out the reality – and then decide. In or out of it.'

'We could retreat to my island, for a spin. I doubt the President is using it to shoot into the coracle,' says Chip.

'No, no,' says Sylvie. 'That's just the skill you need in war.'

We reflect, briefly.

Then Chip says, 'You guys – this is from the funnies. All I want – is my cash back.'

'Oh,' says Sylvie. 'I saw them at the bank. It's all quite regular, no longer having it.'

'I love this!' Roxanne says. 'After the fantasy – there's the fantasy.'

'And are you sure you ever had the cash?' Omar asks Chip. 'You always seemed so calm. No work was evident.'

'If there's trouble,' Sylvie says, 'the Chinese will sort it out for us.'

'Maybe we should check it out, see if there's a civil war,' says Chip. 'Though good info's hard to come by now.'

'We've Chip, we must take care of him,' says Sylvie. 'Chip! You're a burden now, you and your powerful friends....'

Chip's island: we wanted to see the Chinese junks go sailing up the Hudson, bringing a respite, and some order that we didn't want. I hoped to see the coracle guy cheering them on, and being cheered; those guys in white baker's caps, saluting, ranged along the ship's side like beading on tea trolleys.

'The mechanism's broke,' says Chip. 'My island doesn't spin no more.'

'Send Omar down,' says Sylvie, full in charge.

There's no one in the coracle: it's a nest of tiny balls, like turtle eggs.

Omar dives to check the motor, and we see his bald head going down, the water colours it, first tanned, then dark jade, then disappeared, 'Like a medusa,' Roxanne says, in wonder – and I realise, it's Omar is the sea, not I.

So what am I?

Omar doesn't reappear. We hadn't asked if he could swim – it's not a thing you ask. He just changed elements.

The island doesn't turn.

Those water colours – maybe one was the colour Chip sent me to seek out

'Should we tell someone?' Roxanne asks.

'Who? What?' Sylvie says. 'If there's a war, they'll need some unknown guys for the memorials. That's Omar's noble destiny. The good thing is,' and she pulls the four of us together, close. 'There is no general conflict. Big beasts die, their parts are carried off, then some fresh things hold the centre stage. We see an end, but it is not the end. Just repositioning.'

'That's the philosophy, then?' asks Chip.

'Oh no,' says Sylvie. 'Philosophy is what we do. We don't do much. Your cash had crimped our minds. Now, from your ashes, we shall rise....' And she flaps long wings.

'Omar was the immortal type,' says Roxanne, wiping a salty tear. 'It's all salt water now – the brokers in Manhattan go about on stilts; for now, it's just for practice. Omar's safe, a pickled fish in an enormous barrel.'

Ah yes – those barrels, full of fish. Moscow – when it was the new land, we from outside, riding and singing, into the storm of dust.... My father – must be chuckling somewhere, embracing Omar. Their last grasp.

'Come on you!' says Sylvie, pinching me. 'Remember the judgement: "soft". No pickled dreams. Toughen up.'

'I'd hoped for more,' I say. 'Where shall we go, Sylvie? A militia in the woods, Trots armed at last?'

'Oh no,' she says, majestic. 'I might set up a band, but not a *bande*, not *dessinée*: nothing comic. And you? You want love? The hurricane?' And she's all over me. 'Pouf!' she says, a seadrift of spit comes over. 'I'll blow you far away!'

'No, Sylvie,' I say, 'not love. It's being loved I want. Not the warmth, the certainty, my father sought – but something that makes up for him, the vacuum.'

'All my friends – all the people here – are spies,' she says. 'It's nothing. It is all the same, and has been always. It's civil war, but all the pieces, most of them, stay on the board. One day, a lot will disappear.'

She's still on top of me, I see Chip, his face grimacing, as if he's peeking through an *oblò*.

'Poor Chip,' says Sylvie. 'All his bloom's rubbed off. Not much when he'd cash. And now – a wooden Indian with a smirk.' Chip gestures, without words.

'We're off!' says Roxanne. 'Sylvie and me. My daughter isn't safe here. They can't pay the soldiers. It's the end. We'll take her off – Greece, China. Leave her there.'

'Where there are nomads,' Sylvie says. 'The richest experience I can think of. Packing up the yurts. The lucky girl. Yes, here it's hit the wall. Now, it's the crumble.'

'Ours is a girls' trip,' Roxanne says to me. 'You can't come. And I resent that you don't like me.'

'I don't want to come,' I say. 'I'm seeing Larissa. We were babies together.'

'Talk to Chip,' Sylvie says to me. 'He may be missing Omar.'

'I doubt it,' I say. 'He just needs a happy pill.'

Sylvie and Roxanne choose a song, and leave; the child is packed away on someone's back.

*

Larissa's here.

She's dark and anxious, Larissa is, head down, jerking like a bird, pecking at where she puts her feet.

She says, 'Your father parked us close, thought we would bond. It wasn't so. Two bundles in a Georgian park.'

'My father wanted the true faith. When he saw it wasn't there, he sought the truth. Disappointed once again, he ended up, longing to be wise,' I say.

'That is exactly it,' Larissa says. 'Your father came to Moscow at the very end. He wasn't wise at all.'

'It seems beyond our understanding now,' I say. 'Things started falling down. They didn't stop, they haven't stopped. He'd nothing he could sell, and they'd no cash to buy. And then things fell down everywhere.'

Larissa's always expectant, waiting to be found. Parked in a park, and now, 'You live well here,' she says, 'doing nothing but some commenting.... I could stay here, all quiet and good with you—'

'No,' I say. 'It's not a good idea. You're earlier than my memory – and so, I'm bound to love you, but that's it. The end. Goodbye, Larissa,' and she goes. She's not contented.

She comes back at once, carrying a weight. 'No Larissa,' I say. 'If that's your baby in a basket – I've nothing in exchange. The one baby that I know's evacuated, gone to China. Here, it's all smashed up, there's strife....'

'You should reproduce,' she says. 'Better than socialism. Shows faith in future things.'

'That one's gone to China,' I say. 'It'll get toughened up there. But it's safe. In China they've got everything – socialism, capitalism, armies, dissent. I guess it sounds like here, a bit, but more confident.'

'My, you're banal!' Larissa says. 'Is that your best? I hope they put it with the nomads – that way it has a little chance....'

'There's no food or water, and it's hot,' I say.

'It's the way of life, you useless idiot!' Larissa says. 'Remember what they say – 'man never sets himself a problem he can't solve', or something like. Besides – they've television, so the kid will sit and watch, like all the rest.'

'I don't know who sets the problems now,' I say, 'But if the saying has it wrong....and you might say it often is....'

Then – here's Roxanne and Sylvie, back again and joyful, 'Yes!' they say. 'The Chinese have a thing about too many kids – the nomads took our little one without a word.'

'You trafficked her!' Larissa says.

'Oh pooh!' says Roxanne. 'She was glad to go. And here's another one, I see....' She whispers, close to Sylvie. Then she says, 'Chip should take one. Take his mind off cash, and give him company.'

'Of course!' Larissa says. 'that's the ideal. He'd teach her how to ride and paint her face and buy and sell the real estate.'

It's all girls' talk, but it's decided; I'm relieved. A good deed's being done, a problem solved. I think of Aliye, her tale: I say,

'Before you go, Larissa, you should tell a tale that makes us think, and possibly rejoice.'

'No, no!' says Chip, 'First we must sort our families out. You're gross, you two, you're pigs! Those stereotypes!'

'Chip,' Sylvie says, 'You haven't understood. We're naturalists. We're working out the new – what you must want, what you must do, all that. The structure and the urge. Experience, but no metaphysics. The principles for all cohabitation.'

Larissa says, 'It seems to me that here – it's going strong. There's life that's going on...'

'No, no,' says Sylvie, 'You see the bars and clubs are full – it's just because the rest is falling – if it hasn't fallen – down.'

'You're moralists as well as pigs,' shouts Chip. 'You want another set of rules to suit yourselves. I don't want this woman! Or her child!'

'Well,' Larissa says, 'I won't go back, so there. Sylvie, you're right! We need new structures, and new rules, and who should go with who, and tell them what to do – and whether you should steal or booze or take some pills.... We never loved the state, and now all round it's falling down, and we must make things up ourselves. It all was cash. When the state can't pay its guys – that is the end. No regrets – into the whirlwind we shall go, determined, proud....'

'And with eyes closed,' says Chip. 'Someone still has my cash they stole. That's nothing new.'

'Tell us a tale, Larissa, then we'll sort you out,' I say, 'Chip too. There's nothing we can do, when all is crumbling, and there's no Aphrodite, taking sides and nudging spears, turning aside the blades. The heroes – they have all gone down. And no one cares to carry their cadavers off....'

'Not all things fall apart,' Larissa says. She tells her tale. 'Beside me, when I had just been born, there was another basket, with a little boy. Time passed. He had a dog, then lovers, order and ambition, a degree in architecture.... I remember – those dogs with bushy tails, the village lads who walked them down the track – it's asphalt now, and lined with bricks and lo-rise buildings.... What were we to do, when he was ready to be conscripted in the army? How could we get him out? – for he was marked "soft" at birth, and he was mine, my destiny, my beginning and my end.'

'Oh no,' I say, 'that wasn't me. And your child's not mine, Larissa. I wasn't there for long, besides, they can't conscript a foreigner.'

She's blank. 'It's just a tale,' she says. 'It isn't you. It hasn't been for years.'

'If that's your tale,' says Chip, 'Larissa, you'd better stay well clear of all creative trades.'

She doesn't care. 'Your father,' she says to me, 'knew everything. He was the best of spies. He couldn't do a thing with it. All the knowledge – some of it the truth... he couldn't warn the bosses. Couldn't praise them. Couldn't say, "History's against you, your end is more than nigh." Instead, he left a Moses basket, right beside me. That was to be my history—'

'I know all this,' I interrupt. 'I too know everything. It is a curse. You can't accomplish anything. No one listens, no one hires or fires you. You're undercover, quite invisible, sat in the park. My father left me there, abandoned. He'd got bored. Like Roxanne. Except – my story isn't yours, Larissa. Your tale's invented. I am not your destiny. My father – he returned. Carried me off. I wasn't born beside you. The child's not ours.'

'This stuff is dense and deep,' says Roxanne. 'I just dumped my child – now, here's another to sort out. Then, there's the moral base of everything we've to decide. All this while Armageddon's moiling up the road....'

'It's always so, Roxanne,' says Sylvie. 'The future's all planned out and written down, you find the project long long after, in the ruins, as a scroll or book, when you've tacked together something else...

'America: it's the metaphor for everywhere, the point of union where the world's played out. The molecules – they dance, and then they clash. Turn into bombs. It mustn't trouble us, the ultimate war is not the end. It's dialectics, friends. We must anticipate the finish, and thereafter....'

'But Sylvie,' Chip complains, 'We've lost our scientist, our engineer. Omar: the sea, engulfed, sunk into the pickling. Now – to protect ourselves: – do we dig, or do we climb? The pit? The tree?'

'The people here,' says Sylvie, 'Live in the metaphor. They think that where they are, is all the world. It's like Chip's people thought, when they had only bows and arrows to kill each other with...'

'Oh come!' says Chip. 'That's simplified! Larissa – just leave your child and basket here. We are survivors – on our tippy-toes we'll leave.... The ancients said the child would speak in Hebrew if you let it be. The linguists think that's so today. It speaks no Russian yet, so we shall see....'

'That way it will avoid the Schul,' says Roxanne.

All is resolved – posterity, all that. I'm free to be the sea again, absorbing everything. Anger and calm, following each other like big and little waves.

'The whole thing, the future, is to be decided here, and now,' says Chip. 'Sylvie! The moral order you're concocting – it's more than bleak. There's punishments for sure, but no rewards. "All men are brothers" – but there is no family. "Respect for all" – but you've none for yourself, still less for me....'

'No, Chip,' says Sylvie, angrily. 'It's good you're firming up. But what you want is going backwards, to those fictions – exactly what has got us here. Exhortations no one will obey.'

'Sylvie,' I say, 'both you and Chip are stuck. People do what they can get away with – useless giving them more rules. See – they got away with all Chip's money....'

'Money's not a skin,' Roxanne says. 'You can't wear it like the suit you came in.'

'Yes you can,' says Chip. 'That's why I got depilated. Cash on me is like a carapace, a shell. Or a tattoo.'

'We need more stories, that's for sure,' says Roxanne. 'I could put a coda on Larissa's effort – you two, brother, sister – seek each other; and there's a quest for Chip – his treasure, his sparkling roots, the colour he aspired to....'

'You guys!' says Sylvie. 'Stop inventing. Look what's coming!'

Larissa's overwhelmed: she says to me, 'There was a war when first we met. We were young, to be its casualties.'

'There's nothing terrible in that,' I say. 'War is our condition, like wolves have to eat carrion, poor noble things. Here, they found some mechanisms, so's they didn't need to fight at home, but it was always there, and coming; in the past as well.... Now – the question is, what's to be done?'

*

Chip has more pasts to cancel than the rest of us.

'Hey, guys,' he shouts, in military mode. 'Energy fruits – now, that'd be the thing! New colours that would stretch your eyes? Occupation? Civil war? I can't wait for all those things!'

'He means – to simulate,' Sylvie says. 'It's good we settled with those kids. The family's an awful place to start. He'll construct some futures. Like Potemkin, the prince of plywood. He has the tools—'

'No corny stuff,' says Chip, 'No fantasy. No Martians, Thai tanks in the Bronx, coming to my aid.'

'So long as it's simulation, science, not fantasy, I can't object,' Roxanne says. 'Go ahead, Chip. But remember – there's the National Guard. Every state has its army. When things are crumbling, each one goes its own way—'

'Oh no!' says Chip. 'I hadn't thought of that. For sure, I'll find one that'll help me get my money back. One of them will do a deal. Wyoming, do you think?'

Chip's scenarios are fairly stark. 'Sylvie,' he says, 'you can have a little band, and get protection from some guys.

Roxanne – I'd hate to think of you as victim, but those religious types would spit you out – you don't go near to them. Larissa and this uptight guy' – and he points at me – 'you've both got pasts as fellow travellers. You'd better hope you're not found out—'

'Oh Chip!' says Roxanne. 'How you make us suffer. Penned in those tanks, the submarines, the rockets – even when we're not incinerated – the atmosphere is dense and stuffy. I do believe – you get off on our hurt.'

Chip doesn't care: he sketches in a beautiful old Dodge, that's full of nail bombs. 'Better keep your heads down for that one,' he warns us, 'if it hits a bump.'

It's almost beyond imagination, as if Aphrodite's there, making the well-laid guns miss their targets, or she knocks your arm, just as you try to bayonet your awful officer – some guy who worked in advertising....

Sylvie's fulfilled – a warlord, a warlady – working with her militia, working with everyone, punishing those she doesn't like or who can't pay.

'It all ends well, because it ends, and order is restored,' says Chip. 'Although maybe my money's not.'

'Come on, Chip,' Roxanne says. 'Almost everybody says that war is hell, and that's where bad guys ought to go....'

'That's as maybe, Roxanne,' says Chip, swiftly inputting data to his valve-like skull. 'That monotheists' alliance was a dud. Now, what complicates things more, each army issues its own currency.'

'Omar would have brought the calm,' I say, hoping by this to bring it on.

'Omar deserted long ago,' says Sylvie. 'He was a refugee before the battle started.'

'Maybe you'd all better be,' says Chip, still frantic. 'Refugees. These guys will fight it out, then someone will give us cash, and we can buy more arms.'

'This science,' Roxanne says, 'it's more uncomfortable than being shelled, cooped up in Chip's parameters.'

'Where's your spirit of community?' Chip asks. 'At least, of sacrifice, or patience? This is a drill, an exercise – take it in that spirit, as it comes.'

'Where's Aphrodite?' asks Larissa. 'I've heard of her, but she's not up to much. Goddess of providence – she is what we need.'

'She's used to only one big battlefield,' says Chip. 'Now there's too many, and she can't divide. Besides, there's talk of revolutions, and the gods get scared at mention of the word. They jumble it all up.'

'There's no hope here,' I say. 'Chip: find us a mountain – one where they won't dig or drill. A forest, desert – anywhere so's we won't have to flee to Canada.'

'They wouldn't take us,' Sylvie says, 'Our breath would hasten up their melt.'

'The stars!' Larissa says. 'Maybe they'd take sides?'

'The cosmos doesn't give a toss,' says Roxanne, her morale is wilting, her words come from the street...

'No, no,' says Chip. 'She means the actors. Those that aren't just painted on. Italians all take Jewish names – they don't know which side is theirs. No, we can't look to them. With luck, someone will occupy us, or drop us arms.'

Each against all – or was it all against each? My father doesn't give a lead, although it doesn't mean all are the same, or that there's no good choice.

'A safe place, Chip!' I say again. 'I know it's all in fun, nothing means quite what it says, but all the same—'

'No, no,' shouts Sylvie. 'I am in the game, and I will stay there. Chip! Keep them coming, cards and options. Some decent spies I need – not this one here—' and she punches the muscle in my arm, '—as soft as jello.'

'How fortunate my kid is safe and trekking with the yaks,' says Roxanne.

'That's crap,' Larissa says. 'The nomads disappeared before the Jews, and no one cares... and where's the kid I dumped?'

They shout at Sylvie, who shouts back. From someone comes the cry, 'Let's get her!' – maybe from all three.

'Listen!' shouts Sylvie. 'I'll stay here – the Durruti column is my inspiration, though I may change my name. Louise Michel – that comes to mind. I'll find some clean and feisty guys – or gals, for preference – no flab, no therapies....'

'They'll think you're all religious freaks,' says Chip. 'Besides – I love you Sylvie. And remember, this is not a game, it's science, but it isn't happening.'

'But it will,' says Sylvie, 'and thanks, Chip, for the warning of your inner swell. That is your problem. Deal with it.' And to me she says, 'Don't talk to me of politics, coherence – your father'd no adrenal gland, and nor have you. "Soft", both of you. You didn't enter in the storm. You sneaks.'

'They'll inflate you, Sylvie, then they'll cut you down like rhubarb,' Roxanne says. 'That's how it works. They take you at your ambitious word, and then they do for you. It puffs them up.'

'It's all romance,' Larissa says. 'Roxanne is right. They cut you down – your ideas don't die, they go back in Pandora's vase, and they are sealed inside.'

'It doesn't bother me,' says Sylvie. 'All that you say – it doesn't change a thing.'

To that, there is no argument which holds.

'Sylvie's mission... it reconciles her to what comes. And what she does.' Larissa says. 'I don't believe in it myself.'

'Just think,' says Sylvie. 'All those people, wanting to go home to where they've only memories. I can't do anything about all that – I just do what's right. It's true – I'm beautiful – my bones are beautiful, at least. But – what can you do with them? Make soup?'

*

Sylvie leaves.

'She's not a humanist,' says Roxanne. 'That's quite *démodé* now. She wants recruits, not converts. Maybe I shall stay with her. Beauty attracts, you know – so does her lean mind.'

'I know what happens,' says Larissa. 'Sylvie turns malevolent, her gang loses a stand-off, Roxanne gets killed trying to protect her, when she's up and over that wall, already on the run.'

'She's always been malevolent,' says Chip. 'None of us was worth her effort.'

'Look, Chip,' I say. 'Are you quite sure that everything has fallen down? It's all disorder? Suppose it's just got larger? A pact between the guys? Sweep away what doesn't serve, that holds them up – and it's a scheme between the strong, with all their spies, and all the other likewise, from the world entire.... Suppose that, Chip? Then Sylvie's in the maelstrom.... There was so much I had to ask....'

'The only thing you soft guys ever want to ask,' says Chip, 'is "does she love me?" Well, I can answer that. The beautiful are quite incapable of feeling love for any person but themselves. That's what the ancients taught, and they were right. You contemplate the beautiful. That is what it's for. It doesn't fit inside your truckle bed, my dear.'

'Well, yes,' I say, 'that would have been one of those things I'd ask... but I had trusted you, dear Chip, to map it out for us, the future....'

'And you did right,' says Chip. 'Besides, there's no one else to trust. But – my science was a plan, a plot: the simulation... well, in science and in politics, there's bulls, there's bears. The aim is all the same. You knew my aim was one and only one – to get my money back. What was the link with somehow pumping Sylvie up, and living on a mountain with you guys, while all the places where my cash could hide came toppling down?'

'Yes, Chip,' Roxanne says, 'put it like that, we were imprudent. We wanted to believe.'

'Suckers,' Larissa says.

'I may have maybe... misled Sylvie,' Chip says. 'There's gangs and civil war all right – but those guys, all over in America – they're quite rebarbative. You cross them – and they'll drive you mad, and then they'll blow you up. No, not a metaphor alone – but chemically too. Bang bang!'

I say, 'It's all because of Sylvie's beauty – you wouldn't contemplate, but tried to screw... and then you were humiliated....' There's the truth, I think, and although I've told it, that's a thing you never do....

'Well,' says Chip, cool as cool, 'she'll go down fighting. Sylvie rides a horse so thin it can't be targeted. Maybe she wears lucky beads, who knows. It's an intense experience, this struggle for existence. She'll show that Schopenhauer was wrong – she's never bored, and so she must believe in God.'

'So what?' Larissa asks. Chip has no reply. I think he's often bored.

'I ought to follow Sylvie, tell her these truths,' says Roxanne, much disturbed. 'In my own way – not beautiful – I loved her. For sure, the truth will save her.'

'From what?' asks Chip. 'And why? She can't help being beautiful, and when that ends – she ends as well.'

Who knows of Chip's perfidy? To promote is to expose. Encouraging Sylvie to ride her papery horse is to sacrifice her. Who knows of Sylvie's perfidy? Not even Sylvie.

*

She writes to us:

'I need a touch from Aphrodite – I'm maybe her only true believer here. The wars – civil and less so – are so loud! I'm made for being seen, not heard. The people here are used to noise, it's their asbestos blanket.'

'Oh no!' Roxanne says. 'She's so confused. It's the racket, all around. She comes from here, but, returning, it's quite another scene. They eat and drink – dormice and larks' tongues isn't the half of it. All painting their little shapes and opening strange restaurants.... the pyramid, the cube, the wavy line, something to do with Gauss. They build them all, especially the pyramids... stones and cement, so high they block the light....'

'We know all that, Roxanne,' Chip says. 'It's because the price of land is high, the buildings must be high as well. We've lived there, in the canyons; makes you want the stars.'

'Oh yes,' Larissa says, 'you want the stars, and they will have them, bottled.'

'Larissa, what have they told you?' Roxanne asks.

'Well,' Larissa says, stretching out, 'they take a little drift of star, and when one dies, they make a new one, to the size they want.'

'What nonsense,' Chip says.

Sylvie writes, '*I'm the only one here without hope. The others – busy, trying not to be destitute, or even poor – they don't see how desperate it is, how it's all going down.... They wander through the ruins, eating rich foods. Don't they see the sky? Feel the cold, the heat?*'

'Poor Sylvie,' Roxanne says. 'It can't be just her autobiography. She's lost her hope, because there is no hope.'

Should I feel responsible? I didn't merely contemplate. I was intimate – she, much less. She – not at all. I don't bring this up with Chip.

'*They'll surely find me and my comrades,*' Sylvie writes.

She's so much time to write – a will, an epitaph. She doesn't have a cause, so they can pick her off the street, or leave her there, broken, abandoned.

She says, '*The state – it seemed to be disintegrating, but it's what all these people need, to make them whole. They're bubbles, released into it, the state, like bubbles in champagne. Smaller and smaller it gets, but – there are scores of them, a hatch of mini-states, all tributary to the massive one that we can't see. We hear it, though. My band.... It's different – we are a nest of bees or ants, and I'm the queen, the only one with wings....'*

'I must find her, help her,' Roxanne says. 'At least I'll spy on her.'

'No, no,' says Chip, 'She's gone. Gone in the head. She says all this to have you come to her, Roxanne.'

What Sylvie says – they're things you say when you're about to disappear, and start again as something else. I don't say so, but I've seen it all before.

Roxanne goes to look for Sylvie: Larissa says, 'That's great, Roxy.'

Roxanne says, 'No one was closer to me, ever.'

She doesn't come back.

Chip says, 'Sylvie will have gone under. Underground. But they'll know where she is. Besides, a group like hers, there's always someone who will spy. And come to that, they'll know where we are too – not that it does them good.'

I ask Larissa, 'Whatever happened to your kid?'

'Oh,' she says, 'Roxanne placed it. I didn't think Chip was quite suitable – I didn't like his views on money. I hope it goes with the nomads. I had no special plans for it.'

'Those agencies,' says Chip. 'They don't like taking prisoners. They're not interested anyway in what you've done – it's networks they are after.'

'My father said where we were, some people used to hide,' Larissa says. 'But mostly they were working where they oughtn't.'

'My father knew some people who did hide,' I say. 'If you're well hidden, you don't count for anything.'

Chip seems discomforted. 'I don't expect Sylvie did anything except some metaphoric statement. No real damage, nothing they might track back to me – not that it's all about my cash...'

Larissa says, 'You're not involved in all that jacquerie, I hope? That so-called spontaneity? Common sense, know-nothings?'

'I didn't think you cared, Larissa,' Chip says, embarrassed, 'about the detail, the quality, all the theory stuff...'

She turns away from Chip, 'His superficiality...' she says.

I think – if Omar was the sea, and everything that's in it – to reproduce his medusa shape, he makes a journey of ten thousand kilometres, up to the New Siberian islands. Seeming to drift, but pulsing with determination, there to divide, a hundred stinging mushroom canopies, and on and on, to the world's end. An enterprise so far beyond me....

'Omar's drowned,' says Chip, intervening. 'On his first ever helpful gesture. That shows you! That should make you think!'

'You shouldn't just drift,' Larissa says. 'You need to have a plan, like I do.'

'Everybody plans now,' Chip says, 'I planned.'

'No,' Larissa says. 'Plans with an aim. Not forecasts. Forecasts know there's storms. Everyone already knows it.'

'That sounds like communism,' Chip says, 'then, Larissa, you're another carbuncle on our collective toe. Imagine who was in Sylvie's gang – not counting spies! People making gestures, people who read; relativists and dogmatists. All of them,' and he glows red with frustration. 'Exactly the kind who cancel each other out, and are explosions waltzing down the street.'

'Chip,' I say, 'no one has joined those ends together. Being a suspect's nothing. It's the last thing that would make you stand out.'

'Fuck it all,' says Chip, 'we'll all be guillotined for being terrorists. Let's go to my mountain before it's all shipped off.'

'That's a Seventies thing to do,' I say. 'But none of us can play an instrument, so I guess it's all right now.'

178

'None of us can express themself,' says Chip. 'Instrument or nothing. Not even Sylvie.'

'I can,' says Larissa loudly, 'and you'll all of you hear me pretty soon.'

'All I know is, I was robbed,' says Chip. 'That puts me on the side of justice. But not equality.'

*

Chip's mountain glows. 'I like big stuff,' says Chip. 'It's tailings. It's other mountains stripped and dumped – but, see! This greenish yellow here is cobalt. Don't touch the red – it's slag, or maybe artificial rubies, anyway, it's hot. You see, I don't do little things like nose jewels, writing songs and such. This blue and purple – looks like feldspar, but it chars your feet. Don't breathe too deep – you may be stuck with crystals growing in your lungs....'

'It's magical, your mountain, Chip,' I say. 'It's quite unique, and not a metaphor for anything.'

'Usually it's pyrites, those lumps, but sometimes they dump gold, to steady up the price and keep it high,' says Chip, dribbling a ball of lapis lazuli. 'It's a dirty job, picking through, making a fortune from the dirt. I prefer to cool myself, and watch it burn and glitter. It's not everyone has a pile like this.'

We sit around. Sylvie writes: '*Sex, drugs, and what comes after rock. You'd think they were calm – I've done those three myself, and added gambling and drink. In its own way, each is a blessing. All together – you can find them in the same spot. You can go through them all in an afternoon, and in the evening read your Schopenhauer. But here – they're distributed with violence. Beatings and flagellations. Biting off a rooster's head – it's nothing to what guys put guys through here. My theory? – I guess it's all for cash and influence. What interests me is the real tough stuff – the power, the metaphysics. What my gang is for. But – a little debt can have you lose a leg: a kicking's just routine. The soldiers and the agencies – what happens between comrades! Imagine when they're let loose on all the rest....'*

'She's really soft,' Larissa says. 'The barrack's where it starts, of course. They have some officers – they set it off.'

'Sylvie's tasty to look at,' Chip admits. 'She wants to move things on. It signifies for her, I guess. The most she'll get's a good death – a quick one. You can't read much into that.'

'Striving's the thing,' Larissa says. 'The end will disappoint, but that's the way it is.'

Chip seems to find Larissa cute. He says, 'This mountain here's a pile of junk – but people covet it – that gives it sparkle.'

'Oh Chip,' Larissa hugs him. 'It's so full of energy, your hill. Poor Roxanne – she'll have gone trotting down the street, there's doorways, people, all is normal, then – she's snatched! Small rooms, without a mirror. "Come clean – you're one-dimensional. We'll suck your lymph, from now, your life is just a paper sack." That's what they say, the good guys and the not. We shan't see her again,' and Larissa snaps her knees into the vertical, and leaps like Sylvie did – over the jasper blocks where we are sat – somersaulting up and down, sounding that kletzmer doodling as she goes.

'No, no,' shouts Chip, as she showers us with chalcedony drops, 'Not kletzmer – sing us a song like in the olden times...' Larissa stands majestic, sings,

'Everywhere is corners
Every stair leads down –
Down among the jazzmen, singing like a frog,
Singing like a princess, waiting for the kiss,
Kissing in the mirror, changing all the shapes,
Being something different, every time you sing....'

'Ah,' says Chip, almost tearful, 'Those Soviet ballads! They may have been butchers there, but they knew all about writing songs.' He turns to me, 'Brings it back, no doubt? Not like my cash! Nothing brings that back.'

I'm not much moved. 'Spying's quite against new things, going back and moving forward,' I say, coolly.

'Anyway,' he says, 'Roxanne won't reappear, but her sort's immortal. She'll reproduce, like Omar. You won't tell her kids apart. Sylvie – she won't waste gestures; not for her a slogan and crazy shooting. She's in the war, she'll slog it through. No second lives for her. First time's the last time – that's her.'

'Does Sylvie have it?' Larissa asks. 'The Idea? If you don't have It, there's the maximum – of "frightfulness and terror". That's what the philosopher says. Of course, you may have It, and It may be crap.'

'Oh, Sylvie knows philosophy,' says Chip. 'That's why she's gone to war.'

'The trouble with God,' says Larissa, 'is that the appearances are quite arbitrary. But you can't be arbitrary too – you must be humble. Follow, and submit. Philosophy's quite arbitrary, but there's lots of them. War is arbitrary, when it happens to you. I shouldn't say that God is quite like war, like what Sylvie's got mixed up in. But – it is so.'

'Well, Larissa, I think that nonetheless you've left things out,' says Chip. 'It doesn't bother me. I believe in lots of gods, including gods of war – but they don't say what I should do, because they're arbitrary, just as you say, Larissa. It's true they want some visibility, but there's so many of them – and they reproduce – they settle for respect, not love. And not obedience. They don't tell you what they want until it's all been settled, done.'

'You may be right,' Larissa says. 'But mine was a hypothesis. I'm a sceptic, but once you think you've sighted the divinity and made your pact, you're off the map, to put it philosophically.'

I feel quite lost. Those two can argue in the void, while I – my father too – just hung around, and gave bent guys some cash to snoop for us. Now, like Omar, my father floats in the sea. They are the sea. Expanses remembered, like yourself, your life, over, sucked to the pips. Maybe in memory there's a dance – no song. Just empty mouths. And nothing about the rest, nothing at all. My father said the bad things – all those, were over by that time... and then, besides, everything had changed, changed utterly. Now, I'm here: bad things all over.

'You never plugged into anything,' says Chip to me. 'Just turned stuff down – and turned your nose up.'

'No, it's the fear,' I say. 'We used to fool ourselves it all would turn out good. Now, it's the fear....'

*

'These little movies,' Chip says, 'you can't see a thing. This one sent to us – there's dust.... That swirl could be my secret colour? It's apricots and gooseberries, mixed together....'

'Of course you can't make it out,' I say. 'It's what happened to Sylvie and Roxanne. It's over like a spit. It's war photography – things travel fast. Too fast to see and count.'

'It says there's an "unnamed",' Larissa says.

'Oh, that'll be Roxanne,' says Chip. 'You mustn't think I sent her out for reasons selfish or banal. It was her false hope that did for her.'

'Hopefulness is just an attitude,' Larissa says. 'My granny had it. It's not really hope. It's more a call for luck to perch on you.'

'You killed them both, Chip. You had them killed. You knew they could be killed....' I say.

'We need to be precise,' says Chip. 'So far – it's just a storm of dust. At any time, and anywhere.'

'I've seen these images before,' I say. 'There is no hope. Not for Sylvie, not Roxanne.'

'Well, now,' says Chip. 'Responsibility's an idea that's quite more complicated. But – death – that is simpler... in a complicated sort of way. We have religions – they see death quite differently from you…. Resurrection, then an Armageddon. Sacrifice, then paradise. Rebirth, all that. Recycling. Believe or not, it's up to you. Then – there's the ghosts. And concepts – they're immortal. Having a thousand jellyfish, that look and act identically to you… they breed. Has the medusa died? No, no – it's species being. There's no head jellyfish, no living one, and so there's no cadaver. The values – lots of talk of them. They're immortal too, of course. And Sylvie – when we didn't see her, she could write. We saw, we read her words. There she was. And Roxanne: didn't write, and didn't speak. She was invisible. But, there's no corpse….'

'Chip!' I say. 'You set them up. They're dead. No argument.'

'Relax!' he says. 'Beauty fades. It settles. What it was, goes into the soil. I'm like that – a deep one. Like Proust – remember him coming in your store, looking for Magdalenes, sweet ones? Maybe he'd have found Larissa!' Larissa shrugs and pulls away. 'Remember, there's another French guy who's appropriate, who talks of "*l'étoile stalinienne du bonheur*". There's a thought!'

Larissa says, 'You're bleak, Mister Chip.'

He laughs, and says, 'I see you're always hungry for my marvels. I've the one left – a stand of trees, quite central.'

There it is: it says 'Reserved'. 'I hate those guys,' says Chip, 'who occupy the nature, crowd round, sell their caribu sandwiches and their tangled artwork….'

There's straight black trees: branches like scimitars. 'The branches chime,' he says. 'It's all tuned steel. When there is wind – there's always wind, of course, because we're voyaging – they make a carillon.' And so they do. They jangle to and fro.

'If only history had paused at 1913,' Chip says, ears cocked and hand wagging roughly in time to the sound. 'Berg's three orchestral pieces – they would have shown another way.'

Larissa and I consider this, quite lost in ignorance.

Some guys in sporty clothes climb in the garden. At once, Chip breaks off a branch, and, whirling round, uses it as a scythe to menace them. They tell him to fuck off, but it is they who run. 'It's just the way I am,' says Chip. 'It's really all quite arbitrary, but sometimes it's well-aimed as well.'

The intruders shout insults. 'See?' says Chip to us. 'You want a new society for scum like that? You know all about new societies, Larissa, back there in Moscow... So do I – they paid us back all right! We flying chips got a new society, and then another, and another! Sylvie will discover – you too,' he swings his scythe at me, without rancour or intent, 'You go to fight – the old you'll not get back, the new – your bones will go to pickle if it comes.'

'Chip, I didn't realise you identified,' I say. 'It's not just about Indians, it's everyone.'

'No, no,' Larissa says. 'There's change, improvement, even through the fighting. That's why we send our kids to nomad bands. To wait it out.'

'They said that after the emperors would come the *intelligenty*. But it was all bandits and soldiers,' I say.

'And never my turn,' says Larissa.

'You mean what was new, along with those musicians?' asks Chip, disdainfully. 'They didn't ride horses – they put the horse inside themselves.'

'Oh,' says Larissa, 'Not that sort – I mean, when educated guys drank coffee *mit Schlag* and ate tiny cakes – where they make the chocolate, like Linz. And places that changed their name, like Agram.'

'Rich kids,' says Chip. 'Like I was.'

'My father said the toiling masses—' I begin.

'They toil. By definition,' Chip says. 'Like your father didn't.'

'That's cheap,' says Larissa. 'When you two were on the mountain, on your judges' thrones – I thought *How fine their minds, how small the meshes of their nets.* Nothing can escape those well-tempered minds.'

'Ah yes,' I say. 'We were tranquil back there – judges, with no crime laid out before us like a mess of entrails. But now it's brought it back. Omar. How Chip manoeuvred him – *o mar* – becoming sea, and drowning in it.'

'Nonsense,' says Chip. 'Omar had studied an expansion, assimilation, of all things thrown overboard, whipped into storm and sea-drift. Including him. He knew his destiny! ... It was his element, you fool! He went where he had striven to end up – the sea!'

'And yet,' Larissa says, 'he took that mucoid form. A jelly. Strange.'

'Yes, well,' says Chip. 'He had to move around, of course. In the deep, you can't use legs.'

We see our accusation hanging over Chip – the axe that longs to fall, but doesn't manage it, to cut through the doubt, the neck, the bridge that links the head to all the rest, clarifying all. Guilt without recourse.

Just then – a wind arises. Every branch seeks out its note. 'I didn't plan all this,' says Chip, 'The architect arranged that we should hear those pieces every time a breeze tuned up. I'm not a fan of Berg myself – and now a note won't sound, the branch I broke.... Reminds me of my iceberg, melting right away. Still, I have my mountain, glowing, precious.... But – if only we had followed Berg, there'd be no pistol shot, no Sarajevo tumbling it all down.'

The sound is massive, hot and cool, it stirs my memory. It bears me and Larissa back to our baskets in the park. *Calme, luxe...* before us – our whole untouched lives, a path. A fantasy. I say aloud, 'If only we had taken it, that path – upward and onward....'

For a moment, Larissa leans against me. But I am not the father of our child. I watch, I don't walk along the path, its flowers and stones, its steep inclines.

Chip struggles, trying to reattach his scythe.

He's anxious to be away. 'I'll check on what is left of mine,' he says, 'Then I'll come back for you.'

We are alone. Larissa, not much loved, or sought....

'Hey!' Larissa says. 'All the guys here are actors! This city's all a theme park, with some dressed up as animals, and some as chorus....'

'You go fight in places no one's heard of, it's clear it'll all come back on you,' I say. 'The guys here – should have thought of that. Maybe they hadn't read of what they'd done. There will be *casseurs* – they come first. And then the civil war that guys here haven't heard about.'

Chip is a threat for us, for both of us. Perhaps Sylvie left a word?

How can you escape, fleeing before the warriors who fuel themselves with their own horses' blood? Those Romans....

'Lots went to Armenia,' Larissa says. 'And some elsewhere, to wait until the Prophet came along.'

'Well,' I say, 'We should leave quick. I know how these things work. Sylvie would have discovered that.'

'If you're quite sure...' Larissa says. 'But I'd be sorry to leave Chip, a man who has a garden with steel trees that chime with 1913 music, from Vienna too.'

'It's clever, I admit,' I say, 'but very limited.'

'But,' Larissa says, 'you're soft. It's written into you. I think of all these strident people here – whatever they now fear and suffer – you know, they'll suffer ten times worse. They think they're safe. They've escaped from somewhere, and now they're bunkered up. They think, "It will not happen here, we'll never have to choose – resistance, collaboration, lose your stuff and cash, no food or drink, no sleep... we've passed all that to other guys, in places we have never heard of."'

'Chip won't get his money back,' I say. 'It's no good choosing him, Larissa.'

'Oh, it's not about the money,' she says. 'It was that insult: Magdalenes. I'm not his biscuit, sweet or bitter. Nor his cup of tea.'

'We'll leave,' I say. 'Find a safer place, and then I'll say farewell to you.'

'I feel quite safe enough right here,' Larissa says. 'Although you said this here was the world, and not a proper country.'

I assure her, 'Larissa, we won't leave the world. Don't stickle over definitions.'

There's a message from Sylvie. 'That means she's alive,' Larissa says.

Of course, it doesn't.

It says, 'There must be a better place. And if there's not? My companions here are Korean, most of them. *Juche*. That's what you need, iron self-reliance. People in this city – each one has a ghost upon their shoulder, some stranger. Some unacknowledged guilt. A corpse in their name. A responsibility not taken.

'This expanse – for so long, it's been an easy place to rule. Lots of odd guys take the wheel.... So, it starts small, the war of each, the war of all, the one you should avoid. It can go on for lifetimes.'

We pause. I say to Larissa, 'Chip says you are a communist.'

She says, 'We all would like a better place,' and then, 'Poor Roxy.'

I say, not much convinced, 'She was obedient to beauty. They used to say you can't do better than serving beauty.'

'Sylvie will fight, resist,' says Larissa. 'But, why did Chip pick on her? What must she think she's doing there?'

'She saw Chip as he was,' I say, 'that's always hard for guys to take. He made her take a side. Then, he wanted to toughen me, so's it was worthwhile his being dominant. You, Larissa – he wanted clean and pure. You could not imagine that. We weren't malleable, and so – he dropped us both. I'll be pushing you along from now. There's no future in my being soft. Besides, there's only you left. The rest have spun away.'

We think about our prospects: I say, 'Spying – for me, it's completely done with.'

'Chip never spoke to me,' Larissa says.

'It's not important, if you're him. Cash, history – that communicates as well,' I say.

'There's no war, no fighting here,' Larissa says, 'I guess it's still in the periphery.'

'We could try Wyoming,' I tell her. 'Look for your child. Our child, if that's how you see things.'

'It surely wouldn't end up in a place like that,' she says. 'Though people drift away.'

'Yes,' I say. 'Like Omar. Just float away. Even Aphrodite's quite indifferent, or absent as she always seems to be.'

Parade Armour

You can see he's a metaphysician by the way he looks out the train window. He never glances at his hard neighbour, who counts her every word.

'I'm drawing up the tennis championships,' he says. 'Each year, there's lots of lies and walkovers, of course.'

'You must think you know who wins,' she says.

'Oh,' he says, 'it's always me. Another year, I get to keep the cup.'

'That seems a hollow victory,' she says.

'Oh, aren't they all, my dear?' he says. 'But being champion – that's still something.'

'But if you never play?' she says.

'It deals with problems. It's part of my down-to-earth metaphysics. My passion. Not playing, but winning, wanting to win – that's passion too. There's limitations, and transcendence. Those are professional concerns, of course, for us philosophers. Winning by not taking part – that goes beyond your small reality. Then – victory! That's not given by experience: it's a state of quality you don't attain by lobbing balls. The "something new" – that is the hardest. Making sense of our perceptions, reasoning, then going that little step beyond....'

'You might find the step is huge, and lands you in some sticky pit,' she says, hoping.

'Well, we shan't know that until we fall,' he says, coolly.

All three, we stare out the window. There's broken clods and trees: they're digging for wealth, or foundations. Or else some surge has swept it all away, what there was.

The guy who doesn't play tennis says, 'It's your perception. Your finite province of significance. Some see annihilation in the landscape, some see natural gas. From the train, you can't tell which. My vantage point's – I'm rich. As the books say, "a poor man's like a dead man". Most people – especially the poor – are dead already.'

His companion, who looks as if she lectures, says, 'It was the Europeans. When they finished killing blacks and browns and started on each other – that was the end. It's a virus, swirling round the world.'

She leaves, and clumps across the boardwalk. We watch her buttocks as they shrug and bulge, self-conscious as she herself recedes.

'Not much conversation, that one,' the rich non-athlete says. 'But the symbolism's always present. A woman, in a train. It excites – like when they had the 'ladies only' seating. Untouchables – a special privilege.'

'I'm not into that,' I say. 'I'm cool. I don't differentiate.'

'I should have followed her, I guess,' he says. 'Women have lots of catching up to do.'

It's hard to answer that. I hum, 'the Bowery's up and the Battery's down'. He says,

'Yes, and the people all ride in a hole in the ground. A sinister ring to that. Partition's the answer, of course. Probably everywhere, but in America, there's no other way. Exchange of populations. Everyone with who they want, until they want a change.'

There's hunters here, to clear the site. And hooded guys, jerking around on pogo sticks, bringing the old times back. They're in every space, jousting around.

He snarls at me, this rich guy, 'Hey! Surely you don't consort with me because I've got the cash? Divide it with you – then we'd both be poor.'

'No,' I say. 'I'm not into that at all.'

'If you need work,' he goes on, 'The most I've got for you is stacking boxes.'

'That's too bad,' I say. 'That's the one thing I can't do, is stack boxes.'

We're both relieved. 'I give talks too,' he says, 'on how to succeed. They pay well, so it comes true, instantly. You have to objectify yourself. The end of the world, you see, is only of your world. If it happens to the rest, you're quite indifferent. The thing is – not to wait. Have it end in civil war, not the long hot summers of pollution, reaming out your lungs. You're only memory, and when it goes – there isn't you. You're somewhere else. It's just you don't remember where you were before.'

'That's a comfort,' I say.

'Oh no,' he says, 'not comfort. Striving. That's what the Buddha tried to say.'

'What's your line?' I ask: it's been leading to that.

'I speed up your messages,' he says. 'If you know your physics, the faster they go, the more the content changes. Modulates, even. Speed and content, they're the same. It's easy, because what you say – it has no mass.'

'That's quite evident,' I say.

'You're not a Catholic, I hope,' he says. 'That's not the mass I meant.'

'Your profits can be infinite,' I say.

'Like prophecy itself,' he says, spelling out the wordplay on the window, steamed over by our discourse.

'Did you find that woman attractive?' he asks. 'The one with the bum?'

'No,' I say.

'There!' he says. 'A victory! There goes your humanism, your respect.... The fakery! The body, the sex, everything that makes a human – "No!" you say. "Not attractive." Good for you. She was a cypher, occupying a train seat. Do you believe in armour?'

'I guess so,' I say.

'I see it in you,' he says. 'Armour with a hole in it – that's no good at all. If you wear it, hot and heavy – no holes! It should be guaranteed. You need be sure you don't see sunlight, not coming in, nor going out.'

'It figures,' I say.

'That could be a subject of my talk,' he says. 'How to succeed. What's that worth, do you think? Set out price and value.'

'I always skipped that chapter,' I say. 'When we were waiting for socialism. I thought it would be clear. I know there's a difference and a key to the big door. But I've forgotten the rest.'

'Anyway, you weren't going to pay me,' he says. 'Not price, not value.'

'No,' I say. 'Not at all. That's my armour working.'

'I like it that you're primitive,' he says. 'I know a girl, you'd fall in love with her at once. And she'd crawl up your bones like a jigger. Maybe you wouldn't thank me?'

'Maybe I'm gay,' I say, pulling away from him, his offers.

'Love, I said,' he says, 'not sex. D'you think I wanted to peek? When you're rich, you see, you get company. When you're poor, you get family. I know people who'd curl up with you, for free.'

'That sounds good,' I say. 'I might try it.'

The train stops. He says, 'We get out here. You're new to New York. The trains don't go to main stations now – they think we may be bombed. Or converted. Some people say the experience is similar. I don't go with that. The guys here had made an everyday we can all share – they're not giving it up – not to bombs, not to religion. There's enough of both already.'

We jump down and follow the tracks. Is this storm damage? Or construction sites?

'What happens here and now,' the rich guy says, loping along, 'Changes the lifeworld. Changes it without a bomb – and lets us bomb wherever we've a mind.'

'Who's with this "us"?' I ask. 'I've spent years running. Now even trains don't have a destination.'

'You're much too smart to stack those boxes,' says the guy. 'I see you've nothing to do, except seek your fortune.'

I trot after him. I explain the battles I've seen, earthquakes anticipated, wonders.... He's not interested.

He says, 'It's controlling the everyday. Making things change, but not too fast. Getting the normal well-established. That's what matters. That is power, real power. Innovation: determining the speed at which the normal changes. Repainting your lifeworld, recalibrating your common sense. It's a process quite involuntary, that needs a great collective enterprise. All those guys working on it... the bastards.'

He walks into a room, a lounge, well-upholstered. There's people sitting round, like they're plaster, in an installation.

'I could say I devised all this,' he says. 'All these idlers sitting; and ask you to participate. But it would be a fraud. You see the scene, and I pretend you're taking part, an actor, free to speak. You aren't. I put you in, you're the decor. It's all mine, the idea.'

It's an invite – to step outside the frame, by stepping in. He says, 'This here's the woman, this is the one for you. A beauty. She'll break your heart, if you have one.'

'We're all here to do a movie, an ad,' says Juni.

I'm in love with her, at once, of course.

'You want a starring part?' she asks. 'Todd might be behind the camera. It's not that you take a part in it – he gives the part. It rather binds you. If I were you, I should refuse. You're not into little telephones, I hope?'

'Oh no,' I say.

'The physical world,' she says, 'is just a start. Experience is so much more. That's what is interesting. Money encysts a sampling of those things – desire, your labour, what you think while you are doing it, and what you'll do right after.'

'I know all that, Juni,' I say. 'We went through it on the train.'

'Having cash and losing it – it's all beyond the physical,' she says. 'You shouldn't fret about it.'

'Oh, I don't,' I say. 'I've seen the battles and the wonders....' and I'd tell her everything. She isn't interested.

'I bet your women made you dance some complicated figures,' she says, and laughs. 'No reproduction there – each one a novelty.'

'Is Todd really rich?' I ask. 'You all sitting here....'

'He knows rich people who will give him cash. This finite provinces of meaning stuff – they think he has a way to save their money when their bit of the lifeworld ends.'

'It's always like that, Juni,' I tell her.

My love for her – there's no way, it seems, to turn it off, not ever, it's a plague sore that eats like phosphorus.

'Don't show me your tattoos,' she shouts.

'No, no,' I say, 'I've none, and none where you would look.'

'That whiff of flesh, the drawings – that kitsch, we all did those at school. I'm vegan, and the smell of branded animals, the scorch, the claggy meat....' she says.

'You're beautiful, that's why,' I say. 'Your sensibility....'

'You don't say anything,' she says. 'That's good. Good, but not interesting.'

Beautiful people – they have a plan. 'I have a plan,' she says, 'but you're not in it.'

'I bet Todd has a plan to spread the cash around, do good,' I say. 'Arm the oppressed, all that.'

'There's no special merit in feeling extra guilt,' she says. 'The doling out, one day at a time, your drips of charity – you'd better take the desperate as maids and gardeners, be useful, that's the thing. Todd talks – that's his utility.'

Later, I say to Todd, 'Juni's beautiful – I'm in love. But it's disaster.'

'Isn't that too bad?' he says. 'Juni's in love too – with another mismatch. Still, you've yourselves to blame. If you're suffering – that is your choice. Involuntary – it's all the same. Besides, I need people around me with no qualities. Qualities have got us in this mess. If mess you see it as.

'Those big munitions, the warm hearths. It's turned against you. Other guys would want them – couldn't you have guessed? And now we must be selfish, you and I. Save our little lifeworlds – you don't need a gun or rocket, if you're cold – just wear more clothes. The rest – I'm working on.' He talks on, about his studio, the messages – 'I don't give fuck all what people say, it's all without an interest': the rich guys looking for a hole to hide in. 'All designs in silver point, so's you can't erase. Hard edge. Like Leonardo – that coprophiliac!' he says.'But much much cleaner.'

Juni takes me aside. The rest are clowning before the lens. 'We rely on Todd,' she says, 'to stop it happening to us.'

'You mean, stop what's happening all over happening here?' I ask.

'No, no,' she says, 'of course it's happening over here. To stop it happening to us.'

She hoists her skirt high up her thigh. 'See that?' she says. 'You're quite a special friend, to see it.'

'You've made a garden there, in miniature,' I say. 'It's spoiled your body. But it's neatly done, razored in, I'd say. It must be for eating from, the rows are straight, the hedges well hatched in..... There's beets and radishes....'

'It's cuts,' she says. 'A little garden of self-mutilation. There. Now you've seen it; not too many have. No one, but you and I.'

'I imagine reasons of all kinds,' I say.

'Yes,' she says, 'all those, and more.'

In fact, it doesn't at all communicate, this penance. Maybe a hidden call to be exempt, saved, to avoid the destiny...

'You're wrong,' she says. 'It doesn't hurt at all. Not penance, nor a pleasure. A secret, something to be shared. It's all you'll have from me.' That way, it's settled.

Then, Juni says, 'Nature's a bitch. I hate her. Let her croak.'

She's the star of the ad. 'Todd makes tiny movies of us all,' she says. 'Almost completely motionless.'

Tod cranks the handle on the camera. 'Just a few frames each,' he shouts.

'Don't leave your face,' Juni tells me. 'If you don't want to be tracked.'

The others crowd around, some with masks and wigs, pouting and preening. They're copyright- and patent-advocates, assistants of assistants all – 'Todd'll get us out of here,' they shout.

'You could take a course in shamanism,' Juni tells me.

'No,' I say. 'The shaman I knew is dead. No changing horse. They're jealous of each other, down below.'

'If he's any good, he'll come and visit you,' says Juni, but Todd has overheard – 'No goddam courses, you're last in, and so I need you close to me.'

I ask Juni, 'Do you think Todd has a way to save you? All he has in mind is limiting your worlds, while all the rest goes on outside, melting and shattering—'

'Oh no,' she says. 'There's much more than that. We're not a sect! We are a corporation, we make a heap of cash.'

I say, 'People don't trust you, Juni. You're in their city, but to survive, you have to find a strategy to leave....You're suspect.'

'Well, we can't run,' she says. 'Not like they used to. And surviving too – that's maybe not so great.... That's why we must rely on Todd. Perhaps he'll find the way....'

'Hide where you like, Juni. Hide inside yourself, hide with your friends. Find a place where you can hide. What you believe – it's quite irrelevant. None of this will work. In the past, they singled out a group, a thought, and nailed them to the trees. Now – all that is of no avail at all. There's not a tree for each....' I say.

'Well done,' says Todd. 'That is exactly it. This guy,' he pulls at me, tearing my clothes, 'is back from exile. So he knows it all. He's all alone – so his friends, left back, over there.... they must be doing well. Or else got tired of him.'

The company has gathered round, they gesture doubt, hostility. I've no defence, and Juni puts them off the scent.

'Mister Todd, the fox,' says Juni, 'who scares the chicks, and runs and runs. And smells quite bad,' and she pretends to sniff at him. He doesn't smell of fox, he smells of musk, a smell of woman, you don't know if it's from him, or someone he's been close to.

The guys here – they say they're lawyers, experts in some stuff. They get it easy, off their screens. I say to Todd, 'I don't see much going on. It's like a squat here, but you pay the rent. The only rich guy's you – the rest get paid, and then they give it back. And if you fire them, or they quit – there's nothing they can take....'

'Oh yes,' laughs Todd. 'There is to take! Each has a box, like those you came to stack. And – we make the cash by buying out another bunch of guys like us, and selling on. You should feel shame, if you didn't know it worked this way.'

'Not everybody likes you, Todd,' I say.

I wonder if he's Juni's mismatch. It would explain him, and what he does, putting people with her.

'I don't believe in having enemies,' says Todd. 'Not that I feel respect for everyone. But enemies – that brings reprisals. It will never end. Friends too – you can hate your family, but you're only free to criticise your friends. That's why they never last for long. Juni now – she thrives on enemies. My dear – you could have joined that Fraktion, the red army one....' and he laughs.

'That was over, and I didn't yet exist,' says Juni, not amused.

'Oh well,' says Todd, labouring on, 'we're always born too soon or late for things.'

I ask Juni, 'All these groups, militias, undergrounds, that Todd speaks of – why does he think you're suitable?'

'Oh, nothing,' Juni says. 'It's just he feels he must explore. Resistance, flight – he mentions everything. 'If you don't fight, you must avoid the camps. "Someone should bear witness." That's where you find reprisals, so Todd says.'

'You're all too tentative,' I say. 'And what Todd and you guys want – it isn't possible. To stay on the outside....'

'No, no, this is the time, the space,' says Todd, who overhears. 'Before it starts to spread and creep up to your door. I have a plan....'

And so he does: he takes us to the shore. A little boat, its timbers blue and grey, the sails once red, their sunset's past – 'They wash the sails in manganese, to give them strength,' says Todd.

'Can that thing float?' asks Juni. 'It's much smaller than a whale – that rig.... You can't go about, you have to run before the wind....'

'Yes, yes,' says Todd. 'That's just the point. You run before the wind – one day the wind will ease, but then you don't. You have escaped. Forget the whales – those brown humps in the swell – they're empty whisky barrels, sign of how we once did well. The people here had water piped into their homes for fifty years. Now – that's all stopped. It's history, it's challenges. Adapt, adjust.'

We raise the sails – they crack with age. There's space between the boards – 'A Norfolk rig,' shouts Todd. 'That is the best.'

A guy on shore shouts, 'Fother and thrum!'

'Ah yes,' says Todd, 'that's what life is for, to teach. Or to remind. Juni – trample down that lateen sail, to stop the leaks.'

'This one?' she asks. 'This sail is full of holes.'

'Ah yes,' says Todd, 'That's better for the wind. Change them about, my dear, we'll skim away, a caravelle....'

'It still comes in,' I say. 'The sea.'

'It's better so,' says Todd. 'Without the sea the next course, the fish, couldn't succeed the soup we're in,' and he laughs like a tempest. 'If you don't take it serious,' he says, 'it may well disappear. The evolution – just like Lenin said – Juni will recognise the quote – goes one step forward, two steps back, or even more.'

The sea, the sea, all grey and green, huge brushfuls all around us, as we nail ourselves upon the mast, Juni above, myself and Todd tricked out with blue and white, like sailors' duds, the water hustling around our necks.

I shout, 'Take to the raft!' and Juni says, 'we haven't time to build us one! And who'll unnail us from this mast, this tree?'

'In those billows, there is cod,' shouts Todd, and then he laughs. 'And down and down, among the shells, the worms inedible, when things with eyes like dinner plates and fronds for arms appear – there's always lessons being taught.'

We cannot question him – our curiosity has done for us, our inner whale... it trusted him. Mister Todd, the teacher.... Now, we're beached and on the strand. He says,

'I could have told you,' he says. 'That is not the way!'

We sit upon the sand, we laugh, we cry, Juni hugs me, almost my destiny is reached, her tears, her tears.... 'Juni,' I say, 'your tears are salt,' and she replies, 'We drank those waves, they did for us. This is not resolution, it is plenitude. We're tiny troubled seas, all three. We'll weep until we're dry, upon this shore, where memories of boats wash up....'

'And we shall make a fire,' says Todd, decisively, 'with all that decking, till we're truly hot, and dry as dry.'

We lie like stockfish in the heat, our clothes arch up and wrinkle, like baccalà upon our backs. Some guys swarm round to tell us that our boat would sink. 'We know, we know all that,' says Todd. 'You take things as a metaphor, and every time you're saved, you try again – the lesson's never done and never clear, but see! Unfurling like a butterfly, out from its pod, it's revelation! There, it lies along the yards with promise of another trip, another voyage – fresh faces on the shore.... Do we enslave them, do we take them off and shackle them below? Or have them teach us songs and charms to calm the waves? Sailing the seas – it's throwing dice, and betting lives. And being castaways, without a trace... those pebbles on the beach, they will not register a print, you're quite alone, you chant the psalms, and no one hears.' He turns to us, pale, aghast. 'No one! No one hears!'

'Well,' says Juni, 'I'll not go boating with you, Todd. Never no more!'

Todd repeats, 'No one! What kind of lesson is that? They're not indifferent – they just don't hear!'

'Fuck you, Todd,' says Juni, 'I could have drowned.'

He seems embarrassed. 'Oh, you take it serious, but you're alive. If you'd died, you could be excused for feeling glum. You two – you could have made love here on the shore.... The danger done! Some fun for you, a spectacle for us.'

'That's not the lesson, Todd, no, not at all,' says Juni – so full of love for someone else, unknown and unrequited too, no doubt. 'You set things up, and when they fall, you say that's what you've been intending....'

'Well, Juni,' brightening, Todd says. 'That is my signature. But you – do you have one? Are you a literate in life?'

'I was too late,' she says. 'It was all over and gone. Politics with the gun – I'd have been a comrade who's mistaken. Push it to the limit. Find something, try it out; and so – it doesn't work, then, suffer for it. Not wait for compromise and long defeats. Now, the guys who think they're hard – they've no idea. They don't know what to do—'

'That's exactly my position. Hasten it along. Try everything, not to resolve, but for its shape,' says Todd, excited. 'But my dear, action is not for you. Hard guys wouldn't take you on. Dear Juni, you are beautiful, so you exist, but only for beholders. That is what they say, for once they're right.'

Lifeworlds. I have one. Todd has many. Or else, his is elastic. Finding a lifeworld where you can escape, avoid what happens to the rest – it's chancy. Nearly got us drowned. What next? A volcano? Flying on an eagle's back? Fire, water, air – then, there's the atomic ones.

'I have an answer,' Todd tells us. 'A gladiators' school. A life-and-death world. Not to fight with nets and stuff. Mahagonny, city of nets... that must be Rome, those awful buildings, brown with blood. No, not there, not that. A lifeworld, though, that has its terminus. The guys who train... who jump... who drive the cars, who test the planes, funambulists, the guys who leap from space and land in Kirghistan.... Singers who screw with jealous guys who smash their heads.... The drinkers.... Ah yes – look in the bars – they don't know where that day they'll travel, or with who, and where they wake, if they may wake at all. Fallen. Fallen on tracks, on mattresses, in garbage alleys, down the cellar steps, playing with those guns, down the tracks, shooting up.... Out in the yard, pop off your shooter, pop a red pill – watch out! Pop your neighbour, his head – oh no, right through the ear and out the eye, another in the mouth to stop the shouts – hey, call the cops, is there a death row in this state? Oh no, what have I done – please, shoot me too, officer – I've paid for your bullets, here – here are my eyes – you surely cannot miss.... Steady your hand, brace against this venerable apple tree, do your duty, no regrets, remember the oath... you are a soldier, remorse is yours, not ours....'

'Yes, Todd,' says Juni. 'The idea is plain. Macabre too. Is it conclusive, though? These guys, they seem to want the death, the good death. Resolution, tears, applause. A conclusion that stamps and seals their fame, their daring – all that's so. But – is it death they want? Or eternity? An eternal, an infinite, lifeworld.'

'Don't be so smart,' says Todd. 'We'll work that out when we are there.'

'Do you teach the gladiators something?' Juni asks.

'Of course not,' Todd says. 'It's a school of metaphysics. We don't observe, we reason. We mistrust experience. And yet.... You see, the future! That's a province, in the frame, but where experience misleads. My expertise... you may have guessed – it's things that are, but hard to say experience can guide or help. Death is my favourite case: it is, but no one says they have experienced it. Death sounds like my name, but – I am not it, you see, and death is not its sound!'

'I can come in there,' I say. 'My family has specialised in death. Death is like the tennis you will not have played.'

Juni persists. 'Suicide bombers? Have a handle on the future, and on death. So, if they already have another lifeworld just ahead...?'

'Oh Juni! Don't be so eager. Picky, picky, pick! I've not classified the world,' says Todd. 'There's boxers, soldiers – altogether in a lower stream, I think. The more appealing crowd are singers, pop stars – I look forward to grading their exams. All the unsuitable matches that they try to make....'

'You're an old Tory, Todd,' says Juni. 'I see moralism and convention sticking from your mouth like spiders' legs.'

The gladiators' school is laid out like a camp. You hear the singers, but no doubt there's fighters training. Todd's walking up and down. There's guys who're trying on masks and makeup, ogling the camera, fooling about.

'The boy singers make much more than girls,' says Juni. 'But I still think it's crass – their falsetto. The whole business, with those words – being left by lovers, or sometimes not. As if it counted.'

She does a little dance, miming the boys – I guess it's pop, she waves her thin backside, tautens it up, and strikes that ballet pose, the broken swan, the right arm raised, the left crooked and useless. It's a difficult position, quite inconclusive, but the right leg, forward – I guess it shows the breasts, the pelvic engine. 'Oh don't leave me,' Juni sings. 'And if you do I don't care a tiny bit – but I'll cry just the same, always the same....'

'Juni,' says Todd, 'there's no one here for you. And – your music doesn't scan.'

'Scan!' says Juni. 'I knew you were reactionary, Todd. Your camp here – it's like where every human unit ends up – with their lookalikes. What binds us all is death. You can't get away from that, Mister Todd. Run how you like, and gobble down the chicks; they'll run you down with dogs and chew you up.'

The school – transmits the feeling that it's all precarious. It's not about cosmology, it's all about careers. Todd's, and his riches – just the same.

'Todd's my lifeworld,' Juni says. 'It's become a jail. I want away. I want my lover. Todd wants to spend his money faster than it tumbles in. Then he'll complain, and start again.'

I tell Todd, 'I stay because of Juni,' and he says, 'Love requited – that's what you want, although you don't much like her. I like that, striving for the impossible and undesirable. What you want does not exist. That's its attraction, I know...'

Juni interrupts, 'You know how it goes – love unrequited is just dope in your head. Love requited – is a dope in your bed. What would it change, except bring misery?'

'Listen,' says Todd, 'I'm in a hole. These guys – fixers control their boundaries. There's no eternity – it's fashion. Singers and fighters. All they know is sing and fight – no metaphysics, just replicants. This place could last for ever. They steal and deal. And how they sing! "*Oh Lord, we know / no remedy / be merciful to us / in our sins.*" They all end like that. Operas. Crap. The lifeworld – that's when you have your rituals, a sacred mountain, a code of revenge to take, a paradise that waits silent beneath the earthly disc. Or – you sing, you win a prize, you cut a disc, but not an earthly one.

Guys take your cash and marry you. Your voice goes bad. You're done. That's your lifeworld too. The first is resignation, the second ought to be – instead, it's fame and disillusion, the great fall. And I'm stuck with these guys! Fighters. Dancers. The pectorals like pregnant trout. The prancing like the floor is spiked....'

'You hadn't worked the problematic out before the start. Todd, you're a dilettante,' Juni says. 'We've used up our resources, the gold and diamonds too, but you've discovered – singing and fighting! For those, you don't need dig nor suck nor hoe. Well done, Todd. You've failed in metaphysics, but solved another puzzle. What to do, for ever: consuming nothing.'

'My, Juni!' Todd says. 'You're so caustic.'

'We don't want to leave, Todd,' Juni says. 'We just want you to be different.'

'That's up to you,' he says. 'Your vision. Maybe it won't change a thing – but things are not our business. As they say – "things are". You – must become.'

'All right,' says Juni, 'we'll try out your games.' She jumps up on the low wire. 'This is my first time... why! It's like walking on a mattress, like you were a kid.' It sags and bends and billows: she bends like a leaf upon its bough. 'You need know the angulation,' Juni says. 'Now – I'll go higher. Todd, build me some towers!'

A guy says, 'She must sing while she's up there,' maybe she does – she's so high up, it sounds like nothing, or like breeze or bird.

'It's the fear that makes you fall,' says Todd. Juni's so high, so fluent up there, the guys soon tire of watching her.

He fits me with a net, a trident.

I'm afraid.

My opponent's tall, his legs are yellowy, he has no calves. His sword goes swishing overhead. I crouch, the net catches the arm, the sword, I thrust the trident.... Did he staple on his shoulder plate? I twist, the rivets spring, the

204

plate hangs down, and all the wires and cords that keep our arms from falling are exposed.

'Goddam,' says Todd. 'That means he'll need to convalesce. These guys get so attached, they'd stay forever here.'

'You see!' Juni says to me. 'You play your luck, that way, some guy gets hurt.'

'I didn't hear you sing,' I say. 'That's why the guys got bored.'

'I sang. I heard,' she says. 'You – you didn't conquer anything or anyone. Just poked in the dark.'

I stand, my bloody trident and my net, king Neptune on parade.

Juni says to Todd, 'What you call metaphysics – it's just the huge expanse, banal, of love for the absent, longing for absence, fear of death; your plan, and your regret. It's just what can't be reasoned out, it's the effect without a cause, a cause without a clear effect. Todd! see it! – no key. No door.'

'I know all that,' he says, downcast. 'I'm just an amateur. Maybe this palestra is the best thing I can make....'

The guy I pinked – he'll need to go from battle into baritone, and sing. I hear him swishing with his voice, disarmed, his real arm sharp – the wound exposed, and in a sheath, the bones are nicely fretted out and damascened.

'You might have cut my lover down,' says Juni. 'If my lover had been that warrior: makes a nice turn, the story tweaking tails. A word, a tale – like rollmops, the end in the beginning. But this guy, quite unknown to you and me – his crazy skeleton, his wobbly swordplay – no doubt he's loved somewhere, maybe has kids.... I'm glad; he's nothing to me, not at all.'

'Enough of that!' says Todd. 'He has no country you can steal or occupy. There is no moral mess that you can meddle in. Don't psychologise – not him, not you, not Neptune here. It's just a game, just one on one. Just as you say – no door, no key, no conscience, nothing is revealed, there is no enemy.

Forget the literary stuff – there's thousands of the dead around – who knows where they are stored? – no pottery warriors guard, no gold lies in their graves.... It's all collateral, they say, no one you know who grieves, who suffers, who regrets. Collateral for some loan, or some commodity, some moral gain, they say....'

And on and on – the singers sing, the warriors grunt and tumble. Maybe it'll turn to opera. Todd has success, he can't avoid his genius – his is the lucky thrust, not mine.

I tell Juni, 'You could make a living, walking the wire.'

'Oh no,' she says. 'Crushingly dull! The people who do well at that – they're terrified, that's why. They hate it, inching along the line, they dream of falls – down, down, no time even to pee your pants... the fear, that, they transmit: that's why you watch. Me – it's just a few yards on a rod of steel, a stroll. Too easy. Who'd want to do it twice?'

I turn to Todd. 'The state – it seemed so in control, loved, hated, just about in perfect equilibrium....'

'Oh no,' says Todd, 'protect me from large things! You see, the biggest animals – they reach their end. They're strong, imposing, their trampling, trumpeting – their authority – is uncontested by the lesser beasts. And yet – they're weak, their fat inhibits breath, their boots – too massive.

'Faded are their eyes. Death. That's what awaits. And it is clear to all: you're free, and yet you are oppressed. Justice, injustice – in perfect equilibrium – but.... The beast is like the hippo, braced against the flow. The years drone on, the muscles slacken – and – it lets go: over the falls it drops! The oppressed – they most mistrusted it, the mastodon. Could they believe it might be on their side? Naturally not – they're the first to rise. Now, that's what they always say....'

'Todd, it wasn't quite that way,' says Juni, 'but it will do.'

*

'I have no trouble with this civil war,' says Juni. 'And I don't think what Todd is looking for – a safer place – is of much use. It started when you might just want to take a side. But on it goes.... You'd want a different start, and different ends. Seeing what happens – that's the thing. You cannot stand aside – but, best not join in.'

'You're never in love, Juni, are you?' I ask.

'I'm not like you,' she tells me. 'I keep things to myself. You,' she pulls my sleeve, 'you think you're public. You put yourself up for sale, but never name a price. No – civil war, it's just like having lovers; they do, and then they don't. Or maybe you do, and then you don't. And friends, neighbours – it's the same.'

'But the torture? The wounds? Losing the lot?' I ask.

'Oh yes,' she says. 'You have to keep alert. It doesn't always work. But – you're in the context, so you know what's what. You'd been expecting how it will break out. How it might end.'

'This is all hard stuff, that Todd can't get a hold on,' I say. 'The everyday is disassembled, and then you want it back. Things don't speed up – they slow right down. But – are you sure it's all already happening? It's not just round the corner?'

'Oh no,' she says. 'It's here. They keep on saying – be prepared, or it will happen. Well, it is happening, already.'

The water comes in everywhere. There's bombing, all sorts, in our heads. I guess some have it worse.

'You should go be a soldier,' Juni tells me. 'Somewhere. You have the knack. Todd – he'd be in intelligence – that's his slot. Once in, you never leave.'

'The neolithic,' Todd sums things up. 'That's when we last had the panorama, had the common vision. Then we started to distribute everything. Now, maybe, we're at that point again. But I'm not convinced this time they'll do it better.'

Juni says again to me, 'Go, be a soldier. It'll keep your love on edge – yours, and the whoever's. The *bien-aimée*. If you like, don't call it war. Just say it's competition. You can't do it for religion, so you should think of water, fire and earth. We need all those, and cash to match.'

'I guess,' says Todd, 'this camp could be a castle. Carved beerstone gates, all that. But – you defend a place, it's an invite to attack. And then, the first guys who're against you, you fight back, and it defines both you and them. There's no money in the enterprise, and, you know, if there's no fraud, there is no spice.'

'Come, Todd,' says Juni, 'a person builds things up – they get knocked down. Besides, you're too big a person to have enemies.'

'It's true,' he says. 'That stuff is boring – friends, enemies. Don't modify your line, let it march on.'

'You're not reliable, Todd,' says Juni. 'Nor am I, but I'm not fearful. You, though, could build a castle that's made to be knocked down. That's bold.'

'You don't need be reliable,' I say. 'Especially Todd. I don't stand anywhere, there's nowhere that I could. I suppose I could write poetry, about silversmiths, their craft... some images to take minds off.'

'I doubt that,' Todd says, 'You're not a timeless guy.'

'I don't have qualities,' I say. 'Does that make me a soldier?'

'When the guys here lost the big war,' Juni says. 'Of course, it would go civil. It always does.'

'Once, they let Todd into every house,' I say. 'They died early, lived in hope. Carving. That's what you need. Walls, steps. Clay – everyone wants to press their prints. It's our only characteristic. Todd could provide the space where you could leave your aphorism. Now – he puts on the only things that leave no mark – duelling and music.'

Juni's about to object. My love for her is just as strong. I'm glad we're not requited, don't have to live alongside.

'No, Juni,' I say. 'No casuistry. Duelling leaves no mark, and death leaves none. There you are.'

'I could leave a structure, I suppose,' says Todd. 'Empty, for if guys want to write their name. Are you sure the spirit marks its passing so? I need to think I can go beyond myself, in spaces where there is uncertainty and doubt. A total recast of myself.'

'Once Todd brought money that was fresh and bright,' says Juni. 'Not now. But philosophy? The end not being end? The war forever, the forever war – that's not what's coming next? Of course – he's stuck. I'm tired of telling him, and seeing how he bumbles, slips – a bee trapped in its bottle, unable to get out. It's hard to leave his influence, I know, he's infinitely inventive, sometimes nearly fun.'

'Leaving the physical,' I say. 'You and I, Juni. See if there's an after after that.'

'I'm always here,' says Todd. 'You can always rely on me.'

'Beyond the physical world,' says Juni dreamily, 'you won't need friends to hide you – or disappoint you, if they don't. No space for foreign guys to occupy, no boots to bull or springs to ease. It's paradise – yet paradise must be the only place where there's no hope, no change....'

'No democracy,' says Todd, and laughs. 'Come, Juni – this leads you up wrong paths....'

*

Juni and I, we walk a way down the road. 'Todd'll send us money,' Juni says. 'That way, we can be both poor and rich. That's in the spirit of himself.'

The guys have laid out what is here like little countries. Here's a Montenegro. We eat some of their dry cheese.

'You could have been a dancer, Juni,' I say.

We don't want to wash down the curly scraps of cheese with maraschino, though that's what they have.

'Further on, there's buttermen,' a guy says. 'They'll have access to some cows, or goats. It's craft.'

'I could have been a dancer,' Juni says. 'My balance. And my lower back. Being sharp, that comes in too. But – think of all the years it takes the lesser gifted ones to get on stage and stay upright! A bore, you'd say!'

'Control, Juni, that's enough,' I say. She's not controlled, not at all.

'These guys,' she says, 'they say they had "just" wars – it's hard to tell that from just wars.'

'It's over now,' I say. 'These guys are trying something else.'

Here's a bar, open to the street. A guy is sorting papers. 'Hey,' he says, 'this archive! It shows how Stalin stayed a member of a Georgian gang. He was their guy in Moscow. But its base was in the States – one of the gangs run by the FBI, not for the cash, but killing commies. Trots especially.'

'How do you know?' asks Juni.

'Oh,' says the guy, 'the tattoos, of course. They show the hierarchy.'

'And this stuff?' asks Juni. 'We're drinking it.'

'It's what they have, a Titograd Farewell. Banana skin wine and sliv,' he says.

It bears us back. Up the flinty track, past the cut trees, heaped like cigars. Grey mountains. There's a guy, beckoning us – there's yellowy cheese, and things of red, leathery and thin, maybe toadstools.

'Dried hearts,' this second guy says, 'but not yours.'

'We must leave,' I say to Juni. 'There's nothing here, not left, nor to transport to any other place.'

'I don't know how to leave,' she says. 'This is like home was....'

Todd's philosophy – that should be a help, carry us around. I concentrate.

'You're back!' says the first guy. 'Trips don't take long these days.'

'We know all about the gladiatorial craft,' says Juni. 'We learned all the moves.'

The guy, Marvin his name – it's on his uniform – laughs. 'Those Southern armies are so large – poor guys, and everything frontloads. The North has fewer guys, but better arms. We're in the middle here. This is our bar. We used all to be a bikers' gang....' And on he talks.

'Your skill is wasted here,' I say to Juni.

'They're generous with their eats, these Montenegrins,' Juni says. 'Best not to touch it. But – a bikers' gang: I've always wondered if I'd rise to be their queen....'

'No, no,' says Marvin. 'You've not understood. You have to join the food wars, otherwise you'll starve. Here, there's the buttermen, down there – it's oilmen. Up it's yellow, down it's red. The pigs go head to head against the sheep and goats. Us here – we're the synthesis. We drink.'

'Look, Marvin,' Juni says, 'I don't much care what you guys are fighting for. I'm sure it won't be for priorities of mine, or even a belief. We're here to test out philosophical ideas. "Beyond the physical", is us.'

'I told you, Marvin, she's quite uncontrollable. I'm the speculative one,' I say. 'Juni seeks the truth.'

'She seems to treat things very light,' says Marvin. 'They're serious. I hope you're not just pacifists, albatrosses who'll be eaten by the sharks?'

'Oh no,' says Juni, 'I'm quite serious. If guys steal my stuff or hurt me, I'll push my shuttle in their ear, and catch it coming out the other.'

'No, no,' I say, 'we're into finite provinces. It's groups, concocting their everyday reality. Then blocking it off, defending it. It doesn't say you should or shouldn't, just the how and why.'

'That's all right, then,' Marvin says. 'Banality can wear you down, you know. The given, common sense! The univocal! The merely physical! Just so long's you two don't feel superior....'

211

'Of course we're superior,' Juni says. 'If not, there'd be no point.'

'Todd's more superior still,' I say. 'Because he has a heap more cash, and purer motives, I dare say.'

'What you guys are on to,' Marvin says. 'Is nothing but a dons' delight. Meaning and understanding – it's all up to you. Relative or absolute – the earth is maybe flat and maybe round, and maybe carried by a monster toad.... We all have points of view on that. It's act-react. It's up to you – to throw the ball back, or to drop it.'

'No, no,' says Juni. 'That's why Todd has the gladiators – they give tit for tat. That's no uncertainty. The singers, though – they interpret, mastering the genres.'

'It doesn't mean just what you want it,' Marvin says. 'Meaning, that is. What I mean, believe, intend – my little province, home, my carapace – bear it in mind, or you won't understand. I know that's mine, my little world: – it's precious to me, and it works. And yours – can just fuck off.'

'Marvin,' Juni says, 'you're a biker with no bike. What's to understand?'

'Well,' he says, 'We used to run tight ships.'

But he comes along with us.

Here's Todd's encampment, the dusty field beyond the walls.

There seem more fighters on the plain. The gladiators, as they thrust and fall, sing what they can.

'Well,' says Todd, 'How is it, down the road?'

'It's all laid out in tiny countries,' Juni says. 'Each has their special food. The bikers – they have special drinks. But what it means – well, you can guess. That's not what I want to say: it's clear what they all mean, but not what it amounts to.'

'Why should you care?' asks Todd. 'Guys come for you, they get you. Here – I've had to can the opera. Too much invention. Each music turned out different from itself, you understand.'

'That's too bad,' I say. 'Some scenes you'd hate to be without. Madame B – "farewell, my little love...."'

'Yes,' says Todd, 'but listen to what those swordsmen sing, between, beneath, their breaths. Sentiments of the lesser sort of people. Sweet and raw.'

'OK, Todd,' says Juni. 'I see you've given up. No more the quest, no more the things you don't quite understand. No more the championships, the walkovers – the cup you get to keep. You're just an ordinary organiser of the bully boys. Like them, you are locked in, you think you'll face it down.'

'Courage?' asks Todd, quizzically. 'Me? No. I don't think so. I'll visit prisons, but don't plan a stay. We'll wait and see, obedient to our principles.'

'That's nonsense, Todd,' says Juni. 'Inaction. That way the worst will come. We know you are the master, whatever you undertake.'

In the night, there's an alarm. 'Marvin attacked me,' Juni shouts.

'No, no, I'm not like that,' he says. 'Juni attacked me,' and they glare.

'I'm sure it's all pre-emptive,' Todd says. 'Whatever, and on who.'

'It's not a tragedy,' I say. 'What happened to that guy I struck? That went to be a baritone?'

'Oh him,' says Todd, smoothing most things. 'He fell down on his mordents. We had to rake him off the stage. You know what they say – "the pig satisfied ends in the bacon factory". He rested on his hocks. He had to go. Singing's like diplomacy – often you must perform in French, it's not just slash and poke.'

'Should I feel bad?' I ask. 'My prowess with the fork?'

'I covered for you, and your patchy pacifism,' Todd says.

'There must be lots of deaths, here in this camp?' says Marvin.

'We don't call them that,' says Todd. 'There's always an enquiry.'

'Todd,' I say. 'Love. You promised me. Instead, it's like a boil. And death....'

'You killed that warrior, a singer burst from his pod and into life,' he says. 'Like a Monsieur Butterfly.'

'What really is your game?' I ask Todd. 'The physical – it's remorseless – you can't go beyond. The wispy things – the thoughts, beliefs, are all encysted in it.' He yawns. He is not tired, nor bored. 'That's what they all say, out of fear,' he says, 'The things most intimate, most "you" – are those you can't control at all.'

'This idiot,' Marvin shouts. 'She smashed her shield boss in my face.'

It's true. The bones are crimped.

'He tied his bike chain round my neck,' Juni shouts back. You see the mark.

'That's crap,' says Todd. 'It's her tattoo.'

Juni and Marvin scuffle round. They seem to have a bond. Up on their hind legs, they spar and hug. I ask Todd, 'What's your plan?'

'Oh,' he says, 'I train soldiers. Like I always did. Not mercenaries, not a militia. I'm into pedagogy. Metaphysical stuff – it's all around, like air. The pros can't do a thing with it – to them, it's all invisible. And yet – whatever isn't physical, it permeates. What to do with it? I don't know. It doesn't survive you, that I'm certain of. Ephemeral. No immortality. That's why – the soldiers! I don't do it for the countries, or the beliefs. Beliefs are metaphysical, soldiers aren't. You need the troops, though, so's you can do the interesting things. Especially if there's fighting. Just a reserve, a company, that's what you want. An army of your own. Those guys from out the East, the far, far East – they hate each other. When they come here, you can't do anything to stop them, and they're not listening to you.... So, a bunch of well-trained guys, like mine—' He breaks off. 'Marvin – don't hurt her face. She's beautiful. That's all you ever need to know.' He turns back to me, 'No politics, you understand: there is no place....'

'To me, you sound quite fascist, Todd,' I say, and Juni laughs.

Todd says, 'There's places orderly, and those that aren't. Order will make you bow your neck. Disorder – you must bend your knee. That's all there is to it, unless you're unlucky, or an optimist.'

'Todd doesn't need to pay some hulk protection, so's he can stay in business,' Marvin says. Maybe that's all there is to know.

'An airship, that's the thing,' says Todd, quite out of nowhere. 'Some countries base themselves on rivers. That does for China, India – others on mountains, like Korea, and Japan. We here – we improvise, wait for some new thought to strike. The last thing we say we need, is fighting – but it turns out that's the best thing we can do, the only thing. Of course, we live here, so our place, it must be in, and yet above. An airship, now: you can live on that, where the physical begins to end, the mind goes lighter, and you're in and out yourself. Ship in the air – it needs no river and no sea. It needn't move, becalmed up there, like on a mountain quite imaginary. And yet – it's martial too. It threatens, and it lurks. Silent. No slogan and no shout. What holds it up? Just air. That's it. It lives from life itself, and yet its life is cold as cold....'

'Yes, Todd,' says Juni. 'But there's no story moving there. I won't go, and nor will Marvin here.'

'Time and space don't move,' says Todd. 'There's nothing wrong with that. Everything is not all fable, false resolution. Going here and there, elaboration. Animal chatter.'

'Don't be so sure, Todd,' Marvin says, cuddling Juni. 'It all moves. Even the fire must go somewhere.'

'It goes into the cold, you idiot,' says Todd. 'But it doesn't move.'

'You've got it wrong, the both of you,' I say, but they're not listening. I mumble. 'This interminable, distant conflict, creeping nearer.'

Todd reacts: he says, 'You're wrong. I thought you were open to my novelties.... Escaping the past defeats, the persecutions, and the end. Going beyond, leaving behind.'

We climb on board the airship, Todd and I. Juni and Marvin stay behind, we see them frolicking, as we rise. We take some bottles filled with heavy air, in case the breeze is too refined as we rise higher.

'Up here,' says Todd, 'they used to see the monsters – transposed by the fantasies of those odd early folks, flipping up from marine depths – filmy jelly things, with eyes like Minnie Mouse.'

We stare around, hoping at least there's monsters here.

I ask Todd what he wants of me. 'Oh,' he says, 'Admiration, naturally. You're my representative. That first meeting on the train! Delicious – you, at loose ends.... Who doesn't want an admirer? And – you're almost my "admiral",' and he laughs at the wordplay. 'Juni – a lovely person. She could even be that pig, satisfied,' he laughs. 'She won't do, doesn't reflect my quiddity, even though you feel that love for her... and know she doesn't think of you.'

And we look down, through the lumpy air, invisible support, holding on to each other lest we fall, down to the meadow where those two, Juni and Marvin, are lying supine in their pastoral....

'They're in a danger zone down there,' says Todd. 'It's not a place for baring flesh.'

Scattered about, you see there's warehouses, on their roofs – 'Todd's Apparel', 'Todd's Pills'.

'Up here there's peace,' says Todd. 'We can continue with our work.'

'How do we get down?' I ask.

'I haven't worked that out,' says Todd. 'Maybe there's no way to go in peace. But look – how bright the earth is! Blue, green and grey. Umber and rust.'

Inside the ship, there's rows of desks. Deals are being done. Outside, on the deck, there's gladiators sparring. There is no rail.

'Going higher yet,' says Todd. 'We come to where you walk around, just wear a suit. There is nowhere you can fall. You need no container, nothing to keep you safe. Just look – here are the suits.'

It's sets of armour, full, and bright. Parade armour. 'What a sight we'll make!' says Todd. 'Up in the sky, like silver birds, or angels. A picture. Hand in hand, so confident. No one would think to shoot us down.'

'Todd, it's magnificent,' I say. 'And yet – I have a feeling I have failed. Not reached potential, in some way.'

'Juni?' he asks. 'Don't think of it. Your love's inside you, in its crucible. You feel it roar. You are the furnace – she is not the flame. Love is always singular – while it persists. As for potential – to get there, you need other people, interaction. People, you find, are changeable. They transmogrify – inside, in how they greet you, and besides – there's a procession of them. They flow. Flow down to the sea. Then, they are the waves. How can you realise some thing with them? They never are the same. It's buttocks, clambering off the train.'

I've no response. Is it possible I have no qualities, possible to be so devoid of them, a husk? It seems I pay the price of Juni being beautiful. Her form, I mean: you can't see inside.

From beauty, I have no benefit, and no delight.

'Of course, you feel responsible,' says Todd. 'Guilty, at least, for what you haven't done, have not achieved. That's why you're silent, though we might be interested in what you did, or saw, or read, or thought. You're too young to have fought, or dodged. It's all to come. Choosing sides, or seeing things decay and rot – it's all to come. You'd like to stay up here? Watch the armies fight it out below? The innocent a-scurry, looking for a hole. The massacres?'

'No, Todd,' I say. 'This is your place, and your invention.'

He resolves everything – and yet, the past is unchanged. I shall not see the future. Juni the beautiful – no love. A frolic. Not with me.

'You can still have sentiments,' he says. 'Despite this love thing you've been stuck with. Still, whatever you can do down there, your thoughts, intentions, even your horizon – there is space up here for everything. And – I am here.'

He holds me, as if I had been about to fall, or to escape. I'd like to leave, I can't think how to avoid him, Todd: drifting down, back to land.

He says, 'Your encounter with the beauty, Juni – I imagine, it must chill. Listen – I'll make some pepper soup, for both of us. Up here, the air is thin – stuff heats up before you know.'

About the author

John Fraser has lived in Rome since 1980. Previously, he worked in England and Canada.